Pied Piper

There was no time to do anything, to go anywhere, nor was there anywhere to go. Howard caught Sheila and Ronnie and pulled them close to him, flat upon the ground. He shouted to Rose to lie down, quickly.

Then the machines were on them, low-winged, single engined monoplanes with curious bent wings, dark green in colour. A burst of fire was poured into the bus from the machines to right and left; a stream of tracer-bullets shot forward up the road from the centre aircraft. A few bullets lickered straight over Howard and his children on the grass and spattered in the ground a few yards behind them.

For a moment Howard saw the gunner in the rear cockpit as he fired at them. He was a young man, not more than twenty, with a keen, tanned face. He wore a yellow students' corps cap, and he was laughing as he fired.

Nevil Shute

Pied Piper

Mandarin

A Mandarin Paperback

PIED PIPER

First published in Great Britain 1942
by William Heinemann Ltd
This edition published 1990
by Mandarin Paperbacks
an imprint of Reed Consumer Books Limited
Michelin House, 81 Fulham Road, London SW3 6RB
and Auckland, Melbourne, Singapore and Toronto

Reprinted 1991, 1992, 1993

Copyright © by the Trustees of
the Estate of the late Nevil Shute Norway

A CIP catalogue record for this book
is available from the British Library
ISBN 0 7493 0411 1

Printed and bound in Great Britain
by Cox & Wyman Ltd, Reading, Berks.

I

His name is John Sidney Howard, and he is a member of my club in London. I came in for dinner that night at about eight o'clock, tired after a long day of conferences about my aspect of the war. He was just entering the club ahead of me, a tall and rather emaciated man of about seventy, a little unsteady on his feet. He tripped over the door mat as he went in and stumbled forward; the hall porter jumped out and caught him by the elbow.

He peered down at the mat and poked it with his umbrella. 'Damned thing caught my toe,' he said. 'Thank you, Peters. Getting old, I suppose.'

The man smiled. 'Several of the gentlemen have caught their foot there recently, sir,' he said. 'I was speaking to the Steward about it only the other day.'

The old man said: 'Well, speak to him again and go on speaking till he has it put right. One of these days you'll have me falling dead at your feet. You wouldn't like that to happen – eh?' He smiled quizzically.

The porter said: 'No, sir, we shouldn't like that to happen.'

'I should think not. Not the sort of thing one wants to see happen in a club. I don't want to die on a door mat. And I don't want to die in a lavatory, either. Remember the time that Colonel Macpherson died in the lavatory, Peters?'

'I do, sir. That was very distressing.'

'Yes.' He was silent for a moment. Then he said: 'Well, I don't want to die that way, either. See he gets that mat put right. Tell him I said so.'

'Very good, sir.'

The old man moved away. I had been waiting behind him while all this was going on because the porter had my letters. He gave them to me at the wicket, and I looked them through. 'Who was that?' I asked idly.

He said: 'That was Mr Howard, sir.'

'He seemed to be very much concerned about his latter end.'

The porter did not smile. 'Yes, sir. Many of the gentlemen talk in that way as they get on. Mr Howard has been a member here for a great many years.'

I said more courteously: 'Has he? I don't remember seeing him about.'

The man said: 'He has been abroad for the last few months, I think, sir. But he seems to have aged a great deal since he came back. Getting rather frail now, I'm afraid.'

I turned away. 'This bloody war is hard on men of his age,' I said.

'Yes, sir. That's very true.'

I went into the club, slung my gas-mask on to a peg, unbuckled my revolver-belt and hung it up, and crowned the lot with my cap. I strolled over to the tape and studied the latest news. It was neither good nor bad. Our Air Force was still knocking hell out of the Ruhr; Rumania was still desperately bickering with her neighbours. The news was as it had been for three months, since France was overrun.

I went in and had my dinner. Howard was already in the dining-room; apart from us the room was very nearly empty. He had a waiter serving him who was very nearly as old as he was himself, and as he ate his dinner the waiter stood beside his table and chatted to him. I could hardly help overhearing the subject of their conversation. They were talking about cricket, re-living the Test Matches of 1925.

Because I was eating alone I finished before Howard, and went up to pay my bill at the desk. I said to the cashier: 'That waiter over there – what's his name?'

'Jackson, sir?'

'That's right. How long has he been here?'

'Oh, he's been here a long time. All his life, you might say. Eighteen ninety-five or ninety-six he come here, I believe.'

'That's a very long time.'

The man smiled as he gave me my change. 'It is, sir. But Porson – he's been here longer than that.'

I went upstairs to the smoking-room and stopped before a table littered with periodicals. With idle interest I turned over a printed list of members. Howard, I saw, had joined the club in 1896. Master and man, then, had been rubbing shoulders all their lives.

I took a couple of illustrated weeklies, and ordered coffee. Then I crossed the room to where the two most comfortable chairs in my club stand side by side, and prepared to spend an hour of idleness before returning to my flat. In a few minutes there was a step beside me and Howard lowered his long body into the other chair. A boy, unasked, brought him coffee and brandy.

Presently he spoke. He said quietly: 'It really is a most extraordinary thing that you can't get a decent cup of coffee in this country. Even in a club like this they can't make coffee.'

I laid down my paper. If the old man wanted to talk to me, I had no great objection. All day I had been working with my eyes in my old-fashioned office, reading reports

7

and writing dockets. It would be good to take off my spectacles for a little time and un-focus my eyes. I was very tired.

I felt in my pocket for my spectacle-case. I said: 'A chap who deals in coffee once told me that ground coffee won't keep in our climate. It's the humidity, or something.'

'Ground coffee goes off in any climate,' he said dogmatically. 'You never get a proper cup of coffee if you buy it like that. You have to buy the beans and grind it just before you make it. But that's what they won't do.'

He went on talking about coffee and chicory and things like that for a time. Then, by a natural association, we talked about the brandy. He approved of the club brandy. 'I used to have an interest in a wine business,' he said. 'A great many years ago, in Exeter. But I disposed of it soon after the last war.'

I gathered that he was a member of the Wine Committee of the club. I said: 'It must be rather interesting to run a business like that.'

'Oh, certainly,' he said with relish. 'Good wine is a most interesting study – most interesting, I can assure you.'

We were practically the only people in the long, tall room. We spoke quietly as we lay relaxed beside each other in our chairs, with long pauses between sentences. When you are tired there is pleasure in a conversation taken in sips, like old brandy.

I said: 'I used to go to Exeter a good deal when I was a boy.'

The old man said: 'I know Exeter very well indeed. I lived there for forty years.'

'My uncle had a house at Starcross.' And I told him the name.

He smiled. 'I used to act for him. We were great friends. But that's a long time ago now.'

'Act for him?'

'My firm used to act for him. I was a partner in a firm of solicitors, Fulljames and Howard.' And then, reminiscent, he told me a good deal about my uncle and about the family, about his horses and about his tenants. The talk became more and more a monologue; a word or two from me slipped in now and then kept him going. In his quiet vôice he built up for me a picture of the days that now are gone for ever, the days that I remember as a boy.

I lay smoking quietly in my chair, with the fatigue soaking out of me. It was a perfect godsend to find somebody who could talk of other things besides the war. The minds of most men revolve round this war or the last war, and there is a nervous urge in them which brings the conversation round to war again. But war seems to have passed by this lean old man. He turned for his interests to milder topics.

Presently, we were talking about fishing. He was an ardent fisherman, and I have fished a little. Most naval officers take a rod and a gun with them in the ship. I had fished on odd afternoons ashore in many parts of the world, usually with the wrong sort of fly and unsuccessfully, but he was an expert. He had fished from end to end of these islands and over a great part of the Continent. In the old days the life of a country solicitor was not an exacting one.

When he spoke of fishing and of France, it put me in mind of an experience of my own. 'I saw some chaps in France doing a damn funny sort of fly fishing,' I said. 'They had a great bamboo pole about twenty-five feet long with the line tied on the end of it – no reel. They used wet flies, and trailed them about in rough water.'

He smiled. 'That's right,' he said. 'That's how they do it. Where did you see them fishing like that?'

'Near Gex,' I said. 'Practically in Switzerland.'

He smiled reflectively. 'I know that country very well – very well indeed,' he said. 'Saint-Claude. Do you know Saint-Claude?'

I shook my head. 'I don't know the Jura. That's somewhere over by Morez, isn't it?'

'Yes – not very far from Morez.' He was silent for a few moments; we rested together in that quiet room. Presently he said: 'I wanted to try that wet fly fishing in those streams this summer. It's not bad fun, you know. You have to know where the fish go for their food. It's not just a matter of dabbing the flies about anywhere. You've got to place them just as carefully as a dry fly.'

'Strategy,' I said.

'That's the word. The strategy is really just the same.'

There was another of those comfortable pauses. Presently I said: 'It'll be some time before we can go fishing out there again.' So it was I who turned the conversation to the war. It's difficult to keep off the subject.

He said: 'Yes – it's a great pity. I had to come away before the water was fit to fish. It's not much good out there before the very end of May. Before then the water's all muddy and the rivers are running very full – the thawing snows, you know. Later than that, in August, there's apt to be very little water to fish in, and it gets too hot. The middle of June is the best time.'

I turned my head. 'You went out there this year?' Because the end of May that he had spoken of so casually was the time when the Germans had been pouring into France through Holland and Belgium, when we had been retreating on Dunkirk and when the French were being driven back to Paris and beyond. It didn't seem to be a terribly good time for an old man to have gone fishing in the middle of France.

He said 'I went out there in April. I meant to stay for the whole of the summer, but I had to come away.'

I stared at him, smiling a little. 'Have any difficulty in getting home?'

'No,' he said. 'Not really.'

'You had a car, I suppose?'

'No,' he said. 'I didn't have a car. I don't drive very well, and I had to give it up some years ago. My eyesight isn't what it used to be.'

'When did you leave Jura, then?' I asked.

He thought for a minute. 'June the eleventh,' he said at last. 'That was the day, I think.'

I wrinkled my brows in perplexity. 'Were the trains all right?' Because, in the course of my work, I had heard a good deal about conditions in France during those weeks.

He smiled. 'They weren't very good,' he said reflectively.

'How did you get along, then?'

He said: 'I walked a good deal of the way.'

As he spoke, there was a measured *crump . . . crump . . . crump . . . crump*, as a stick of four fell, possibly a mile away. The very solid building swayed a little, and the floors and windows creaked. We waited, tense and still. Then came the undulating wail of the sirens, and the sharp crack of gunfire from the park. The raid was on again.

'Damn and blast,' I said. 'What do we do now?'

The old man smiled patiently: 'I'm going to stay where I am.'

There was good sense in that. It's silly to be a hero to evade discomfort, but there were three very solid floors above us. We talked about it, as one does, studying the ceiling and wondering whether it would support the weight of the roof. Our reflections did not stir us from our chairs.

A young waiter came into the room, carrying a torch and with a tin hat in his hand.

He said: 'The shelter is in the basement, through the buttery door, sir.'

Howard said: 'Do we have to go there?'

'Not unless you wish to.'

I said: 'Are you going down there, Andrews?'

'No, sir. I'm on duty, in case of incendiary bombs, and that.'

'Well,' I said, 'get on and do whatever you've got to do. Then, when you've got a minute to spare, bring me a glass of Marsala. But go and do your job first.'

Howard said: 'I think that's a very good idea. You can bring me a glass of Marsala, too – between the incendiary bombs. You'll find me sitting here.'

'Very good, sir.'

He went away, and we relaxed again. It was about half-past ten. The waiter had turned out all the lights except for the one reading-lamp behind our heads, so that we sat there in a little pool of soft yellow light in the great shadowy room. Outside, the traffic noises, little enough in London at that time, were practically stilled. A few police whistles shrilled in the distance and a car went by at a high speed; then silence closed down upon the long length of Pall Mall, but for some gunfire in the distance.

Howard asked me: 'How long do you suppose we shall have to sit here?'

'Till it's over, I suppose. The last one went on for four hours.' I paused, and then I said: 'Will anyone be anxious about you?'

He said, rather quickly: 'Oh, no. I live alone, you see – in chambers.'

I nodded. 'My wife knows I'm here. I thought of ringing

her up, but it's not a very good thing to clutter up the lines during a raid.'

'They ask you not to do that,' he said.

Presently Andrews brought the Marsala. When he had gone away, Howard lifted up his glass and held it to the light. Then he remarked: 'Well, there are less comfortable ways of passing a raid.'

I smiled. 'That's true enough.' And then I turned my head. 'You said you were in France when all this started up. Did you come in for many air raids there?'

He put his glass down, seven-eighths full. 'Not real raids. There was some bombing and machine-gunning of the roads, but nothing very terrible.'

He spoke so quietly about it that it took a little time for me to realise what he had said. But then I ventured:

'It was a bit optimistic to go to France for a quiet fishing holiday, in April of this year.'

'Well, I suppose it was,' he replied thoughtfully. 'But I wanted to go.'

He said he had been very restless, that he had suffered from an urge, an imperious need to get away and to go and do something different. He was a little hesitant about his reasons for wanting to get away so badly, but then told me that he hadn't been able to get a job to do in the war.

They wouldn't have him in anything, I imagine because he was very nearly seventy years old. When war broke out he tried at once to get into the Special Constabulary; with his knowledge of the Law it seemed to him that police duty would suit him best. The police thought otherwise, having no use for constables of his age. Then he tried to become an Air Raid Warden, and suffered another disappointment. And then he tried all sorts of things.

It's very difficult for old people, for old men particularly, in a war. They cannot grow accustomed to the fact that there is little they can do to help; they suffer from frustration, and the war eats into them. Howard fell into the habit of ordering his life by the news bulletins upon the wireless. Each day he got up in time to hear the seven o'clock news, had his bath, shaved, and dressed and was down to hear the eight o'clock, and went on so all day till after the midnight news, when he retired to bed. Between the bulletins he worried about the news, and read every paper he could lay his hands upon till it was time to turn the wireless on again.

He lived in the country when the war broke out. He had a house at Market Saffron, not very far from Colchester. He had moved there from Exeter four years previously, after the death of his wife; as a boy he had been brought up in Market Saffron and he still had a few acquaintances in the neighbourhood. He went back there to spend the last years of his life. He bought an old country house, not very large, standing in about three acres of garden and paddock.

His married daughter came back from America and lived with him in 1938, bringing her little boy. She was married to a New York insurance man called Costello, Vice-President of his corporation and very comfortably off. She'd had a spot of bother with him. Howard didn't know the ins and outs of it and didn't bother about it much; privately, he was of the opinion that his daughter was to blame for the trouble. He was fond of his son-in-law, Costello. He didn't understand him in the least, but he liked him very well.

That's how he was living when the war broke out, with his daughter Enid and her little boy Martin, that his father would insist on calling Junior. That puzzled the old man very much.

Then the war broke out, and Costello began cabling for them to go back home to Long Island. And in the end they went. Howard backed up Costello and put pressure on his daughter, in the belief that a woman who is separated from her husband is never very happy. They went, and he was left to live alone at Market Saffron, with occasional week-end visits from his son John, a Squadron-Leader in the Royal Air Force.

Costello made a great effort, in cables many hundreds of words long, to get the old man to go too. He wasn't having any. He said that he was afraid of being in the way, that a third party would have spoilt the chance of reconciliation. But his real reason, he admitted, was that he didn't like America. He had crossed the Atlantic to stay with them when they had first been married, and he had no desire to repeat the experience. After nearly seventy years in a more equable climate he found New York intolerably hot and desperately cold in turns, and he missed the little courtesies to which he was accustomed in our feudal life. He liked his son-in-law, he loved his daughter, and her boy was one of the great interests in his life. Not all these motives were sufficient to induce him to exchange the comfort and security of England grappling in battle to the death for the strange discomforts of the land that was at peace.

So Enid and her boy sailed in October. He took them to Liverpool and saw them on the boat, and then he went back home. From then onwards he lived very much alone, though his widowed sister came and stayed with him for three weeks before Christmas, and John paid him several visits from Lincolnshire, where he had a squadron of Wellington bombers.

It was lonely for the old man, of course. In the ordinary way he would have been content with the duck-shooting and with his garden. He explained to me that he found his garden really more interesting in the winter than in the summer, because it was then that he could make his alterations. If he wanted to move a tree, or plant a new hedge, or dig out an old one – that was the time to do it. He took great pleasure in his garden, and was always moving things about.

The war spoilt all that. The news bulletins penetrated every moment of his consciousness till he could no longer take pleasure in the simple matters of his country life. He fretted that he could get nothing to do, and almost for the first occasion in his life the time hung heavily upon his hands. He poured his mind out irritably to the vicar one day, and that healer of sick souls suggested that he might take up knitting for the troops.

After that, he took to coming up to London for three days a week. He got himself a little one-room flat in bachelor chambers, and took most of his meals at the club. That made things easier for him. Travelling up to London on Tuesday absorbed the best part of a day, and travelling down again on Friday absorbed another one; in the meantime odd duties had accumulated at Market Saffron so that the week-end was comparatively busy. In this way he created the illusion that he had enough to do, and he grew happier in consequence.

Then, at the beginning of March, something happened that made a great change in his life. He didn't tell me what it was.

After that, he shut up the house at Market Saffron altogether, and came to London permanently to live mostly at the club. For two or three weeks he was busy enough, but after that time started to lie heavy on his hands again. And still he could get nothing to do in the war.

It was spring by then, and a most lovely spring it was. After the hard winter we had had, it was like opening a door. Each day he went for a walk in Hyde Park and Kensington Gardens, and watched the crocuses as they came out, and the daffodils. The club life suited him. He felt as he walked through the park during that marvellous spring that there was a great deal to be said for living in London, provided that you could get away from it from time to time.

As the sun grew stronger, the urge came on him to get away from England altogether for a while.

And really, there didn't seem to be any great reason why he should remain in England. The war in Finland was over, and on the western front there seemed to be complete stalemate. Matters in France were quite normal, except that upon certain days of the weeks you could only have certain kinds of food. It was then that he began to think about the Jura.

The high alpine valleys were too high for him; he had been to Pontresina three years previously and had been very short of breath. But the spring flowers in the French Jura were as beautiful as anything in Switzerland, and from the high ground up above Les Rousses you can see Mont Blanc. He wanted passionately to get where he could see mountains. 'I will lift up mine eyes unto the hills,' he said, 'from whence cometh my help.' That's how he felt about it.

He thought that if he went out there he would be just in time to see the flowers come thrusting through the snow; if he stayed on for a month or two he would come in for the fishing as the sun got warmer. He looked forward very much to fishing in those mountain streams. Very unspoilt they were, he said, and very fresh and quiet.

He wanted to see the spring, this year – to see as much of it as ever he could. He wanted to see all that new life coming on, replacing what is past. He wanted to soak himself in that. He wanted to see the hawthorn coming out along the river-banks, and the first crocuses in the fields. He wanted to see the new green of the rushes by the water's edge poking up through the dead stuff. He wanted to feel the new warmth of the sun, and the new freshness of the air. He wanted to savour all the spring there was this year – the whole of it. He wanted that more than anything else in the world, because of what had happened.

That's why he went to France.

He had much less difficulty in getting out of the country than he had expected. He went to Cook's, and they told him how to set about it. He had to get an exit permit, and that had to be done personally. The man in the office asked him what he wanted to leave the country for.

Old Howard coughed at him. 'I can't stand the spring weather in England,' he said. 'I've been indoors most of the winter. My doctors says I've got to get into a warmer climate.' A complacent doctor had given him a certificate.

'I see,' said the official. 'You want to go down to the south of France?'

'Not right down to the south,' he said. 'I shall spend a few days in Dijon and go to the Jura as soon as the snow is off the ground.'

The man wrote out a permit for three months, upon the grounds of health. So that wasn't very difficult.

Then the old man spent a deliriously happy two days with Hardy's, the fishing tackle makers in Pall Mall. He took it gently, half an hour in the morning and half an hour in the afternoon; in between he fingered and turned over his purchases, dreamed about fishing, and made up his mind what he would buy next . . .

He left London on the morning of April the 10th, the very morning that the news came through that Germany had invaded Denmark and Norway. He read the news in his paper in the train on the way to Dover, and it left him cold. A month previously he would have been frantic over it, jumping from wireless bulletin to newspaper and back to the wireless again. Now it passed him by as something that hardly concerned him any more. He was much more concerned whether he had brought with him enough gut casts and points. True, he was stopping for a day or two in Paris, but French gut, he said, is rotten stuff. They don't understand, and they make it so thick that the fish can't help seeing it, even with a wet fly.

His journey to Paris was not very comfortable. He got on to the steamer in Folkestone harbour at about eleven in the morning, and there they sat till the late afternoon. Trawlers and drifters and paddle-steamers and yachts, all painted grey and manned by naval ratings, came in and out of the harbour, but the cross-Channel steamer stayed at the quay. The vessel was crowded, and there weren't enough seats for lunch, and not enough food if there had been seats. Nobody could tell them what they were stopping for, although it was a pretty safe guess that it was a submarine.

At about four o'clock there were a number of heavy explosions out at sea, and soon after that they cast off and got away.

It was quite dark when they got to Boulogne, and things were rather disorganised. In the dim light the Douane took an age to pass the luggage, there was no train to meet the boat, and not enough porters to go round. He had to take a taxi to the station and wait for the next train to Paris, at about nine o'clock. It was a stopping train, crowded, and running very late. It was after one o'clock when they finally did get to Paris.

They had taken eighteen hours over a journey that takes six in normal times. Howard was tired, very tired indeed. His heart began to trouble him at Boulogne and he noticed people looking at him queerly; he knew that meant that he had gone a bad colour. However, he had a little bottle with him that he carried for that sort of incident; he took a dose of that when he got into the train and felt a good deal better.

He went to the Hotel Girodet, a little place just off the Champs Elysées near the top, that he had stayed at before. Most of the staff he knew had been called up for military service, but they were very kind to him and made him comfortable. He stayed in bed till lunch-time the first day and rested in his room most of the afternoon, but next morning he was feeling quite himself, and went out to the Louvre.

All his life he had found great satisfaction in pictures – real pictures, as he called them, to distinguish them from impressionism. He was particularly fond of the Flemish school. He spent some time that morning sitting on a bench in front of Chardin's still life of pipes and drinking-vessels on a stone table. And then, he told me, he went and had a look at the artist's portrait of himself. He took great pleasure in the strong, kind face of the man who had done such very good work, over two hundred years ago.

That's all he saw that morning at the Louvre. Just that chap, and his work.

He went on next day towards the Jura. He was still feeling a little shaky after the fatigue of the crossing, so that day he only went as far as Dijon. At the Gare de Lyons he bought a paper casually and looked it over, though he had lost all interest in the war. There was a tremendous amount of bother over Norway and Denmark, which didn't seem to him to be worth quite so much attention. It was a good long way away.

Normally that journey takes about three hours, but the railways were in a bad state of disorganisation. They told him that it was because of troop movements. The *Rapide* was an hour late in leaving Paris, and it lost another two hours on the way. It was nearly dinner-time when he reached

Dijon, and he was very thankful that he had decided to stop there. He had his bags carried to a little hotel just opposite the station, and they gave him a very good dinner in the restaurant. Then he took a cup of coffee and a *cointreau* in the café and went up to bed at about half-past nine, not too tired to sleep well.

He was really feeling very well next day, better than he had felt for a long time past. The change of air, added to the change of scene, had done that for him. He had coffee in his room and got up slowly; he went down at about ten o'clock and the sun was shining, and it was warm and fresh out in the street. He walked up through the town to the Hôtel de Ville and found Dijon just as he remembered it from his last visit, about eighteen months before. There was the shop where they had bought their berets, and he smiled again to see the name, *AU PAUVRE DIABLE*. And there was the shop where John had bought himself a pair of skis, but he didn't linger there for very long.

He had his lunch at the hotel and took the afternoon train on into the Jura: he found that the local trains were running better than the main line ones. He changed at Andelot and took the branch line up into the hills. All afternoon the little engine puffed along its single track, pulling its two old coaches through a country dripping with thawing snow. The snow slithered and cascaded off the slopes into the little streams that now were rushing torrents for a brief season. The pines were shooting with fresh green, but the meadows were still deep in a grey, slushy mess. In the high spots of the fields where grass was showing, he noticed a few crocuses. He'd come at the right time, and he was very, very glad of it.

The train stopped for half an hour at Morez, and then went on to Saint-Claude. It got there just at dusk. He had sent a telegram from Dijon to the Hôtel de la Haute

Montagne at Cidoton asking them to send a car down for him, because it's eleven miles and you can't always get a car in Saint-Claude. The hotel car was there to meet him, a ten-year-old Chrysler driven by the *concierge*, who was a diamond-cutter when he wasn't working at the hotel. But Howard only found that out afterwards; the man had come to the hotel since his last visit.

He took the old man's bags and put them in the back of the car, and they started off for Cidoton. For the first five miles the road runs up a gorge, turning in hairpin bends up the side of the mountain. Then, on the high ground, it runs straight over the meadows and between the woods. After a winter spent in London, the air was unbelievably sweet. Howard sat beside the driver, but he was too absorbed in the beauty of that drive in the fading light to talk much to him. They spoke once about the war, and the driver told him that almost every able-bodied man in the district had been called up. He himself was exempt, because the diamond dust had got into his lungs.

The Hôtel de la Haute Montagne is an old coaching-house. It has about fifteen bedrooms, and in the season it's a ski-ing centre. Cidoton is a tiny hamlet – fifteen or twenty cottages, no more. The hotel is the only house of any size in the place; the hills sweep down to it all round, fine slopes of pasture dotted here and there with pinewoods. It's very quiet and peaceful in Cidoton, even in the winter season when the village is filled with young French people on their skis. That was as it had been when he was there before.

It was dark when they drew up at the hotel. Howard went slowly up the stone steps to the door, the *concierge* following behind him with the bags. The old man pushed open the heavy oak door and went into the hall. By his side, the door leading into the *estaminet* flew open, and there was Madame Lucard, buxom and cheerful as she had been the year before, with the children round her and the maids grinning over her shoulder. Lucard himself was away with the *Chasseurs Alpins*.

They gave him a vociferous French welcome. He had not thought to find himself so well remembered, but it's not very common for English people to go deep into the Jura. They chattered at him nineteen to the dozen. Was he well? Had he made a good crossing of the *Manche*? He had stopped in Paris? And in Dijon also? That was good. It was very tiring to travel in this *sale* war. He had brought a fishing-rod with him this time, instead of skis? That was good. He would take a glass of Pernod with Madame?

And then, *Monsieur votre fils*, he was well too?

Well, they had to know. He turned away from her blindly. '*Madame*,' he said, '*mon fils est mort. Il est tombé de son avion, au-dessus de Heligoland Bight.*'

2

Howard settled down at Cidoton quite comfortably. The fresh mountain air did him a world of good; it revived his appetite and brought him quiet, restful sleep at night. The little rustic company of the *estaminet* amused and interested him, too. He knew a good deal of rural matters and he spoke good, slightly academic French. He was a good mixer and the farmers accepted him into their company, and talked freely to him of the matters of their daily life. It may be that the loss of his son helped to break the ice.

He did not find them noticeably enthusiastic for the war.

He was not happy for the first fortnight, but he was probably happier than he would have been in London. While the snow lasted, the slopes were haunted for him. In his short walks along the road before the woodland paths became available, at each new slope of snow he thought to see John come hurtling over the brow, stem-christie to a traverse, and vanish in a white flurry that sped down into the valley. Sometimes the fair-haired French girl, Nicole, who came from Chartres, seemed to be with him, flying along with him in the same flurry of snow. That was the most painful impression of all.

Presently as the sun grew stronger, the snow went away. There was the sound of tinkling water everywhere, and bare grass showed where there had been white slopes. Then flowers began to appear and his walks had a new interest. As the snow passed his bad dreams passed with it; the green flowering fields held no memories for him. He grew much more settled as the spring drew on.

Mrs Cavanagh helped him, too.

He had been worried and annoyed to find an English woman staying in the hotel, so far from the tourist track. He had not come to France to speak English or to think in English. For the first week he sedulously avoided her, together with her two children. He did not have to meet them. They spent a great part of their time in the salon; there were no other visitors in the hotel in between time. He lived mostly in his bedroom or else in the estaminet, where he played innumerable games of draughts with the habitués.

Cavanagh, they told him, was an official in the League of Nations at Geneva, not more than twenty miles away as the crow flies. He was evidently fearful of an invasion of Switzerland by the Germans, and had prudently sent his wife and children into Allied France. They had been at Cidoton for a month; each week-end he motored across the border to visit them. Howard saw him the first Saturday that he was there, a sandy-haired, worried-looking man of forty-five or so.

The following week-end Howard had a short talk with him. To the old solicitor, Cavanagh appeared to be oddly unpractical. He was devoted to the League of Nations even in this time of war.

'A lot of people say that the League has been a failure,' he explained. 'Now, I think that is very unfair. If you look at the record of that last twenty years you'll see a record of achievement that no other organisation can show. Look at what the League did in the matter of the drug traffic!' And so on.

About the war, he said: 'The only failure that can be laid to the account of the League is its failure to inspire the nations with faith in its ideals. And that means propaganda. And propaganda costs money. If the nations had spent one-tenth of what they have spent in armaments upon the League, there would have been no war.'

After half an hour of this, old Howard came to the conclusion that Mr Cavanagh was a tedious fellow. He bore with him from a natural politeness, and because the man was evidently genuine, but he made his escape as soon as he decently could. The extent of his sincerity was not made plain to Howard till the day he met Mrs Cavanagh in the woods, and walked a mile back to the hotel with her.

He found her a devoted echo of her man. 'Eustace would never leave the League,' she said. 'Even if the Germans were to enter Switzerland, he'd never leave Geneva. There's still such great work to be done.'

The old man looked at her over his spectacles. 'But would the Germans let him go on doing it if they got into Switzerland?'

'Why, of course they would,' she said. 'The League is international. I know, of course, that Germany is no longer a member of the League. But she appreciates our non-political activities. The League prides itself that it could function equally well in any country, or under any government. If it could not do that, it couldn't be said to be truly international, could it?'

'No,' said Howard, 'I suppose it couldn't.'

They walked on for a few steps in silence. 'But if Geneva really were invaded by the Germans,' he said at last, 'would your husband stay there?'

'Of course. It would be very disloyal if he didn't.' She paused, and then she said: 'That's why he sent me out here with the children, into France.'

She explained to him that they had no ties in England. For ten years they had lived in Geneva; both children had been born there. In that time they had seldom returned to England, even on holiday. It had barely occurred to them that she should take the children back to England, so far away from him. Cidoton, just across the border into France, was far enough.

'It's only just for a few weeks, until the situation clears a little,' she said placidly. 'Then we shall be able to go home.' To her, Geneva was home.

He left her at the entrance to the hotel, but next day at *déjeuner* she smiled at him when he came into the room, and asked him if he had enjoyed his walk.

'I went as far as the Pointe des Neiges,' he said courteously. 'It was delightful up there this morning, quite delightful.'

After that they often passed a word or two together, and he fell into the habit of sitting with her for a quarter of an hour each evening after dinner in the salon, drinking a cup of coffee. He got to know the children too.

There were two of them. Ronald was a dark-haired little boy of eight, whose toy train littered the floor of the salon with its tin lines. He was mechanical, and would stand fascinated at the garage door while the *concierge* laboured to induce ten-year-old spark-plugs to fire the mixture in the ten-year-old Chrysler. Old Howard came up behind him once.

'Could you drive a car like that?' he asked gently.

'*Mais oui – c'est facile, ça.*' French came more easily to this little boy than English. 'You climb up in the seat and steer with the wheel.'

'But could you start it?'

'You just push the button, *et elle va*. That's the 'lectric starter.' He pointed to the knob.

27

'That's right. But it would be a very big car for you to manage.'

The child said: 'Big cars are easier to drive than little ones. Have you got a car?'

Howard shook his head. 'Not now. I used to have one.'

'What sort was it?'

The old man looked down helplessly. 'I really forget,' he said. 'I think it was a Standard.'

Ronald looked up at him, incredulous. 'Don't you *remember*?'

But Howard couldn't.

The other child was Sheila, just five years old. Her drawings littered the floor of the salon; for the moment her life was filled with a passion for coloured chalks. Once as Howard came downstairs he found her sitting in a heap upon the landing at a turn of the staircase, drawing industriously on the fly-leaf of a book. The first tread of the flight served as a desk.

He stooped down by her. 'What are you drawing?'

She did not answer.

'Won't you show me?' he said. And then: 'The chalks are lovely colours.'

He knelt down rheumatically upon one knee. 'It looks like a lady.'

She looked up at him. 'Lady with a dog,' she said.

'Where's the dog?' He looked at the smudged pastel streaks.

She was silent. 'Shall I draw the dog, walking behind on a lead?' he said.

She nodded vigorously. Howard bent to his task, his knees aching. But his hand had lost whatever cunning it might once have had, and his dog became a pig.

Sheila said: 'Ladies don't take pigs for a walk.'

His ready wit had not deserted the solicitor. 'This

28

one did,' he said. 'This is the little pig that went to market.'

The child pondered this. 'Draw the little pig that stayed at home,' she said, 'and the little piggy eating roast beef.' But Howard's knees would stand no more of it. He stumbled to his feet. 'I'll do that for you tomorrow.'

It was only at that stage he realised that his picture of the lady leading a pig embellished the fly-leaf of *A Child's Life of Jesus*.

Next day after *déjeuner* she was waiting for him in the hall. 'Mummy said I might ask you if you wanted a sweet.' She held up a grubby paper bag with a sticky mass in the bottom.

Howard said gravely: 'Thank you very much.' He fumbled in the bag and picked out a morsel which he put into his mouth. 'Thank you, Sheila.'

She turned, and ran from him through the *estaminet* into the big kitchen of the inn. He heard her chattering in there in fluent French to Madam Lucard as she offered her sweets.

He turned, and Mrs Cavanagh was on the stairs. The old man wiped his fingers furtively upon the handkerchief in his pocket. 'They speak French beautifully,' he said.

She smiled. 'They do, don't they? The little school they go to is French-speaking, of course.'

He said: 'They just picked it up, I suppose?'

'Oh yes. We didn't have to teach it to them.'

He got to know the children slightly after that and passed the time of day with them whenever he met them alone; on their side they said: 'Good morning, Mr Howard,' as if it was a lesson that they had been taught – which indeed it was. He would have liked to get to know them better, but he was shy, with the diffidence of age. He used to sit and watch them playing in the garden underneath the pine-trees sometimes, mysterious games that he would have liked to have known about, that touched dim chords of memory sixty years back. He did have one success with them, however.

As the sun grew warmer and the grass drier he took to sitting out in the garden after *déjeuner* for half an hour, in a deck-chair. He was sitting so one day while the children played among the trees. He watched them covertly. It seemed that they wanted to play a game they called *attention* which demanded a whistle, and they had no whistle.

The little boy said: 'I can whistle with my mouth,' and proceeded to demonstrate the art.

His sister pursed up her immature lips and produced only a wet splutter. From his deck-chair the old man spoke up suddenly.

'I'll make you a whistle, if you like,' he said.

They were silent, staring at him doubtfully. 'Would you like me to make you a whistle?' he enquired.

'When?' asked Ronald.

'Now. I'll make you one out of a bit of that tree.' He nodded to a hazel bush.

They stared at him, incredulous. He got up from his chair and cut a twig the thickness of his little finger from the bush. 'Like this.'

He sat down again, and began to fashion a whistle with the pen-knife that he kept for scraping out his pipe. It was a trick that he had practised throughout his life, for John first and then for Enid when they had been children, more recently for little Martin Costello. The Cavanagh children stood by him watching his slow, wrinkled fingers as they worked; in their faces incredulity melted into interest. He stripped the bark from the twig, cut deftly with the little knife, and bound the bark back into place. He put it to his lips, and it gave out a shrill note.

They were delighted, and he gave it to the little girl, 'You can whistle with your mouth,' he said to Ronald, 'but she can't.'

'Will you make me one tomorrow?'

'All right, I'll make you one tomorrow.' They went off together, and whistled all over the hotel and through the village, till the bark crushed beneath the grip of a hot hand. But the whistle was still good for taking to bed, together with a Teddy and a doll called Mélanie.

'It was so very kind of you to make that whistle for the children,' Mrs Cavanagh said that night, over coffee. 'They were simply thrilled with it.'

'Children always like a whistle, especially if they see it made,' the old man said. It was one of the basic truths that he had learned in a long life, and he stated it simply.

'They told me how quickly you made it,' she said. 'You must have made a great many.'

'Yes,' he said, 'I've made a good many whistles in my time.' He fell into a reverie, thinking of all the whistles he had made for John and Enid, so many years ago, in the quiet garden of the house at Exeter. Enid who had grown up and married and gone to live in the United States. John, who had grown up and gone into the Air Force. John.

He forced his mind back to the present. 'I'm glad they liked it,' he said. 'I promised Ronald that I'd make him one tomorrow.'

Tomorrow was the tenth of May. As the old man sat in his deck-chair beneath the trees carving a whistle for Ronald, German troops were pouring into Holland, beating down the Dutch Army. The Dutch Air Force was flinging its full strength of forty fighting planes against the Luftwaffe. A thousand traitors leapt into activity; all through the day the parachutists dropped from the sky. In Cidoton the only radio happened to be switched off, and so Howard whittled at his hazel twig in peace.

It did not break his peace much when they switched it on. In Cidoton the war seemed very far away; with Switzerland to insulate them from the Germans the village was able to view the war dispassionately. Belgium was being invaded again, as in the last war; the *sale Boche!* This time Holland, too, was in it; so many more to fight upon the side of France. Perhaps they would not penetrate into France at all this time, with Holland to be conquered and assimilated first.

In all this, Howard acquiesced. He could remember very clearly how the war had gone before. He had been in it for a short time, in the Yeomanry, but had been quickly invalided out with rheumatic fever. The cockpit of Europe would take the shock of the fighting as it usually did; there was nothing new in that. In Cidoton, it made no change. He listened to the news from time to time in a detached manner, without great interest. Presently fishing would begin; the snow was gone from the low levels and the mountain streams were running less violently each day.

The retreat from Brussels did not interest him much; it had all happened before. He felt a trace of disquiet when Abbeville was reached, but he was no great strategist, and did not realise all that was involved. He got his first great shock when Leopold, King of the Belgians, laid down his arms upon the 29th May. That had not happened in the last war, and it upset him.

But on that day nothing could upset him for very long. He was going fishing for the first time next morning, and the evening was occupied in sorting out his gear, soaking his casts and selecting flies. He walked six miles next day and caught three blue trout. He got back tired and happy at about six o'clock, had dinner, and went up immediately to bed. In that way he missed the first radio broadcasts of the evacuation of Dunkirk.

Next day he was jerked finally from his complacence. He sat by the radio in the *estaminet* for most of the day, distressed and worried. The gallant retreat from the beaches stirred him as nothing had for months; for the first time he began to feel a desire to return to England. He knew that if he went, there would be nothing for him to do, but he wanted to be back. He wanted to be in the thick of things again, seeing the British uniforms in the streets, sharing the tension and anxiety. Cidoton irked him with its rustic indifference to the war. .

By the 4th June the last forces had left Dunkirk, Paris had had its one and only air-raid, and Howard had made up his mind. He admitted as much that night to Mrs Cavanagh.

'I don't like the look of things at all,' he said. 'Not at all. I think I shall go home. At a time like this, a man's place is in his own country.'

She looked at him, startled. 'But surely, you're not afraid that the Germans will come here, Mr Howard? They couldn't get as far as this.' She smiled reassuringly.

'No,' he said, 'they won't get much farther than they are now. But at the same time, I think I shall go home.' He paused, and then he said a little wistfully: 'I might be able to get into the A.R.P.'

She knitted on quietly. 'I shall miss having you to talk to in the evenings,' she said. 'The children will miss you, too.'

'It has been a great pleasure to have known them,' he said. 'I shall miss them.'

She said: 'Sheila enjoyed the little walk you took her for. She put the flowers in her tooth-mug.'

It was not the old man's way to act precipitately, but he gave a week's notice to Madame Lucard that night and planned to leave on the eleventh. He did it in the *estaminet*, and provoked a lively discussion on the ethics of his case, in which most of the village took part. At the end of an hour's discussion, and a round of Pernod, the general opinion was favourable to him. It was hard on Madame Lucard to lose her best guest, the gendarme said, and sad for them to lose their English *Camarade*, but without doubt an old soldier should be in his own country in these times. Monsieur was very right. But he would return, perhaps?

Howard said that he hoped to return within a very few weeks, when the dangerous stage of the war had passed.

Next day he began to prepare for his journey. He did not hurry over it because he meant to stay his week out. In fact, he had another day's fishing and caught another two blue trout. There was a lull in the fighting for a few days after the evacuation from Dunkirk and he went through a day of indecision, but then the Germans thrust again upon the Somme and he went on preparing to go home.

On the ninth of June Cavanagh appeared, having driven unexpectedly from Geneva in his little car. He seemed more worried and distrait than usual, and vanished into the bedroom with his wife. The children were sent out to play in the garden.

An hour later he tapped upon the door of Howard's bedroom. The old man had been reading in a chair and had dropped asleep, the book idle on his lap. He woke at the second tap, settled his spectacles, and said: 'Come in!'

He stared with surprise at his visitor, and got up. 'This is a great pleasure,' he said formally. 'But what brings you out here in the middle of the week? Have you got a holiday?'

Cavanagh seemed a little dashed. 'I've taken a day off,' he said after a moment. 'May I come in?'

'By all means.' The old man bustled round and cleared a heap of books from the only other chair in the room.

Then he offered his guest a cigarette. 'Won't you sit down?'

The other sat down diffidently. 'What do you think of the war?' he asked.

Howard said: 'I think it very serious. I don't like the news at all.'

'Nor do I. I hear you're going home?'

'Yes, I'm going back to England. I feel that at a time like this my place is there.'

There was a short silence. Then Cavanagh said: 'In Geneva we think that Switzerland will be invaded.'

Howard looked at him with interest. 'Do you, now! Is that going to be the next thing?'

'I think so. I think that it may happen very soon.'

There was a pause. Then Howard said: 'If that happened, what would you do?'

The little sandy-haired man from Geneva got up and walked over to the window. He stood for a moment looking out over the meadows and the pinewoods. Then he turned back into the room. 'I should have to stay in Geneva,' he said. 'I've got my work to do.'

'Would that be very – wise?'

'No,' said Cavanagh frankly. 'But it's what I have made up my mind to do.'

He came back and sat down again. 'I've been talking it over with Felicity,' he said. 'I've got to stay there. Even in German occupation there would still be work for us to do. It's not going to be pleasant. It's not going to be profitable. But it's going to be worth doing.'

'Would the Germans allow the League to function at all?'

'We have positive assurances that they will.'

'What does your wife think about it?' asked Howard.

'She thinks that it's the proper thing to do. She wants to come back to Geneva with me.'

'Oh . . .'

The other turned to him. 'It's really about that that I looked in to see you,' he said. 'If we do that, things may go hardly with us before the war is over. If the Allies win they'll win by the blockade. There won't be much to eat in any German territory.'

Howard stared at the little man in wonder. 'I suppose not.' He had not credited Cavanagh with such cool courage.

'It's the children,' the other said apologetically. 'We were thinking – Felicity was wondering . . . if you could possibly take them back to England with you, when you go.'

He went on hurriedly, before Howard could speak: 'It's only just to take them to my sister's house in Oxford, up on Boars Hill. As a matter of fact, I could send her a telegram and she could meet you at Southampton with the car, and drive them straight to Oxford. It's asking an awful lot, I'm afraid. If you feel you couldn't manage it . . . we'll understand.'

Howard stared at him. 'My dear chap,' he said, 'I should be only too glad to do anything I can to help. But I must tell you, that at my age I don't stand travel very well. I was quite ill for a couple of days in Paris, on my way out here. I'm nearly seventy, you know. It would be safer if you put your children in the care of somebody a little more robust.'

Cavanagh said: 'That may be so. But as a matter of fact, there is nobody. The alternative would be for Felicity to take the children back to England herself.'

There was a pause. The old man said: 'I see. She doesn't want to do that?'

The other shook his head. 'We want to be together,' he said, a little pitifully. 'It may be for years.'

Howard stared at him. 'You can count on me to do

anything within my power,' he said. 'Whether you would be wise to send the children home with me is something that you only can decide. If I were to die upon the journey it might cause a good deal of trouble, both for your sister in Oxford and for the children.'

Cavanagh smiled. 'I'm quite prepared to take that risk,' he said. 'It's a small one compared with all the other risks one has to take these days.'

The old man smiled slowly. 'Well, I've been going seventy years and I've not died yet. I suppose I may last a few weeks longer.'

'Then you'll take them?'

'Of course I will, if that's what you want me to do.'

Cavanagh went away to tell his wife, leaving the old man in a flutter. He had planned to stay in Dijon and in Paris for a night as he had done on the way out; it now seemed to him that it would be wiser if he were to travel straight through to Calais. Actually it meant no changes in his arrangements to do that, because he had booked no rooms and taken no tickets. The changes were in his plans; he had to get accustomed to the new idea.

Could he manage the two children by himself, or would it be wiser to engage a village girl from Cidoton to travel with them as far as Calais to act as a *bonne*? He did not know if a girl could be found to come with them. Perhaps Madame Lucard would know somebody . . .

It was only later that he realised that Calais was in German hands, and that his best route across the Channel would be by way of St Malo to Southampton.

He came down presently, and met Felicity Cavanagh in the salon. She caught his hand. 'It's so very, very kind of you to do this for us,' she said. It seemed to him that she had been crying a little.

'Not in the least,' he said. 'I shall enjoy having them as travelling companions.'

She smiled. 'I've just told them. They're simply thrilled. They're terribly excited to be going home with you.' It was the first time that he had heard her speak of England as home.

He broached the matter of a girl to her, and they went together to see Madame Lucard. But Cidoton proved to be incapable of producing anybody willing to go with them to St Malo, or even as far as Paris. 'It doesn't matter in the least,' said Howard. 'After all, we shall be home in twenty-four hours. I'm sure we shall get on famously together.'

She looked at him. 'Would you like me to come with you as far as Paris? I could do that, and then go back to Geneva.'

He said: 'Not at all – not at all. You stay with your man. Just tell me about their clothes and what they say, er, when they want to retire. Then you won't need to worry any more about them.'

He went up with her that evening to see them in bed. He said to Ronald: 'So you're coming back to England with me, eh, to stay with your auntie?'

The little boy looked up at him with shining eyes. 'Yes, *please!* Are we going in a train?'

Howard said: 'Yes, we'll be a long time in the train.'

'Will it have a steam engine, or a 'lectric one?'

'Oh – a steam engine, I think. Yes, certainly, a steam engine.'

'How many wheels will it have?' But this was past the old man's capacity.

Sheila piped up. 'Will we have dinner in the train?'

'Yes,' he said, 'you'll have your dinner in the train. I expect you'll have your tea and your breakfast in it too.'

'Oo . . . Oo,' she said. And then, incredulously, 'Breakfast in the train?'

Ronald stared at him. 'Where will we sleep?'

His father said: 'You'll sleep in the train, Ronnie. In a little bed to yourself.'

'Really sleep in the train?' He swung round to the old man. 'Mr Howard, please – may I sleep next to the engine?'

Sheila said: 'Me too. I want to sleep next to the engine.'

Presently their mother got them settled down to sleep. She followed the men downstairs. 'I'm fixing up with Madame Lucard to pack a hamper with all your meals,' she said. 'It'll be easier for you to give them their meals in the *wagon lit* than to bother with them in the restaurant car.'

Howard said: 'That's really very kind. It's much better that way.'

She smiled. 'I know what it is, travelling with children.'

He dined with them that night, and went early to bed. He was pleasantly tired, and slept very well; he woke early, as he usually did, and lay in bed revolving in his mind all the various matters that he had to attend to. Finally he got up, feeling uncommonly well. It did not occur to him that this was because he had a job to do, for the first time in many months.

The next day was spent in a flutter of business. The children were taking little with them in the way of luggage; one small portmanteau held the clothes for both of them. With their mother to assist him the old man learned the intricacies of their garments, and how they went to bed, and what they had to eat.

Once Mrs Cavanagh stopped and looked at him. 'Really,' she said, 'you'd rather that I came with you to Paris, wouldn't you?'

'Not in the least,' he said. 'I assure you, they will be quite all right with me.'

She stood silent for a minute. 'I believe they will,' she said slowly. 'Yes, I believe they'll be all right with you.'

She said no more about Paris.

Cavanagh had returned to Geneva, but he turned up again that night for dinner. He took Howard aside and gave him the money for their journey. 'I can't tell you how terribly grateful we are to you,' he muttered. 'It just makes all the difference to know that the kids will be in England.'

The old man said: 'Don't worry about them any more. They'll be quite safe with me. I've had children of my own to look after, you know.'

He did not dine with them that night, judging it better to leave them alone together with the children. Everything was ready for his journey; his portmanteaux were packed, his rods in the long tubular travelling-case. There was nothing more to be done.

He went up to his room. It was bright moonlight, and he stood for a while at his window looking out over the pastures and the woods towards the mountains. It was very quiet and still.

He turned uneasily from the window. It had no right to be so peaceful, here in the Jura. Two or three hundred miles to the north the French were fighting desperately along the Somme; the peace in Cidoton was suddenly unpleasant to him, ominous. The bustle and the occupation that his charge of the children had brought to him had changed his point of view; he now wanted very much to be in England, in a scene of greater action. He was glad to be leaving. The peace of Cidoton had helped him over a bad time, but it was time that he moved on.

Next morning all was bustle. He was down early, but the children and their parents were before him. They all had their *petit déjeuner* together in the dining-room; as a last lesson Howard learned to soften the crusts of the rolls for the children by soaking them in coffee. Then the old Chrysler was at the door to take them down to Saint-Claude.

The leave-taking was short and awkward. Howard had said everything that there was to say to the Cavanaghs, and the children were eager to climb into the car. It meant nothing to them that they were leaving their mother, possibly for years; the delicious prospect of a long drive to Saint-Claude and a day and a night in a real train with a steam engine filled their minds. Their father and mother kissed them, awkward and red-faced, but the meaning of the parting escaped the children altogether. Howard stood by, embarrassed.

Mrs Cavanagh muttered: 'Good-bye, my darlings,' and turned away.

Ronald said: 'May I sit by the driver?'

Sheila said: 'I want to sit by the driver, too.'

Howard stepped forward. 'You're both going to sit behind with me.' He bundled them into the back of the car. Then he turned back to their mother. 'They're very happy,' he said gently. 'That's the main thing, after all.'

He got into the car; it moved off down the road, and that miserable business was all over.

He sat in the middle of the seat with one child on each side of him for equity in the facilities for looking out. From time to time one saw a goat or a donkey and announced the fact in mixed French and English; then the other one would scramble over the old man to see the wonder. Howard spent most of the drive putting them back into their own seats.

Half an hour later they drew up at the station of Saint-Claude. The *concierge* helped them out of the car. 'They are pretty children,' he said in French to Howard. 'Their father and mother will be very sad, I think.'

The old man answered him in French: 'That is true. But in war, children should stay quiet in their own country. I think their mother has decided wisely.'

The man shrugged his shoulders; it was clear that he did not agree. 'How could war come to Cidoton?'

He carried their luggage to a first-class compartment and helped Howard to register the portmanteaux. Presently the little train puffed out up the valley, and Saint-Claude was left behind. That was the morning on which Italy declared war on the Allies, and the Germans crossed the Seine to the north of Paris.

3

Half an hour after leaving Morez the children were already bored. Howard was watching for this, and had made his preparations. In the attaché case that he carried with him he had secreted a number of little amusements for them, given to him by their mother. He pulled out a scribbling-pad and a couple of coloured pencils, and set them to drawing ships.

By the time they got to Andelot, three hours later, they had had their lunch; the carriage was littered with sandwich wrappings and with orange peel; an empty bottle that had contained milk stood underneath a seat. Sheila had had a little sleep, curled up by old Howard with her head resting on his lap; Ronnie had stood looking out of the window most of the way, singing a little song in French about numerals –

> *Un, deux, trois,*
> *Allons dans les bois –*
> *Quatre, cinq, six,*
> *Cueillir des cerises . . .*

Howard felt that he knew his numerals quite well by the time they got to Andelot.

He had to rouse Sheila from a heavy slumber as they drew

into the little country station where they had to change. She woke up hot and fretful and began to cry a little for no reason at all. The old man wiped her eyes, got out of the carriage, lifted the children down on to the platform, and then got back into the carriage for the hand luggage. There were no porters on the platform, but it seemed that that was inevitable in France in war-time. He had not expected it to be different.

He walked along the platform carrying the hand luggage, with the two children beside him; he modified his pace to suit their rate of walking, which was slow. At the *Bureau*, he found a stout, black-haired stationmaster.

Howard enquired if the *Rapide* from Switzerland was likely to be late.

The man said that the *Rapide* would not arrive. No trains from Switzerland would arrive.

Dumbfounded, Howard expostulated. It was intolerable that one had not been told that at Saint-Claude. How, then, could one proceed to Dijon?

The stationmaster said that Monsieur might rest tranquil. A train would run from the frontier at Vallorbes to Dijon. It was incessantly expected. It had been incessantly expected for two hours.

Howard returned to the children and his luggage, annoyed and worried. The failure of the *Rapide* meant that he could not travel through to Paris in the train from Andelot, but must make a change at Dijon. By the time he got there it would be evening, and there was no knowing how long he would have to wait there for a train to Paris, or whether he could get a sleeping berth for the children. Travelling by himself it would have been annoying: with two children to look after it became a serious matter.

He set himself to amuse them. Ronnie was interested in the railway trucks and the signals and the shunting engine; apart from his incessant questions about matters that Howard did not understand he was very little trouble. Sheila was different. She was quite unlike the child that he had known in Cidoton, peevish and fretful, and continually crying without energy. The old man tried a variety of ways to rouse her interest, without a great deal of success.

An hour and forty minutes later, when he was thoroughly worn out, the train for Dijon pulled into the station. It was very full, but he managed to find one seat in a first-class carriage and took Sheila on his knee, where she fell asleep again before so very long. Ronnie stood by the door looking out of the window, chattering in French to a fat old woman in a corner.

Presently this woman leaned forward to Howard. She said: 'Your little one has fever, is it not so?'

Startled, he said in French: 'But no. She is a little tired.'

She fixed him with beady black eyes. 'She has a fever. It is not right to bring a child with fever in the train. It is not hygienic. I do not like to travel with a child that has a fever.'

'I assure you, madame,' he said, 'you deceive yourself.' But a horrible suspicion was creeping over him.

She appealed to the rest of the carriage. 'I,' she ejaculated, '– it is I who deceive myself, then! Let me tell you, m'sieur, it is not I who deceive myself. But no, certainly. It is you, m'sieur, truly, you who are deceived. I tell you that your little one has fever, and you do very wrong to bring her in a train with others who are healthy. Look at her colour, and her skin! She has scarlet fever, or chicken-pox, or some horrible disease that clean people do not get.' She turned vehemently to the others in the carriage. 'Imagine, bringing a child in that condition in the train!'

There was a grunt from the other occupants. One said: 'It is not correct. It should not be allowed.'

Howard turned to the woman. 'Madame,' he said, 'you have children of your own, I think?'

She snorted at him. 'Five,' she said. 'But never have I travelled with a child in that condition. It is not right, that.'

He said: 'Madame, I ask for your help. These children are not my own, but I am taking them to England for a friend, because in these times it is better that children should be in their own country. I did not know the little one was feverish. Tell me, what would you do, as her mother?'

She shrugged her shoulder, still angry. 'I? I have nothing to do with it at all, m'sieur, I assure you of that. I would say, let children of that age stay with their mother. That is the place for such children. It is getting hot and travelling in trains that gives children fever.'

With a sinking heart Howard realised that there was some truth in what she said. From the other end of the carriage somebody said: 'English children are very often ill. The mothers do not look after their children properly. They expose them to currents of air and then the children get fever.'

There was general agreement in the carriage. Howard turned again to the woman. 'Madame,' he said, 'do you think this fever is infectious? If it is so, I will get out at the next station. But as for me, I think she is only tired.'

The little beady eyes of the old peasant woman fixed him. 'Has she got spots?'

'I – I don't think so. I don't know.'

She snorted. 'Give her to me.' She reached out and took Sheila from him, settled her on a capacious lap, and deftly removed her coat. With quick fingers she undid the child's clothes and had a good look at her back and front. 'She has no spots,' she said, replacing the garments. 'But fever – poor little one, she is hot as fire. It is not right to expose a child in this condition, m'sieur. She should be in bed.'

Howard reached out for Sheila and took her back; the Frenchwoman was certainly right. He thanked her for her help. 'It is clear to me that she must go to bed when we arrive at Dijon,' he said. 'Should she see a doctor?'

The old woman shrugged her shoulders. 'It is not necessary. A tisane from the chemist, and she will be well. But you must not give her wine while she has fever. Wine is very heating to the blood.'

Howard said: 'I understand, madame. She shall not have wine.'

'Not even mixed with water, or with coffee.'

'No. She should have milk?'

'Milk will not hurt her. Many people say that children should drink as much milk as wine.' This provoked a discussion upon infant welfare that lasted till they got to Dijon.

The station at Dijon was a seething mass of soldiers. With the utmost difficulty Howard got the children and his bags out of the train. He had an attaché case and a suitcase and the tin tube that held his rods with him in the carriage; the rest of his luggage with the little portmanteau that held the children's clothes was registered through to Paris. Carrying Sheila in his arms and leading Ronnie by the hand, he could not carry any of his luggage; he was forced to leave everything in a corner of the station platform and thrust his way with the two children through the crowd towards the exit.

The square before the station was a mass of lorries and troops. He threaded his way through and across the road to the hotel that he had stayed at before, startled and bewildered by the evident confusion of the town. He forced his way through to the hotel with the children; at the desk the girl recognised him, but told him that all the rooms were taken by the military.

'But, mademoiselle,' he said, 'I have a sick child to look after.' He explained.

The girl said: 'It is difficult for you, m'sieur. But what can I do?'

He smiled slowly. 'You can go and fetch Madame, and perhaps it will be possible for us to arrange something.'

Twenty minutes later he was in possession of a room with one large double bed, and apologising to an indignant French subaltern whose capitaine had ordered him to double up with another officer.

The *bonne*, a stout, untidy woman bulging out of her clothes, bustled about and made the room tidy. 'The poor little one,' she said. 'She is ill – yes? Be tranquil, monsieur. Without doubt, she has a little chill, or she has eaten something bad. All will be well, two days, three days, perhaps. Then she will be quite well again.' She smoothed the bed and crossed to Howard, sitting on a chair still holding Sheila in his arms. 'There, monsieur. All is now ready.'

The old man looked up at her. 'I thank you,' he said courteously. 'One thing more. If I put her to bed now, would you come back and stay with her while I go to get a doctor?'

The woman said: 'But certainly, monsieur. The poor little one.' She watched him as he began to undress Sheila on his lap; at the disturbance she began to cry again. The Frenchwoman smiled broadly, and began a stream of motherly French chatter to the child, who gradually stopped crying. In a minute or so Howard had surrendered Sheila to her, and was watching. The *bonne* looked up at him. 'Go and look for your doctor, monsieur, if you wish. I will stay with them for a little.'

He left them, and went down to the desk in the hall, and asked where he could find a doctor. In the thronging crowd the girl paused for a moment. 'I do not know, m'sieur . . . yes. One of the officers dining in the restaurant – he is a *médecin major*.'

The old man pressed into the crowded restaurant. Practically every table was taken by officers, for the most part glum and silent. They seemed to the Englishman to be a fat, untidy-looking lot; about half of them were unshaven. After some enquiry he found the *médecin major* just finishing his meal, and explained the position to him. The man took up his red velvet cap and followed him upstairs.

Ten minutes later he said: 'Be easy, monsieur. She must stay warm in bed tomorrow, and perhaps longer. But tomorrow I think that there will be no fever any more.'

Howard asked: 'What has she got?'

The man shrugged his shoulders indifferently. 'She is not infectious. Perhaps she has been hot, and playing in a current of air. Children, you understand, get fever easily. The temperature goes up quite high and very quickly. Then in a few hours, down again . . .'

He turned away. 'Keep her in bed, monsieur. And light food only; I will tell Madame below. No wine.'

'No,' said Howard. He took out his note-case. 'Without doubt,' he said, 'there is a fee.'

A note passed. The Frenchman folded it and put it in the breast pocket of his tunic. He paused for a moment. 'You go to England?' he enquired.

Howard nodded. 'I shall take them to Paris as soon as she can travel, and then to England by St Malo.'

There was a momentary silence. The fat, unshaven officer stood for a moment staring at the child in the bed. At last he said: 'It may be necessary that you should go to Brest. Always, there will be boats for England at Brest.'

49

The old man stared at him. 'But there is a service from St Malo.'

The doctor shrugged his shoulders. 'It is very near the Front. Perhaps there will be only military traffic there.' He hesitated, and then said: 'It seems that the *sales Boches* have crossed the Seine, near Rheims. Only a few, you understand. They will be easily thrown back.' He spoke without assurance.

Howard said quietly: 'That is bad news.'

The man said bitterly: 'Everything to do with this war is bad news. It was a bad day for France when she allowed herself to be dragged into it.'

He turned and went downstairs. Howard followed him, and got from the restaurant a jug of cold milk and a few little plain cakes for the children and, as an afterthought, a couple of feet of bread for his own supper. He carried these things through the crowded hall and up the stairs to his own room, afraid to leave the children very long.

Ronnie was standing at the window, staring out into the street. 'There's lots and lots of camions and motors at the station,' he said excitedly. 'And guns, too. Real guns, with motors pulling them! May we go down and see?'

'Not now,' said the old man. 'It's time you were in bed.'

He gave the children their supper of cakes, and milk out of a tooth-glass; Sheila seemed cooler, and drank her milk with very little coaxing. Then it was time to put Ronnie to bed in the big bed beside his sister. The little boy asked: 'Where are my pyjamas?'

Howard said. 'At the station. We'll put you into bed in your shirt for a start, just for fun. Then I'll go and get your pyjamas.'

He made a game of it with them, and tucked them up carefully one at each side of the big bed, with a bolster down the middle. 'Now you be good,' he said. 'I'm just going to get the luggage. I'll leave the light on. You won't be afraid?'

Sheila did not answer; she was already nearly asleep, curled up, flushed and tousled on the pillow. Ronnie said sleepily: 'May we see the guns and the camions tomorrow?'

'If you're good.'

He left them, and went down to the hall. The restaurant and the café were more crowded than ever; in the throng there was no hope at all of getting anyone to help him with the luggage. He pushed his way to the door and went out into the street, bewildered at the atmosphere of the town, and more than a little worried.

He found the station yard thronged with lorries and guns, with a few light tanks. Most of the guns were horse-drawn; the teams stood in their harness by the limbers as if ready to move on at any moment. Around them lorries rumbled in the darkness, with much melodious shouting in the broad tones of the southern French.

The station, again, was thronged with troops. They covered all the platforms, smoking and spitting wearily, squatting upon the dirty asphalt in the half-light, resting their backs against anything that offered. Howard crossed to the arrival platform and searched painstakingly for his luggage among the recumbent forms. He found the tin case with his rods and he found the small attaché case; the suitcase had vanished, nor could he discover any trace of the registered luggage.

He had not expected any more, but the loss of the suitcase was a serious matter. He knew that when he got to Paris he would find the registered luggage waiting for him in the *consigne*, were it six months later. But the suitcase had apparently been stolen; either that, or it had been placed in safe keeping by some zealous railway official. In the circumstances that did not seem probable. He would look for it in the morning; in the meantime they must all get on without pyjamas for the night. He made his way back to the hotel, and up to the bedroom again.

Both children were sleeping; Sheila was hot and restless and had thrown off most of her coverings. He spread them over her more lightly, and went down to the restaurant to see if he could get a meal for himself. A tired waiter refused point-blank to serve him, there was no food left in the hotel. Howard bought a small bottle of brandy in the café, and went up to the bedroom again, to dine off brandy and water, and his length of bread.

Presently he stretched himself to sleep uneasily in the arm-chair, desperately worried over what the next day would bring. One fact consoled him; he had his rods, quite safe.

Dawn came at five and found him still dozing uneasily in the chair, half covered by the dust-cover from the bed. The children woke soon after that and began chattering and playing in the bed; the old man stirred and sat up stiffly in his chair. He rubbed a hand over his face; he was feeling very ill. Then the children claimed his attention and he got up and put them right.

There was no chance of any further sleep; already there was much tramping to and fro in the hotel. In the station yard outside his window, lorries, tanks, and guns were on the move; the grinding of the caterpillar tracks, the roar of exhausts, the chink of harness and the stamping of the teams made up a melody of war. He turned back to the children; Sheila was better, but still obviously unwell. He brought the basin to the bed and washed her face and arms; then he combed her hair with the small pocket comb that he had found in the attaché case, one of the few small toilet articles he had. He took her temperature, under the arm for fear that she might chew on the thermometer.

It came out a degree above normal; he tried vainly to recall how much he should add on for the arm. In any case, it didn't matter much; she'd have to stay in bed. He got Ronnie up, washed him, and set him to dress himself; then he sponged over his own face and rang the bell for the *femme de chambre*. He was unshaven, but that could wait.

She came presently, and exclaimed when she saw the chair and coverlet: 'Monsieur has slept so?' she said. 'But there was room in bed for all of you!'

He felt a little foolish. 'The little one is ill,' he said. 'When a child is ill, she should have room. I was quite comfortable.'

Her eyes softened, and she clucked her tongue again. 'Tonight I will find another mattress,' she said. 'Be assured, monsieur, I will arrange something.'

He ordered coffee and rolls and jam; she went away and came back presently with a loaded tray. As she set it down upon the dressing-table, he ventured: 'I must go out this morning to look for my luggage, and to buy a few things. I will take the little boy with me; I shall not be very long. Would you listen for the little girl, in case she cries?'

The woman beamed at him. 'Assuredly. But it will not be necessary for monsieur to hurry. I will bring *la petite* Rose, and she can play with the little sick one.'

Howard said: 'Rose?'

He stood for ten minutes, listening to a torrent of family history. Little Rose was ten years old, the daughter of the woman's brother, who was in England. No doubt monsieur had met her brother? Tenois was the name, Henri Tenois. He was in London, the wine waiter at the Hotel Dickens, in Russell Square. He was a widower, so the *femme de chambre* made a home for *la petite* Rose. And so on, minute after minute.

Howard had to exercise a good deal of tact to get rid of her before his coffee cooled.

An hour later, spruce and shaved and leading Ronnie by the hand, he went out into the street. The little boy, dressed in beret, overcoat, and socks, looked typically French; by contrast Howard in his old tweed suit looked very English. For ten minutes he fulfilled his promise in the market square, letting the child drink in his fill of camions, guns, and tanks. They stopped by one caterpillar vehicle, smaller than the rest.

'*Celui-ci*,' said Ronnie clearly, '*c'est un char de combat.*'

The driver smiled broadly. 'That's right,' he said in French.

Howard said in French: 'I should have called it a tank, myself.'

'No, no, no,' the little boy said earnestly. 'A tank is much bigger, monsieur. Truly.'

The driver laughed. 'I've got one myself just like that, back in Nancy. He'll be driving one of these before he's much older, *le petit chou.*'

They passed on, and into the station. For half an hour they searched the platforms, still thronged with the tired troops, but found no sign of the lost suitcase. Nor could the overworked and worried officials give any help. At the end of that time Howard gave it up; it would be better to buy a few little things for the children that he could carry in the attaché case when they moved on. The loss of a suitcase was not an unmixed disaster for a man with a weak heart in time of war.

They left the station and walked up towards the centre of the town to buy pyjamas for the children. They bought some purple sweets called *cassis* to take back with them for

Sheila, and they bought a large green picture-book called *Babar the Elephant*. Then they turned back to the hotel.

Ronnie said presently: 'There's a motor-car from England, monsieur. What sort is it?'

The old man said: 'I don't suppose I can tell you that.' But he looked across the road to the filling-station. It was a big open touring car, roughly sprayed dull green all over, much splashed and stained with mud. It was evidently weeks since it had had a wash. Around it, two or three men were bustling to get it filled with petrol, oil, and water. One of them was manipulating the air hose at the wheels.

One of the men seemed vaguely familiar to the old man. He stopped and stared across the road, trying to place where they had met. Then he remembered; it was in his club six months before. The man was Roger Dickinson; something to do with a newspaper. The *Morning Record* – that was it. He was quite a well-known man in his own line.

Howard crossed the road to him, leading Ronnie by the hand. 'Morning,' he said. 'Mr Roger Dickinson, isn't it?'

The man turned quickly, cloth in hand; he had been cleaning off the windscreen. Recognition dawned in his eyes. 'I remember,' he said. 'In the Wanderers' Club . . .'

'Howard is the name.'

'I remember.' The man stared at him. 'What are you doing now?'

The old man said: 'I'm on my way to Paris, but I'm hung up here for a few days, I'm afraid.' He told Dickinson about Sheila.

The newspaperman said: 'You'd better get out, quick.'

'Why do you say that?'

The newspaperman stared at him, turning the soiled cloth over in his hands. 'Well, the Germans are across the Marne.' The old man stared at him. 'And now the Italians are coming up from the south.'

He did not quite take in the latter sentence. 'Across the Marne?' he said. 'Oh, that's very bad. Very bad indeed. But what are the French doing?'

'Running like rabbits,' said Dickinson.

There was a momentary silence. 'What did you say that the Italians were doing?'

'They've declared war on France. Didn't you know?'

The old man shook his head. 'Nobody told me that.'

'It only happened yesterday. The French may not have announced it yet, but it's true enough.'

By their side a little petrol flooded out from the full tank on to the road; one of the men removed the hose and slammed the snap catch of the filler cap with a metallic clang. 'That's the lot,' he said to Dickinson. 'I'll slip across and get a few *brioches*, and then we'd better get going.'

Dickinson turned to Howard. 'You must get out of this,' he said. 'At once. You'll be all right if you can get to Paris by tonight – at least, I think you will. There are boats still running from St Malo.'

The old man stared at him. 'That's out of the question, Dickinson. The other child has got a temperature.'

The man shrugged his shoulders. 'Well, I tell you honestly, the French won't hold. They're broken now – already. I'm not being sensationalist. It's true.'

Howard stood staring up the street. 'Where are you making for?'

'I'm going down into Savoy to see what the Italians are doing in that part. And then, we're getting out. Maybe Marseilles, perhaps across the frontier into Spain.'

The old man smiled. 'Good luck,' he said. 'Don't get too near the fighting.'

The other said: 'What are you going to do, yourself?'

'I don't quite know. I'll have to think about it.'

He turned away towards the hotel, leading Ronnie by the

hand. A hundred yards down the road the mud-stained, green car came softly up behind, and edged into the kerb beside him.

Dickinson leaned out of the driver's seat. 'Look, Howard,' he said. 'There's room for you with us, with the two kids as well. We can take the children on our knees all right. It's going to be hard going for the next few days; we'll be driving all night, in spells. But if you can be ready in ten minutes with the other kid, I'll wait.'

The old man stared thoughtfully into the car. It was a generous offer, made by a generous man. There were four of them already in the car, and a great mass of luggage; it was difficult to see how another adult could be possibly squeezed in, let alone two children. It was an open body, with an exiguous canvas hood and no side screens. Driving all night in that through the mountains would be a bitter trial for a little girl of five with a temperature.

He said: 'It's very, very kind of you. But really, I think we'd better make our own way.'

The other said: 'All right. You've plenty of money, I suppose?'

The old man reassured him on that point, and the big car slid away and vanished down the road. Ronnie watched it, half crying. Presently he sniffed, and Howard noticed him.

'What's the matter?' he said kindly. 'What is it?'

There was no answer. Tears were very near.

Howard searched his mind for childish trouble. 'Was it the motor-car?' he said. 'Did you think we were going to have a ride in it?'

The little boy nodded dumbly.

The old man stooped and wiped his eyes. 'Never mind,' he said. 'We'll wait till Sheila gets rid of her cold, and then we'll all go for a ride together.' It was in his mind to hire a car, if possible, to take them all the way from Dijon to St Malo and the boat. It would cost a good bit of money, but the emergency seemed to justify the expense.

'Soon?'

'Perhaps the day after tomorrow, if she's well enough to enjoy it with us.'

'May we go and see the *camions* and the *chars de combat* after *déjeuner*?'

'If they're still there we'll go and see them, just for a little.' He must do something to make up for the disappointment. But when they reached the station yard, the lorries and the armoured cars were gone. There were only a few decrepit-looking horses picketed beneath the tawdry advertisements for Byrrh and Pernod.

Up in the bedroom things were very happy. *La petite* Rose was there, a shy little girl with long black hair and an advanced maternal instinct. Already Sheila was devoted to her. *La petite* Rose had made a rabbit from two of Howard's dirty handkerchiefs and three little bits of string, and this rabbit had a burrow in the bedclothes on Ronnie's side of the bed; when you said 'Boo' he dived back into his burrow, manipulated ingeniously by *la petite* Rose. Sheila, bright-eyed, struggled to tell old Howard all about it in mixed French and English. In the middle of their chatter three aeroplanes passed very low over the station and the hotel.

Howard undid his parcels, and gave Sheila the picture-book about Babar the Elephant. Babar was an old friend of *la petite* Rose, and well known; she took the book and drew Ronnie to the bed, and began to read the story to them. The little boy soon tired of it; aeroplanes were more in his line, and he went and leaned out of the window hoping to see another one go by.

Howard left them there, and went down to the hall of

the hotel to telephone. With great difficulty, and great patience, he got through at last to the hotel at Cidoton; obviously he must do his best to let Cavanagh know the difficulties of the journey. He spoke to Madame Lucard, but the Cavanaghs had left the day before, to go back to Geneva. No doubt they imagined that he was practically in England by that time.

He tried to put a call through to Cavanagh at the League of Nations in Geneva, and was told curtly that the service into Switzerland had been suspended. He enquired about the telegraph service, and was told that all telegrams to Switzerland must be taken personally to the *Bureau de Ville* for censoring before they could be accepted for despatch. There was said to be a very long queue at the censor's table.

It was time for *déjeuner*; he gave up the struggle to communicate with Cavanagh for the time being. Indeed, he had been apathetic about it from the start. With the clear vision of age he knew that it was not much good; if he should get in touch with the parents it would still be impossible for him to cross the border back to them, or for them to come to him. He would have to carry on and get the children home to England as he had undertaken to do; no help could come from Switzerland.

The hotel was curiously still, and empty; it seemed today that all the soldiers were elsewhere. He went into the restaurant and ordered lunch to be sent up to the bedroom on a tray, both for himself and for the children.

It came presently, brought by the *femme de chambre*. There was much excited French about the pictures of Babar, and about the handkerchief rabbit. The woman beamed all over; it was the sort of party that she understood.

Howard said: 'It has been very, very kind of you to let

59

la petite Rose be with *la petite* Sheila. Already they are friends.'

The woman spoke volubly. 'It is nothing, monsieur – nothing at all. Rose likes more than anything to play with little children, or with kittens, or young dogs. Truly, she is a little mother, that one.' She rubbed the child's head affectionately. 'She will come back after *déjeuner*, if monsieur desires?'

Sheila said: 'I want Rose to come back after *déjeuner*, Monsieur Howard.'

He turned slowly: 'You'd better go to sleep after *déjeuner*.' He turned to the woman. 'If she could come back at four o'clock?' To Rose: 'Would you like to come and have tea with us this afternoon – English tea?'

She said shyly: '*Oui, monsieur.*'

She went away and Howard gave the children their dinner. Sheila was still hot with a slight temperature. He put the tray outside the door when they had finished, and made Ronnie lie down on the bed with his sister. Then he stretched out in the arm-chair, and began to read to them from a book given to him by their mother, called *Amelianne at the Circus*. Before very long the children were asleep: Howard laid down the book and slept for an hour himself.

Later in the afternoon he walked up through the town again to the *Bureau de Ville*, leading Ronnie by the hand, with a long telegram to Cavanagh in his pocket. He searched for some time for the right office, and finally found it, picketed by an anxious and discontented crowd of French people. The door was shut. The censor had closed the office and gone off for the evening, nobody knew where. The office would be open again at nine in the morning.

'It is not right, that,' said the people. But it appeared that there was nothing to be done about it.

Howard walked back with Ronnie to the hotel. There were troops in the town again, and a long convoy of lorries blocked the northward road near the station. In the station yard three very large tanks were parked, bristling with guns, formidable in design but dirty and unkempt. Their tired crews were refuelling them from a tank lorry, working slowly and sullenly, without enthusiasm. A little chill shot through the old man as he watched them bungling their work. What was it Dickinson had said? 'Running like rabbits.'

It could not possibly be true. The French had always fought magnificently.

At Ronnie's urgent plea they crossed to the square, and spent some time examining the tanks. The little boy told him: 'They can go right over walls and houses even. Right over!'

The old man stared at the monsters. It might be true, but he was not impressed with what he saw. 'They don't look very comfortable,' he said mildly.

Ronnie scoffed at him. 'They go ever so fast, and all the guns go bang, bang, bang.' He turned to Howard. 'Are they going to stay here all night?'

'I don't know. I expect they will. Come on, now; Sheila will want her tea. I expect you want yours, too.'

Food was a magnet, but Ronnie looked back longingly over his shoulder. 'May we come and see them tomorrow?'

'If they're still here.'

Things were still happy in the bedroom. *La petite* Rose, it seemed, knew a game which involved the imitation of animals in endless repetition—

My great-aunt lives in Tours,
In a house with a cherry-tree

With a little mouse (squeak, squeak)
And a big lion (roar, roar)
And a wood pigeon (coo, coo) . . .

and so on quite indefinitely. It was a game that made no great demand on the intelligence, and Sheila wanted nothing better. Presently, they were all playing it; it was so that the *femme de chambre* found them.

She came in with the tea, laughing all over her face. 'In Touraine I learned that, as a little girl, myself,' she said. 'It is pretty, is it not? All children like "my great-aunt lives in Tours" – always, always. In England, monsieur, do the children play like that?'

'Much the same,' he said. 'Children in every country play the same games.'

He gave them their milk and bread and butter and jam. Near the *Bureau de Ville* he had seen a shop selling ginger-bread cakes, the tops of which were covered in crystallised fruits and sweets. He had bought one of these; as he was quite unused to housekeeping it was three times as large as was necessary. He cut it with his pen-knife on the dressing-table and they all had a slice. It was a very merry tea-party, so merry that the grinding of caterpillar tracks and the roaring of exhausts outside the window passed them by unnoticed.

They played a little more after tea; then he washed the children as the *femme de chambre* re-made the bed. She helped him to undress them and put them into their new pyjamas; then she held Sheila on her capacious lap while the old man took her temperature carefully under the arm. It was still a degree or so above normal, though the child was obviously better; whatever had been wrong with her was passing off. It would not be right, he decided, to travel on the next day; he had no wish to be held up with another illness in less comfortable surroundings. But on the day after that, he thought it should be possible to get away. If they started very early in the morning they would get through to St Malo in the day. He would see about the car that night.

Presently, both the children were in bed, and kissed good night. He stood in the passage outside the room with the *femme de chambre* and her little girl. 'Tonight, monsieur,' she said, 'presently, when they are asleep, I will bring a mattress and make up a bed for monsieur on the floor. It will be better than the arm-chair, that.'

'You are very kind,' he said. 'I don't know why you should be so very, very good to us. I am most grateful.'

She said: 'But monsieur, it is you who are kind . . .'

He went down to the lobby, wondering a little at the effusive nature of the French.

Again the hotel was full of officers. He pushed his way to the desk and said to the girl: 'I want to hire a car, not now, but the day after tomorrow – for a long journey. Can you tell me which garage would be the best?'

She said: 'For a long journey, monsieur? How far?'

'To St Malo, in Normandy. The little girl is still not very well. I think it will be easier to take her home by car.'

She said doubtfully: 'The Garage Citroën would be the best. But it will not be easy, monsieur. You understand – the cars have all been taken for the army. It would be easier to go by train.'

He shook his head. 'I'd rather go by car.'

She eyed him for a moment. 'Monsieur is going away, then, the day after tomorrow?'

'Yes, if the little girl is well enough to travel.'

She said, awkwardly: 'I am desolated, but it will be necessary for monsieur to go then, at the latest. If the little one is still ill, we will try to find a room for monsieur in the town. But we have heard this afternoon, the hotel is to be taken over tomorrow by the *Bureau Principal* of the railway, from Paris.'

He stared at her. 'Are they moving the offices from Paris, then?'

She shook her head. 'I only know what I have told you, monsieur. All our guests must leave.'

He was silent for a minute. Then he said: 'What did you say was the name of the garage?'

'The Garage Citroën, monsieur. I will telephone and ask them, if you wish?'

He said: 'Please do.'

She turned away and went into the box; he waited at the desk, worried and anxious. He felt that the net of circumstances was closing in on him, driving him where he did not want to go. The car to St Malo was the knife that would cut through his difficulties and free him. Through the glass of the booth he saw her speaking volubly into the telephone; he waited on tenterhooks.

She came back presently. 'It is impossible,' she said. 'There is no car available for such a journey. I regret – Monsieur Duval, the proprietor of the garage, regrets also – but monsieur will have to go by train.'

He said very quietly: 'Surely it would be possible to arrange something? There must be a car of some sort or another?'

She shrugged her shoulders. 'Monsieur could go to see Monsieur Duval perhaps, at the garage. If anybody in Dijon could produce a car for such a journey it would be he.'

She gave him directions for finding the garage; ten minutes later he was in the Frenchman's office. The garage owner was quite positive. 'A car, yes,' he declared. 'That is the least thing, monsieur, I could find the car. But petrol – not a litre that has not been taken by the army. Only by

64

fraud can I get petrol for the car – you understand? And then, the roads. It is not possible to make one's way along the road to Paris, not possible at all, monsieur.'

'Finally,' he said, 'I could not find a driver for a journey such as that. The Germans are across the Seine, monsieur; they are across the Marne. Who knows where they will be the day after tomorrow?'

The old man was silent.

The Frenchman said: 'If monsieur wishes to get back to England he should go by train, and he should go very soon.'

Howard thanked him for the advice, and went out into the street. Dusk was falling; he moved along the pavement, deep in thought. He stopped by a café and went in, and ordered a Pernod with water. He took the drink and went and sat down at a table by the wall, and stayed there for some time, staring at the garish advertisements of cordials upon the walls.

Things had grown serious. If he left now, at once, it might be possible to win through to St Malo and to England; if he delayed another thirty-six hours it might very well be that St Malo would be overwhelmed and smothered in the tide of the German rush, as Calais had been smothered, and Boulogne. It seemed incredible that they could still be coming on so fast. Surely, surely, they would be checked before they got to Paris? It could not possibly be true that Paris would fall?

He did not like this evacuation of the railway offices from Paris. That had an ugly sound.

He could go back now to the hotel. He could get both the children up and dress them, pay the bill at the hotel, and take them to the station. Ronnie would be all right. Sheila – well, after all, she had a coat. Perhaps he could get hold of a shawl to wrap her up in. True it was night-time and the

65

trains would be irregular; they might have to sit about for hours on the platform in the night waiting for a train that never came. But he would be getting the children back to England, as he had promised Cavanagh.

But then, if Sheila should get worse? Suppose she took a chill and got pneumonia?

If that should happen, he would never forgive himself. The children were in his care; it was not caring for them if he went stampeding to the station in the middle of the night to start on a long, uncertain journey regardless of their weakness and their illness. That wasn't prudence. That was . . . fright.

He smiled a little at himself. That's what it was, just fright – something to be conquered. Looking after children, after all, meant caring for them in sickness. That's what it meant. It was quite clear. He'd taken the responsibility for them, and he must see it through, even though it now seemed likely to land him into difficulties that he had not quite anticipated when he first took on the job.

He got up and went back to the hotel. In the lobby the girl said to him:

'Monsieur has found a car?'

He shook his head. 'I shall stay here till the day after tomorrow. Then, if the little girl is well, we will go on by train.'

He paused. 'One thing, mademoiselle. I will only be able to take one little bag for the three of us, that I can carry myself. If I leave my fishing-rods, would you look after them for me for a time?'

'But certainly, monsieur. They will be quite safe.'

He went into the restaurant and found a seat for dinner. It was a great relief to him that he had found a means to place his rods in safety. Now that that little problem had been solved, he was amazed to find how greatly it had been distressing him; with that disposed of he could face the future with a calmer mind.

He went up to the bedroom shortly after dinner. The *femme de chambre* met him in the corridor, the yellow, dingy, corridor of bedrooms, lit only by a low-power lamp without a shade. 'I have made monsieur a bed upon the floor,' she said in a low tone. 'You will see.' She turned away.

'That was very kind of you,' he said. He paused, and looked curiously at her. In the dim light he could not see very clearly, but he had the impression that she was sobbing.

'Is anything the matter?' he asked gently.

She lifted the corner of her apron to her eyes. 'It is nothing,' she muttered. 'Nothing at all.'

He hesitated, irresolute. He could not leave her, could not just walk into his bedroom and shut the door, if she was in trouble. She had been too helpful with the children. 'Is it Madame?' he said. 'Has she complained about your work? If so, I will speak to her. I will tell her how much you have helped me.'

She shook her head and wiped her eyes.

'It is not that, monsieur,' she said. 'But –, I am dismissed. I am to go tomorrow.'

He was amazed. 'But why?'

'Five years,' she said. 'Five years I have been with Madame – in all seasons of the year, monsieur – five years continuously! And now, to be dismissed at the day! It is intolerable, that.' She began to weep a little louder.

The old man said: 'But why has Madame done this?'

She said: 'Have you not heard? The hotel is closing tomorrow. It is to be an office for the railway.' She raised her tear-stained face. 'All of us are dismissed, monsieur, everyone. I do not know what will happen to me, and *la petite* Rose.'

He was dumbfounded, not knowing what to say to help the woman. Obviously, if the hotel was to be an office for the railway staff, there would be no need for any chamber-maids; the whole hotel staff would have to go. He hesitated, irresolute.

'You will be all right,' he said at last. 'It will be easy for so good a *femme de chambre* as you to get another job.'

She shook her head. 'It is not so. All the hotels are closing, and what family can now afford a servant? You are kind, monsieur, but it is not so. I do not know how we shall live.'

'You have some relations, or family, that you can go to, no doubt?'

'There is nobody, monsieur. Only my brother, father of little Rose, and he is in England.'

Howard remembered the wine waiter at the Dickens Hotel in Russell Square. He said a word or two of meagre comfort and optimism to the woman; presently he escaped into the bedroom. It was impossible for him to give her any help in her great trouble.

She had made him quite a comfortable bed upon a mattress laid upon the floor. He went over to the children's bed and took a look at them; they were sleeping very deeply, though Sheila still seemed hot. He sat for a little reading in the arm-chair, but he soon grew tired; he had not slept properly the night before and he had had an anxious and a worrying day. Presently he undressed, and went to bed upon the floor.

When he awoke the dawn was bright; from the window there came a great groaning clatter as a tank got under way and lumbered up the road. The children were awake and playing in the bed; he lay for a little, simulating sleep, and then got up. Sheila was cool, and apparently quite well.

He dressed himself and took her temperature. It was

very slightly above normal still; evidently, whatever it was that had upset her was passing off. He washed them both and set Ronnie to dress himself, then went downstairs to order breakfast.

The hotel routine was already disarranged. Furniture was being taken from the restaurant; it was clear that no more meals would be served there. He found his way into the kitchen, where he discovered the *femme de chambre* in depressed consultation with the other servants, and arranged for a tray to be sent up to his room.

That was a worrying, trying sort of day. The news from the north was uniformly bad; in the town people stood about in little groups talking in low tones. He went to the station after breakfast with Ronnie, to enquire about the trains to Paris, leaving Sheila in bed in the devoted care of *la petite Rose*. They told him at the station that the trains to Paris were much disorganised '*à cause de la situation militaire*,' but trains were leaving every three or four hours. So far as they knew, the services from Paris to St Malo were normal, though that was on the Chemin de L'Ouest.

He walked up with Ronnie to the centre of the town, and ventured rather timidly into the children's department of a very large store. A buxom Frenchwoman came forward to serve him, and sold him a couple of woollen jerseys for the children and a grey, fleecy blanket. He bought the latter more by instinct than by reason, fearful of the difficulties of the journey. Of all difficulties, the one he dreaded most was that the children would get ill again.

They bought a few more sweets, and went back to the hotel. Already the hall was thronged with seedy-looking French officials, querulous from their journey and disputing over offices. The girl from the desk met Howard as he went upstairs. He could keep his room for one more night, she said; after that he must get out. She would try and arrange

69

for meals to be sent to the room, but he would understand – it would not be as she would wish the service.

He thanked her and went up upstairs. *La petite* Rose was reading about Babar to Sheila from the picture-book; she was curled up in a heap on the bed and they were looking at the pictures together. Sheila looked up at Howard, bright and vivacious, as he remembered her at Cidoton.

'*Regardez*,' she said, '*voici Jacko* climbing right up the *queue de* Babar on to his back!' She wriggled in exquisite amusement. 'Isn't he *naughty*!'

He stopped and looked at the picture with them. 'He is a naughty monkey, isn't he?' he said.

Sheila said: '*Drefully* naughty.'

Rose said very softly: '*Qu'est-ce que monsieur a dit?*'

Ronnie explained to her in French, and the bilingual children went on in the language of the country. To Howard they always spoke in English, but French came naturally to them when playing with other children. It was not easy for the old man to determine in which language they were most at home. On the whole, Ronnie seemed to prefer to speak in English. Sheila slipped more naturally into French, perhaps because she was younger and more recently in charge of nurses.

The children were quite happy by themselves. Howard got out the attaché case and looked at it; it was very small to hold necessities for three of them. He decided that Ronnie might carry that one, and he would get a rather larger case to carry himself, to supplement it. Fired by this idea, he went out of the bedroom to go to buy a cheap fibre case.

On the landing he met the *femme de chambre*. She hesitated, then stopped him.

'Monsieur is leaving tomorrow?' she said.

'I have to go away, because they want the room,' he replied. 'But I think the little girl is well enough to travel.

I shall get her up for *déjeuner*, and then this afternoon she can come out for a little walk with us.'

'Ah, that will be good for her. A little walk, in the sun.' She hesitated again, and then she said: 'Monsieur is travelling direct to England?'

He nodded. 'I shall not stay in Paris. I shall take the first train to St Malo.'

She turned her face up to him, lined and prematurely old, beseechingly. 'Monsieur – it is terrible to ask. Would you take *la petite* Rose with you, to England?'

He was silent; he did not quite know what to say to that. She went on hurriedly.

'I have the money for the fare, monsieur. And Rose is a good little girl – oh, she is so good, that one. She would not trouble monsieur, no more than a little mouse.'

Every instinct warned the old man that he must kill this thing stone dead – quick. Though he would not admit it to himself, he knew that to win through to England would take all his energy, burdened as he was with two little children. In the background of his mind lurked fear, fear of impending, absolute disaster.

He stared down at the tear-stained, anxious face, and temporised. 'But why do you want to send her to England?' he asked. 'The war will never come to Dijon. She will be quite safe here.'

The woman said: 'I have no money, monsieur. Her father is in England, but he cannot send money to us here. It is better that she should go to England, now.'

He said: 'Perhaps I could arrange to help him to send money.' There was still a substantial balance on his letter of credit. 'You do not want her to leave you, do you?'

She said: 'Monsieur, things are happening in France that you English do not understand. We are afraid of what is coming, all of us . . .'

71

They were silent for a moment.

'I know things are very bad,' he said quietly. 'It may be difficult for me, an Englishman, to get to England now. I don't think it will be – but it may. Suppose I could not get her out of the country for some reason?'

She wrinkled her face up and lifted the corner of her apron to her eyes. 'In England she would be safe,' she muttered. 'I do not know what is going to happen to us, here in Dijon. I am afraid.' She began to cry again.

He patted her awkwardly upon the shoulder. 'There,' he said. 'I will think about it this afternoon. It's not a thing to be decided in a hurry.' He made his escape from her, and went down to the street.

Once out in the street, he quite forgot what he had come for. Absent-mindedly he walked towards the centre of the town, wondering how he could evade the charge of another child. Presently, he sat down in a café and ordered himself a *bock*.

It was not that he had anything against *la petite* Rose. On the contrary, he liked the child; she was a quiet, motherly little thing. But she would be another drag on him at a time when he knew with every instinct of his being that he could tolerate no further drags. He knew himself to be in danger. The sweep and drive of Germany down in France was no secret any longer; it was like the rush through Belgium had been in the last war, only more intense. If he delayed a moment longer than was necessary, he would be engulfed by the invading army. For an Englishman that meant a concentration camp, for a man of his age that probably meant death.

From his chair upon the pavement he stared out upon the quiet, sunlit *Place*. Bad times were coming for the French; he and his children must get out of it, damn quick. If the Germans conquered they would bring with them, inevitably, their trail of pillage and starvation, gradually mounting towards anarchy as they faced the inevitable defeat. He must not let his children be caught in that. Children in France, if she were beaten down, would have a terrible time.

It was bad luck on little Rose. He had nothing against her; indeed, she had helped him in the last two days. He would have found it difficult to manage Sheila if Rose had not been there. She had kept the little girl, hardly more than a baby, happy and amused in a way that Howard himself could never have managed alone.

It was a pity that it was impossible to take her. In normal times he might have been glad of her; he had tried in Cidoton to find a young girl who would travel with them to Calais. True, Rose was only ten years old, but she was peasant-French; they grew up very quickly . . .

Was it impossible to take her?

Now it seemed desperately cruel, impossible to leave her behind.

He sat there miserably irresolute for half an hour. In the end he got up and walked slowly back to the hotel, desperately worried. In his appearance he had aged five years.

He met the *femme de chambre* upon the landing. 'I have made up my mind,' he said heavily. '*La petite* Rose may come with us to England; I will take her to her father. She must be ready to start tomorrow morning, at seven o'clock.'

4

That night Howard slept very little. He lay on his bed upon the floor, revolving in his mind the things he had to do, the various alternative plans he must make if things should go awry. He had no fear that they would not reach Paris. They would get there all right; there was a train every three or four hours. But after that – what then? Would he be able to get out of Paris again, to St Malo for the boat to England? That was the knotty point. Paris had stood a siege before, in 1870; it might well be that she was going to stand another one. With three children on his hands he could not let himself be caught in a besieged city. Somehow or other he must find out about the journey to England before they got to Paris.

He got up at about half-past five, and shaved and dressed. Then he awoke the children; they were fretful at being roused and Sheila cried a little, so that he had to stop and take her on his lap and wipe her eyes and make a fuss of her. In spite of the tears she was cool and well, and after a time submitted to be washed and dressed.

Ronnie said, sleepily: 'Are we going in the motor-car?'

'No,' said the old man, 'not today, I couldn't get a car to go in.'

'Are we going in a *char de combat*?'

'No. We're going in a train.'

'Is that the train we're going to sleep in?'

Howard shook his head patiently. 'I couldn't manage that, either. We may have to sleep in it, but I hope that we'll be on the sea tonight.'

'On a ship?'

'Yes. Go on and clean your teeth; I've put the toothpaste on the brush for you.'

There was a thunderous roar above the hotel, and an aeroplane swept low over the station. It flew away directly in a line with their window, a twin-engined, low-wing monoplane, dark green in colour. In the distance there was a little, desultory rattle, like musketry fire upon a distant range.

The old man sat upon the bed, staring at it as it receded in the distance. It couldn't possibly . . .

Ronnie said: 'Wasn't that one *low*, Mr Howard?'

They'd never have the nerve to fly so low as that. It must have been a French one. 'Very low,' he said, a little unsteadily. 'Go on and clean your teeth.'

Presently there was a tap upon the door, and the *femme de chambre* was there bearing a tray of coffee and rolls. Behind her came *la petite* Rose, dressed in her Sunday best, with a large black straw hat, a tight black overcoat, and white socks. She looked very uncomfortable.

Howard said kindly in French: 'Good morning, Rose. Are you coming with us to England?'

She said: '*Oui, monsieur.*'

The *femme de chambre* said: 'All night she has been talking about going in the train, and going to England, and going to live with her father. She has hardly slept at all, that one.' There was a twist in her smile as she spoke; it seemed to Howard that she was not far from tears again.

'That's fine,' he said. He turned to the *femme de chambre*.

75

'Sit down and have a cup of coffee with us. Rose will, won't you, Rose?'

The woman said: *'Merci, monsieur.* But I have the sandwiches to prepare, and I have had my coffee.' She rubbed the little girl's shoulder. 'Would you like another cup of coffee, *ma petite?'*

She left Rose with them and went out. In the bedroom Howard sat the children down, each with a buttered roll to eat and a cup full of weak coffee to drink. The children ate very slowly; he had finished his own meal by the time they were only half-way through. He pottered about and packed up their small luggage; Rose had her own things in a little attaché case upon the floor beside her.

The children ate on industriously. The *femme de chambre* came back with several large, badly-wrapped parcels of food for the journey, and a very large wine bottle full of milk. 'There,' she said unsteadily. 'Nobody will starve today!'

The children laughed merrily at the poor joke. Rose had finished, and Ronnie was engulfing the last mouthful, but Sheila was still eating steadily. There was nothing now to wait for, and the old man was anxious to get to the station for fear that they might miss a train. 'You don't want that,' he said to Sheila, indicating her half-eaten roll. 'You'd better leave it. We've got to go now.'

'I want it,' she said mutinously.

'But we've got to go now.'

'I want it.'

He was not going to waste energy over that. 'All right,' he said, 'you can bring it along with you.' He picked up their bags and shepherded them all out into the corridor and down the stairs.

At the door of the hotel he turned to the *femme de chambre.* 'If there is any difficulty I shall come back here,' he said.

'Otherwise, as I said, I will send a telegram when we reach England, and Rose is with her father.'

She said quickly: 'But monsieur must not pay for that, Henri will send the telegram.'

He was touched. 'Anyway, it will be sent directly we arrive in London. *Au revoir, mademoiselle.*'

'*Au revoir, monsieur. Bonne chance.*' She stood and watched them as he guided the three children across the road in the thin morning sunlight, the tears running all unheeded down the furrows of her face.

In the station there was great confusion. It was quite impossible to find out the times or likelihood of trains, or whether, amongst all the thronging soldiers, there would be seats for children. The most that he could learn was that trains for Paris came in at *Quai* 4 and that there had been two since midnight. He went to the booking-office to get a ticket for Rose, but it was closed.

'One does not take tickets any more,' a bystander said. 'It is not necessary.'

The old man stared at him. 'One pays, then, on the train, perhaps?'

The man shrugged his shoulders. 'Perhaps.'

There was nobody to check tickets as they passed on to the platform. He led the children through the crowd, Sheila still chewing her half-eaten roll of bread, clutched firmly in a hand already hot. *Quai* 4 was practically deserted, rather to his surprise. There did not seem to be great competition to get to Paris; all the traffic seemed to be the other way.

He saw an engine-driver, and approached him: 'It is here that the train for Paris will arrive?'

'But certainly.'

The statement was not reassuring. The empty spaces of the platform oppressed the old man; they were unnatural, ominous. He walked along to a seat and put down all the

77

parcels and attaché cases on it, then settled down to wait until a train should come.

The children began running up and down the platform, playing games of their own making. Presently, mindful of the chill that had delayed him, he called Ronnie and Sheila to him and took off their coats, thinking to put them on when they were in the train. As an afterthought he turned to Rose.

'You also,' he said. 'You will be better playing without your coat, and the hat.'

He took them off and put them on the seat beside him. Then he lit his pipe, and settled down to wait in patience for the train.

It came at about half-past eight, when they had been there for an hour and a half. There were a few people on the platform by that time, not very many. It steamed into the station, towering above them; there were two soldiers on the footplate of the engine with the train crew.

To his delight, it was not a crowded train. He made as quickly as he could for a first-class compartment, and found one occupied only by two morose officers of the *Armée de l'Air*. The children swarmed on to the seats and climbed all over the carriage, examining everything, chattering to each other in mixed French and English. The two officers looked blacker; before five minutes had elapsed they had got up, swearing below their breath, and had removed to another carriage.

Howard looked at them helplessly as they went. He would have liked to apologise, but he didn't know how to put it.

Presently, he got the children to sit down. Mindful of chills, he said: 'You'd better put your coats on now. Rose, you put yours on, too.'

He proceeded to put Sheila into hers. Rose looked around

the carriage blankly. 'Monsieur – where is my coat? And my hat, also?'

He looked up. 'Eh? You had them when we got into the train?'

But she had not had them. She had rushed with the other children to the carriage, heedless, while Howard hurried along behind her, burdened with luggage. Her coat and hat had been left upon the station bench.

Her face wrinkled up, and she began to cry. The old man stared at her irritably for a moment; he had thought that she would be a help to him. Then the patience borne of seventy years of disappointments came to his aid; he sat down and drew her to him, wiping her eyes. 'Don't bother about it,' he said gently. 'We'll get another hat and another coat in Paris. You shall choose them yourself.'

She sobbed: 'But they were so expensive.'

He wiped her eyes again. 'Never mind,' he said. 'It couldn't be helped. I'll tell your aunt when I send the telegram that it wasn't your fault.'

Presently she stopped crying. Howard undid one of his many parcels of food and they all had a bit of an orange to eat, and all troubles were forgotten.

The train went slowly, stopping at every station and occasionally in between. From Dijon to Tonnerre is seventy miles; they pulled out of that station at about half-past eleven, three hours after leaving Dijon. The children had stood the journey pretty well so far; for the last hour they had been running up and down the corridor shouting, while the old man dozed uneasily in a corner of the compartment.

He roused after Tonnerre, and fetched them all back into the carriage for *déjeuner* of sandwiches and milk and oranges. They ate slowly, with frequent distractions to look out of the window. Sandwiches had a tendency to become

79

mislaid during these pauses, and to vanish down between the cushions of the seats. Presently they were full. He gave them each a cup of milk, and laid Sheila down to rest upon the seat, covered over with the blanket he had bought in Dijon. He made Rose and Ronnie sit down quietly and look at Babar; then he was able to rest himself.

From Tonnerre to Joigny is thirty miles. The train was going slower than ever, stopping for long periods for no apparent reason. Once, during one of these pauses, a large flight of aeroplanes passed by the window, flying very high; the old man was shocked to hear the noise of gunfire, and to see a few white puffs of smoke burst in the cloudless sky far, far below them. It seemed incredible, but they must be German. He strained his eyes for fighters so far as he could do without calling the attention of the children from their books, but there were no fighters to be seen. The machines wheeled slowly round and headed back towards the east, unhindered by the ineffective fire.

The old man sank back into his seat, full of doubts and fears.

He was dozing a little when the train pulled into Joigny soon after one o'clock. It stood there in the station in the hot sunlight, interminably. Presently a man came down the corridor.

'*Descendez, monsieur,*' he said. 'This train goes no farther.'

Howard stared up at him dumbfounded. 'But – this is the Paris train?'

'It is necessary to change here. One must descend.'

'When will the next train leave for Paris?'

'I do not know, monsieur. That is a military affair.'

He got the children into their coats, gathered his things together, and presently was on the platform, burdened with his luggage, with the three children trailing after him. He went straight to the station-master's office. There was an officer there, a *capitaine des transports*. The old man asked a few straight questions, and got straight answers.

'There will be no more trains for Paris, monsieur. None at all. I cannot tell you why, but no more trains will run north from Joigny.'

There was a finality in his tone that brooked no argument. The old man said: 'I am travelling to St Malo, for England, with these children. How would you advise me to get there?'

The young officer stared at him. 'St Malo? That is not the easiest journey, now, monsieur.' He thought for a moment. 'There would be trains from Chartres . . . And in one hour, at half-past two, there is an autobus for Montargis . . . You must go by Montargis, monsieur. By the autobus to Montargis, then to Pithiviers, from Pithiviers to Angerville, and from Angerville to Chartres. From Chartres you will be able to go by train to St Malo.'

He turned to an angry Frenchwoman behind Howard, and the old man was elbowed out of the way. He retired on to the platform, striving to remember the names of the places that he had just heard. Then he thought of his little *Baedeker* and got it out, and traced the recommended course across country to Chartres. It skirted round Paris, sixty miles farther west. So long as there were buses one could get to Chartres that way, but Heaven alone knew how long it would take.

He knew the ropes where French country autobuses were concerned. He went and found the bus out in the station yard, and sat in it with the children. If he had been ten minutes later he would not have found a seat.

Worried and distracted by the chatter of the children, he tried to plan his course. To go on to Montargis seemed the only thing to do, but was he wise to do it? Would it not be better to try and travel back to Dijon? The route that he had been given through Montargis to Chartres was quite a sensible one according to his *Baedeker*; it lay along a good main road for the whole of the hundred miles or so to Chartres. This bus would give him a good lift of thirty-five or forty miles upon the way, so that by the time he left it he would be within sixty miles of Chartres and the railway to St Malo; provided he could get a bus to carry him that sixty miles he would be quite all right. If all went well he would reach Chartres that night, and St Malo the next morning; then the cross-channel boat and he would be home in England.

It seemed all right, but was it really wise? He could get back to Dijon, possibly, though even that did not seem very certain. But if he got back there, what then? With the Germans driving forward into France from the north, and the Italians coming up from the south, Dijon seemed to be between two fires. He could not stay indefinitely in Dijon. It was better, surely, to take courage and go forward in the bus, by north and west in the direction of the Channel and home.

The bus became filled with a hot, sweating crowd of French country people. All were agitated and upset, all bore enormous packages with them, all were heading to the west. Howard took Sheila on his knee to make more room and squeezed Ronnie standing up between his legs. Rose pressed up against him, and an enormous woman with a very small infant in her arms shared the seat with them. From the conversation of the people in the bus Howard learned that the Germans were still pouring on, but that Paris would be defended to the last. Nobody knew how far the Germans had advanced, how near to Joigny they might be. It was wise to move, to go and stay with relations farther to the west.

One man said: 'The Chamber has left Paris. It is now at Tours.' Somebody else said that that rumour was not true, and a desultory argument began. Nobody seemed to take much interest in the Chamber; Paris and the life of cities meant very little to these peasants and near-peasants.

It was suffocatingly hot in the bus. The two English children stood it better than Howard could have expected; *la petite* Rose seemed to be more affected than they were. Howard, looking down, saw that she had gone very white. He bent towards her.

'Are you tired?' he said kindly. She shook her head mutely. He turned and struggled with the window at his side; presently he succeeded in opening it a little and letting in a current of warm, fresh air.

Presently the driver climbed into his seat, and the grossly overloaded vehicle lumbered from the square.

The movement brought a little more air into the bus.

They left the town after a couple of stops, carrying an additional load of people on the roof. They started out along the long straight roads of France, dusty and in poor repair. The dust swirled round the heavy vehicle; it drove in at the open window, powdering them all. Ronnie, standing between the old man's legs, clung to the window, avid for all that he could see; Howard turned Sheila on his lap with difficulty, so that she could see out too.

Beside him, presently, Rose made a little wailing cry. Howard looked down, and saw her face white with a light greenish hue; before he could do anything to help her she had vomited upon the floor.

For a moment he was startled and disgusted. Then patience came back to him; children couldn't help that sort of thing. She was coughing and weeping; he pulled out his handkerchief and wiped her face and comforted her.

'*Pauvre petite chou*,' he said awkwardly. 'You will be better now. It is the heat.'

With some struggling he moved Sheila over and lifted Rose up on his knee, so that she could see out and have more air. She was still crying bitterly; he wiped her eyes and talked to her as gently as he could. The broad woman by him smiled serenely, quite unmoved by the disaster.

'It is the rocking,' she said in soft Midland French, 'like the sea. Always I have been sick when, as a little girl, I have travelled. Always, always. In the train and in the bus, always, quite the same.' She bent down. '*Sois tranquille, ma petite*,' she said. 'It is nothing, that.'

Rose glanced up at her, and stopped crying. Howard chose the cleanest corner of his handkerchief and wiped her eyes. Thereafter she sat very quiet and subdued upon his knee, watching the slowly moving scene outside the window.

'I'm never sick in motor-cars,' said Ronnie proudly in English. The woman looked at them with new curiosity; hitherto they had spoken in French.

The road was full of traffic, all heading to the west. Old battered motor-cars, lorries, mule carts, donkey-carts, all were loaded to disintegration point with people making for Montargis. These wound in and out among the crowds of people pushing hand-carts, perambulators, wheelbarrows even, all loaded with their goods. It was incredible to Howard; it seemed as though the whole countryside were in flight before the armies. The women working in the fields looked up from time to time in pauses of their work to stare at the strange cavalcade upon the highway. Then they bent again to the harvest of their roots; the work in hand was more important than the strange tides that flowed upon the road.

Halfway to Montargis the bus heeled slowly to the near

side. The driver wrestled with the steering; a clattering bump, rhythmic, came from the near back wheel. The vehicle drew slowly to a stop beside the road.

The driver got down from his seat to have a look. Then he walked slowly back to the entrance to the bus. '*Un pneu*,' he said succinctly. '*Il faut descende – tout le monde.* We must change the wheel.'

Howard got down with relief. They had been sitting in the bus for nearly two hours, of which an hour had been upon the road. The children were hot and tired and fretful; a change would obviously be a good thing. He took them one by one behind a little bush in decent manner; a proceeding which did not escape the little crowd of passengers collected by the bus. They nudged each other. '*C'est un anglais . . .*'

The driver, helped by a couple of passengers, wrestled to jack up the bus and get the flat wheel off. Howard watched them working for a little time; then it occurred to him that this was a good opportunity to give the children tea. He fetched his parcel of food from the rack, and took the children a few yards up the road from the crowd. He sat them down upon the grass verge in the shade of a tree, and gave them sandwiches and milk.

The road stretched out towards the west, dead straight. As far as he could see it was thronged with vehicles, all moving the same way. He felt it really was a most extraordinary sight, a thing that he had never seen before, a population in migration.

Presently Rose said she heard an aeroplane.

Instinctively, Howard turned his head. He could hear nothing.

'I hear it,' Ronnie said. 'Lots of aeroplanes.'

Sheila said: 'I want to hear the aeroplane.'

'Silly,' said Ronnie. 'There's lots of them. Can't you hear?'

The old man strained his ears, but he could hear nothing. 'Can you see where they are?' he asked, nonchalantly. A cold fear lurked in the background of his mind.

The children scanned the sky. '*V'là*,' said Rose, pointing suddenly. '*Trois avions – là.*'

Ronnie twisted round in excitement to Howard. 'They're coming down towards us! Do you think we'll see them close?'

'Where are they?' he enquired. He strained his eyes in the direction from which they had come. 'Oh, I see. They won't come anywhere near here. Look, they're going down over there.'

'Oh . . .' said Ronnie, disappointed. 'I did want to see them close.'

They watched the aircraft losing height towards the road, about two miles away. Howard expected to see them land among the fields beside the road, but they did not land. They flattened out and flew along just above the tree-tops, one on each side of the road and one behind flying down the middle. A little crackling rattle sounded from them as they came. The old man stared, incredulous – it could not be . . .

Then, in a quick succession, from the rear machine, five bombs fell on the road. Howard saw the bombs actually leave the aeroplane, saw five great spurts of flame upon the road, saw queer, odd fragments hurled into the air.

From the bus a woman shrieked: '*Les Allemands!*' and pandemonium broke loose. The driver of the little Peugeot car fifty yards away saw the gesticulations of the crowd, looked back over his shoulder, and drove straight into the back of a mule cart, smashing one of its wheels and cascading the occupants and load on to the road. The

French around the bus dashed madly for the door, hoping for shelter in the glass and plywood body, and jammed in a struggling, pitiful mob in the entrance. The machines flew on towards them, their machine-guns spitting flame. The rear machine, its bombs discharged, flew forward and to the right; with a weaving motion the machine upon the right dropped back to the rear centre, ready in its turn to bomb the road.

There was no time to do anything, to go anywhere, nor was there anywhere to go. Howard caught Sheila and Ronnie and pulled them close to him, flat upon the ground. He shouted to Rose to lie down, quickly.

Then the machines were on them, low-winged, single engined monoplanes with curious bent wings, dark green in colour. A burst of fire was poured into the bus from the machines to right and left; a stream of tracer-bullets shot forward up the road from the centre aircraft. A few bullets lickered straight over Howard and his children on the grass and spattered in the ground a few yards behind them.

For a moment Howard saw the gunner in the rear cockpit as he fired at them. He was a young man, not more than twenty, with a keen, tanned face. He wore a yellow students' corps cap, and he was laughing as he fired.

Then the two flanking aircraft had passed, and the centre one was very near. Looking up, the old man could see the bombs slung in their racks beneath the wing; he watched in agony for them to fall. They did not fall. The machine passed by them, not a hundred feet away. He watched it as it went, sick with relief. He saw the bombs leave the machine three hundred yards up the road, and watched dumbly as the debris flew upwards. He saw the wheel of a cart go sailing through the air, to land in the field.

Then that graceful, weaving dance began again, the machine in the rear changing places with the one on the left. They vanished in the distance; presently Howard heard the thunder of another load of bombs upon the road.

He released the children, and sat up upon the grass. Ronnie was flushed and excited. 'Weren't they *close*!' he said. 'I did see them well. Did you see them well, Sheila? Did you hear them firing the guns?'

He was ecstatically pleased. Sheila was quite unaffected. She said: 'May I have some orange?'

Howard said slowly and mechanically: 'No, you've had enough to eat. Drink up your milk.' He turned to Rose and found her inclined to tears. He knelt up and moved over to her. 'Did anything hit you?' he asked in French.

She shook her head dumbly.

'Don't cry, then,' he said kindly. 'Come and drink your milk. It'll be good for you.'

She turned her face up to him. 'Are they coming back? I don't like the noise they make.'

He patted her on the shoulder. 'Never mind,' he said a little unsteadily. 'The noise won't hurt you. I don't think they're coming back.' He filled up the one cup with milk and gave it to her. 'Have a drink.'

Ronnie said: 'I wasn't frightened, was I?'

Sheila echoed: 'I wasn't frightened, was I?'

The old man said patiently: 'Nobody was frightened. Rose doesn't like that sort of noise, but that's not being frightened.' He stared over to the little crowd around the bus. Something had happened there; he must go and see. 'You can have an orange,' he said. 'One-third each. Will you peel it, Rose?'

'*Mais oui, monsieur.*'

He left the children happy in the prospect of more food, and went slowly to the bus. There was a violent and distracted clamour from the crowd; most of the women were in tears of fright and rage. But to his astonishment, there were no casualties save one old woman who had lost two fingers of her left hand, severed cleanly near the knuckles by a bullet. Three women, well accustomed to first aid in accidents upon the farm, were tending her, not inexpertly.

Howard was amazed that no one had been killed. From the right a dozen bullets had entered the body of the bus towards the rear; from the left the front wheels, bonnet and radiator had been badly shot about. Between the two the crowd of peasants milling round the door had escaped injury. Even the crowd in the small Peugeot had escaped, though one of the women in the mule cart was shot through the thigh. The mule itself was dying in the road.

There was nothing he could do to help the wounded women. His attention was attracted by a gloomy little knot of men around the driver of the bus; they had lifted the bonnet and were staring despondently at the engine. The old man joined them; he knew little of machinery, but it was evident even to him that all was not quite right. A great pool of water lay beneath the engine of the bus; from holes in radiator and cylinder casting the brown, rusty water still ran out.

One of the men turned aside to spit. '*Ça ne marche, plus,*' he said succinctly.

It took a moment or two for the full meaning of this to come home to Howard. 'What does one do?' he asked the driver. 'Will there be another bus?'

'Not unless they find a madman for a driver.' There was a strained silence. Then the driver said: '*Il faut continuer à pied.*'

It became apparent to Howard that this was nothing but the ugly truth. It was about four in the afternoon and Montargis was twenty-five kilometres, say fifteen miles, farther on, nearer to them than Joigny. They had passed one or two villages upon the road from Joigny; no doubt one or two more lay ahead before Montargis. But there would be no chance of buses starting at these places, nor was there any reasonable chance of a hotel.

It was appalling, but it was the only thing. He and the children would have to walk, very likely the whole of the way to Montargis.

He went into the wrecked body of the bus and collected their things, the two attaché cases, the little suitcase, and the remaining parcels of food. There was too much for him to carry very far unless the children could carry some of it; he knew that that would not be satisfactory for long. Sheila could carry nothing; indeed, she would have to be carried herself a great deal of the way. Ronnie and Rose, if they were to walk fifteen miles, would have to travel light.

He took his burdens back to the children and laid them down upon the grass. It was impossible to take the suitcase with them; he packed it with the things that they could spare most easily and left it in the bus in the faint hope that one day it might somehow be retrieved. That left the two bulging little cases and the parcels of food. He could carry those himself.

'We're going to walk on to Montargis,' he explained to the children. 'The bus won't go.'

'Why not?' asked Ronnie.

'There's something the matter with the engine.'

'Oh – may I go and see?'

Howard said firmly: 'Not now. We're just going to walk on.' He turned to Rose. 'You will like walking more than riding in the bus, I know.'

She said: 'I did feel so ill.'

'It was very hot. You're feeling better now?'

She smiled. '*Oui, monsieur.*'

They started out to walk in the direction of Montargis. The heat of the day was passing; it was not yet cool, but it was bearable for walking. They went very slowly, limited by the rate at which Sheila walked, which was slow. The old man strolled patiently along. It was no good worrying the children with attempts to hurry them; they had many miles to cover and he must let them go at their own pace.

Presently they came to the place where the second load of bombs had dropped.

There were two great craters in the road, and three more among the trees at the verge. There had been a cart of some sort there. There was little crowd of people busy at the side of the road; too late, he thought to make a detour from what he feared to let the children see.

Ronnie said clearly and with interest: 'Are those dead people, Mr Howard?'

He steered them over to the other side of the road. 'Yes,' he said quietly. 'You must be very sorry for them.'

'May I go and see?'

'No,' he said. 'You mustn't go and look at people when they're dead. They want to be left alone.'

'Dead people do look funny, don't they, Mr Howard?'

He could not think of what to say to that one, and herded them past in silence. Sheila was singing a little song and showed no interest; Rose crossed herself and walked by quickly with averted eyes.

They strolled on at their slow pace up the road. If there had been a side road Howard would have taken it, but there was no side road. It was impossible to make a detour other than by walking through the fields; it would not help him to turn back towards Joigny. It was better to go on.

They passed other casualties, but the children seemed to take little interest. He shepherded them along as quickly as he could; when they had passed the target for the final load of bombs there would probably be an end to this parade of death. He could see that place now, half a mile ahead. There were two motor-cars jammed in the road, and several trees seemed to have fallen.

Slowly, so slowly, they approached the place. One of the cars was wrecked beyond redemption. It was a Citroën front drive saloon; the bomb had burst immediately ahead of it, splitting the radiator in two and blasting in the windscreen. Then a tree had fallen straight on top of it, crushing the roof down till it touched the chassis. There was much blood upon the road.

Four men, from a decrepit old de Dion, were struggling to lift the tree to clear the road for their own car to pass. On the grass verge a quiet heap was roughly covered by a rug.

Pulling and heaving at the tree, the men rolled it from the car and dragged it back, clearing a narrow passage with great difficulty. They wiped their brows, sweating, and clambered back into their old two-seater. Howard stopped by them as the driver started his engine.

'Killed?' he asked quietly.

The man said bitterly: 'What do you think? The filthy Boches!' He let the clutch in and the car moved slowly forward round the tree and up the road ahead of them.

Fifty yards up the road it stopped. One of the men leaned back and shouted at him: 'You – with the children. You! *Gardez le petit gosse!*'

They let the clutch in and drove on. Howard looked down in bewilderment at Rose. 'What did he mean?'

'He said there was a little boy,' she said.

He looked around. 'There's no little boy here.'

Ronnie said: 'There's only dead people here. Under that rug.' He pointed with his finger.

Sheila awoke to the world about her. 'I want to see the dead people.'

The old man took her hand firmly in his own. 'Nobody

goes to look at them,' he said. 'I told you that.' He stared around him in bewilderment.

Sheila said: 'Well, may I go and play with the boy?'

'There's no boy here, my dear.'

'Yes there is. Over there.'

She pointed to the far side of the road, twenty yards beyond the tree. A little boy of five or six was standing there, in fact, utterly motionless. He was dressed in grey, grey stockings above the knee, grey shorts, and a grey jersey. He was standing absolutely still, staring down the road towards them. His face was a dead, greyish white in colour.

Howard caught his breath at the sight of him, and said very softly: 'Oh, my God!' He had never seen a child looking like that, in all his seventy years.

He crossed quickly over to him, the children following. The little boy stood motionless as he approached, staring at him vacantly. The old man said: 'Are you hurt at all?'

There was no answer. The child did not appear to have heard him.

'Don't be afraid,' Howard said. Awkwardly he dropped down on one knee. 'What is your name?'

There was no answer. Howard looked round for some help, but for the moment there were no pedestrians. A couple of cars passed slowly circumnavigating the tree, and then a lorry full of weary, unshaven French soldiers. There was nobody to give him any help.

He got to his feet again, desperately perplexed. He must go on his way, not only to reach Montargis, but also to remove his children from the sight of that appalling car, capable, if they realised its grim significance, of haunting them for the rest of their lives. He could not stay a moment longer than was necessary in that place. Equally, it seemed impossible to leave this child. In the next village, or at any

93

rate in Montargis, there would be a convent; he would take him to the nuns.

He crossed quickly to the other side of the road, telling the children to stay where they were. He lifted up a corner of the rug. They were a fairly well-dressed couple, not more than thirty years old, terribly mutilated in death. He nerved himself and opened the man's coat. There was a wallet in the inside pocket; he opened it, and there was the identity-card. Jean Duchot, of 8 bis, Rue de la Victoire, Lille.

He took the wallet and some letters and stuffed them into his pocket; he would turn them over to the next gendarme he saw. Somebody would have to arrange the burial of the bodies, but that was not his affair.

He went back to the children. Sheila came running to him, laughing. 'He is a funny little boy,' she said merrily. 'He won't say anything at all!'

The other two had stepped back and were staring with childish intensity at the white-faced boy in grey, still staring blankly at the ruins of the car. Howard put down the cases and took Sheila by the hand. 'Don't bother him,' he said. 'I don't suppose he wants to play just now.'

'Why doesn't he want to play?'

He did not answer that, but said to Rose and Ronnie: 'You take one of the cases each for a little bit.' He went up to the little boy and said to him: 'Will you come with us? We're all going to Montargis.'

There was no answer, no sign that he had heard.

For a moment Howard stood in perplexity; then he stooped and took his hand. In that hot afternoon it was a chilly, damp hand that he felt. *'Allons, mon vieux,'* he said, with gentle firmness, 'we're going to Montargis.' He turned to the road; the boy in grey stirred and trotted docilely beside him. Leading one child with either hand, the old man strolled down the long road, the other children followed behind, each with a case.

More traffic overtook them, and now there was noticeable a greater proportion of military lorries mingled with the cars. Not only the civilians streamed towards the west; a good number of soldiers seemed to be going that way too. The lorries crashed and clattered on their old-fashioned solid rubber tyres, grinding their ancient gears. Half of them had acetylene headlamps garnishing the radiators, relics of the armies of 1918, stored twenty years in transport sheds behind the barracks in quiet country towns. Now they were out upon the road again, but going in the other direction.

The dust they made was very trying to the children. With the heat and the long road they soon began to flag; Ronnie complained that the case he was carrying hurt his arm, and Sheila wanted a drink, but all the milk was gone. Rose said her feet were hurting her. Only the limp little boy in grey walked on without complaint.

Howard did what he could to cheer them on, but they were obviously tiring. There was a farm not very far ahead; he turned into it, and asked the haggard old woman at the door if she would sell some milk. She said there was none, upon which he asked for water for the children. She led them to the well in the court-yard, not very distant from the midden, and pulled up a bucket for them; Howard conquered his scruples and his apprehensions and they all had a drink.

They rested a little by the well. In a barn, open to the court-yard, was an old farm cart with a broken wheel, evidently long disused. Piled into this was a miscellaneous assortment of odd rubbish, and amongst this rubbish was what looked like a perambulator.

He strolled across to look more closely, the old woman

watching him, hawk-eyed. It was a perambulator in fact, forty or fifty years old, covered in filth, and with one broken spring. But it was a perambulator, all the same. He went back to the old lady and commenced to haggle for it.

Ten minutes later it was his, for a hundred and fifty francs. She threw in with that a frayed piece of old rope with which he made shift to lash the broken spring. Hens had been roosting on it, covering it with their droppings; he set Ronnie and Rose to pull up handfuls of grass to wipe it down with. When they had finished he surveyed it with some satisfaction. It was a filthy object still, and grossly expensive, but it solved a great many of his problems.

He bought a little bread from the old woman and put it with the cases in the pram. Rather to his surprise nobody wanted to ride, but they all wanted to push it; he found it necessary to arrange turns. 'The youngest first,' he said. 'Sheila can push it first.'

Rose said: 'May I take off my shoes? They hurt my feet.'

He was uncertain, revolving this idea in his head. 'I don't think that's a good idea,' he said. 'The road will not be nice to walk on.'

She said: 'But monsieur, one does not wear shoes at all, except in Dijon.'

It seemed that she was genuinely used to going without shoes. After some hesitation he agreed to let her try it, and found that she moved freely and easily over the roughest parts of the road. He put her shoes and stockings in the pram, and spent the next quarter of an hour refusing urgent applications from the English children to copy her example.

Presently Sheila tired of pushing. Rose said: 'Now it is the turn of Pierre.' In motherly fashion she turned to the little boy in grey. 'Now, Pierre. Like this.' She brought him to the pram, still white-faced and listless, put his hands on the cracked china handles and began to push it with him.

Howard said to her: 'How do you know his name is Pierre?'

She stared at him. 'He said so – at the farm.'

The old man had not heard a word from the little boy; indeed, he had been secretly afraid that he had lost the power of speech. Not for the first time he was reminded of the gulf that separated him from the children, the great gulf that stretches between youth and age. It was better to leave the little boy to the care of the other children, rather than to terrify him with awkward, foreign sympathy and questions.

He watched the two children carefully as they pushed the pram. Rose seemed to have made some contact with the little fellow already, sufficient to encourage her. She chatted to him as they pushed the pram together, having fun with him in childish, baby French. When she trotted with the pram he trotted with her; when she walked he walked, but otherwise he seemed completely unresponsive. The blank look never left his face.

Ronnie said: 'Why doesn't he say anything, Mr Howard? He is funny.'

Sheila echoed: 'Why doesn't he say anything?'

Howard said: 'He's been very unhappy. You must be as nice and as kind to him as ever you can.'

They digested this in silence for a minute. Then Sheila said: 'Have you got to be nice to him, too, Monsieur Howard?'

'Of course,' he said. 'Everybody's got to be as nice as ever they can be to him.'

She said directly, in French: 'Then why don't you make him a whistle, like you did for us?'

Rose looked up. '*Un sifflet?*'

Ronnie said in French: 'He can make whistles ever so well out of a bit of wood. He made some for us at Cidoton.'

She jumped up and down with pleasure. '*Ecoute* Pierre,' she said. '*Monsieur va te fabriquer un sifflet!*'

They all beamed up at him in expectation. It was clear that in their minds a whistle was the panacea for all ills, the cure for all diseases of the spirit. They seemed to be completely in agreement on that point.

'I don't mind making him a whistle,' he said placidly. He doubted if it would be any good to Pierre, but it would please the other children, 'We'll have to find the right sort of bush. A hazel bush.'

'*Un coudrier,*' said Ronnie. '*Cherchons un coudrier.*'

They strolled along the road in the warm evening, pushing the pram and looking for a hazel bush. Presently Howard saw one. They had been walking for three-quarters of an hour since they had left the farm, and it was time the children had a rest; he crossed to the bush and cut a straight twig with his pocket-knife. Then he took them into the field a little way back from the traffic of the road and made them sit down upon the grass, and gave them an orange to eat between them. The three children sat watching him entranced as he began his work upon the twig, hardly attending to the orange. Rose sat with her arm round the little boy in grey; he did not seem to be capable of concentrating upon anything. Even the sections of the orange had to be put into his mouth.

The old man finished cutting, bound the bark back into place and lifted the whistle to his lips. It blew a little low note, pure and clear.

'There you are,' he said. 'That's for Pierre.'

Rose took it. '*Regarde*, Pierre,' she said, '*ce que monsieur t'a fait.*' She blew a note on it for him.

Then, gently, she put it to his lips. '*Siffle*, Pierre,' she said.

There was a little woody note above the rumble of the lorries on the road.

5

Presently they got back to the road and went on towards Montargis.

Evening was coming upon them; out of a cloudless sky the sun was dropping down to the horizon. It was the time of evening when in England birds begin to sing after a long, hot day. In the middle of France there are few birds because the peasant Frenchman sees to that on Sundays, but instinctively the old man listened for their song. He heard a different sort of song. He heard the distant hum of aeroplanes; in the far distance he heard the sharp crack of gunfire and some heavier explosions that perhaps were bombs. Upon the road the lorries of French troops, all making for the west, were thicker than ever.

Clearly it was impossible for them to reach Montargis. The road went on and on; by his reckoning they had come about five miles from where they had left the bus. There were still ten miles or so ahead of them, and night was coming on. The children were weary. Ronnie and Shelia were inclined to quarrel with each other; the old man felt that Sheila would burst into tears of temper and fatigue before so very long. Rose was not so buoyant as she had been and her flow of chatter to the little boy had ceased; she slipped along on her bare feet in silence, leading him by the hand. The little boy, Pierre, went on with her, white-faced and silent, stumbling a little now and then, the whistle held tight in his other hand.

It was time for them to find a lodging for the night.

The choice was limited. There was a farm on the right of the road, and half a mile farther on he could see a farm on the left of the road; farther than that the children could not walk. He turned into the first one. A placard nailed upon a post, *CHIEN MECHANT*, warned him, but did not warn the children. The dog, an enormous brindled creature, leaped out at them to the limit of his chain, raising a terrific clamour. The children scattered back, Sheila let out a roar of fright and tears, and Rose began to whimper. It was in the din of dog and children competing with each other that Howard presented himself at the door of the farm and asked for a bed for the children.

The gnarled old woman said: 'There are no beds here. Do you take this for a hotel?'

A buxom, younger woman behind her said: 'They could sleep in the barn, *ma mère*.'

The old dame said: 'Eh? the barn?' She looked Howard up and down. 'The soldiers sleep in the barn when we billet them. Have you any money?'

He said: 'I have enough to pay for a good bed for these children, madame.'

'Ten francs.'

'I have ten francs. May I see the barn?'

She led him through the cow-house to the barn behind. It was a large, bare apartment with a threshing floor at one end, empty and comfortless. The younger woman followed behind them.

He shook his head. 'I am desolated, madame, but the children must have a bed. I must look somewhere else.'

He heard the younger woman whisper something about the hay-loft. He heard the older woman protest angrily. He

heard the young one say: '*Ils sont fatigués, les petits* . . .'
Then they turned aside and conferred together.

The hay-loft proved to be quite possible. It was a shelter,
anyway, and somewhere where the children could sleep. He
made a bargain for them to sleep there for fifteen francs. He
found that the women had milk to spare, but little food. He
left the children in the loft and went and brought the pram
in past the dog; he broke his bread in two and gave half of
it to the younger woman, who would make bread and milk
for the children.

Half an hour later he was doing what he could to make
the children comfortable upon the hay. The younger woman
came in and stood watching for a moment. 'You have no
blankets, then?' she said.

He shook his head, bitterly regretful that he had left his
blanket in the bus. 'It was necessary to leave everything,
madame,' he said quietly.

She did not speak, but presently she went away. Ten
minutes later she returned with two coarse blankets of
the sort used for horses. 'Do not tell *ma mère*,' she said
gruffly.

He thanked her, and busied himself making a bed for the
children. She stood there watching him, silent and bovine.
Presently the children were comfortable and settled for the
night. He left them and walked to the door of the barn and
stood looking out.

The woman by him said: 'You are tired yourself, monsieur.'

He was deadly tired. Now that his responsibilities were
over for a while, he had suddenly become slack and faint.
'A little tired,' he said. 'I shall have supper and then I shall
sleep with the children. *Bonne nuit*, madame.'

She went back to the farmhouse, and he turned to the
pram, to find the other portion of the loaf of bread. Behind

him the old woman called sharply from the door across the yard.

'You can come and have a bowl of soup with us, if you like.'

He went into the kitchen gratefully. They had a stock-pot simmering upon a charcoal stove; the old woman helped him to a large bowl of steaming broth and gave him a spoon. He sat down gratefully at the bare, scrubbed table to consume it with his bread.

The woman said suddenly: 'Are you from Alsace? You speak like a German.'

He shook his head. 'I'm an Englishman.'

'Ah – an Englishman!' They looked at him with renewed interest. 'But the children, they are not English.'

The younger woman said: 'The bigger boy and the smaller girl are English. They were not talking French.'

With some difficulty he explained the position to them. They listened to him in silence, only half believing what he said. In all her life the old woman had never had a holiday; only very occasionally had she been beyond the market town. It was difficult for them to comprehend a world where people travelled to another country, far away from home, merely to catch fish. And as for an old man who took care of other people's children for them, it simply did not make sense at all.

Presently they stopped bothering him with their questions, and he finished the soup in silence.

He felt better after that, much better. He thanked them with grave courtesy and went out into the yard. Already it was dusk. On the road the lorries still rumbled past at intervals, but firing seemed to have ceased altogether.

The old woman followed him to the door. 'They do not stop tonight,' she said, indicating the road. 'The night before last the barn was full. Twenty-two francs for sleeping soldiers – all in one night.' She turned and went indoors again.

He went up to the loft. The children were all asleep, curled up together in odd attitudes; the little boy Pierre twitched and whimpered in his sleep. He still had the whistle clutched in one hand. Howard withdrew it gently and put it on the chopping machine, then spread the blanket more evenly over the sleeping forms. Finally he trod down a little of the hay into a bed and lay down himself, pulling his jacket round him.

Before sleep came to him he suffered a bad quarter of an hour. Here was a pretty kettle of fish, indeed. It had been a mistake ever to have left Joigny, but it had not seemed so at the time. He should have gone straight back to Dijon when he found he could not get to Paris, back to Switzerland, even. His effort to get through by bus to Chartres had failed most dismally, and here he was! Sleeping in a hay-loft, with four children utterly dependent on him, straight in the path of the invading German Army!

He turned uneasily in the hay. Things might not be so bad. The Germans, after all, could hardly get past Paris; that lay to the north of him, a sure shield the farther west he got. Tomorrow he would reach Montargis, even if it meant walking the whole way; the children could do ten miles in a day if they went at a slow pace and if the younger two had rides occasionally in the pram. At Montargis he would hand the little boy in grey over to the sisters, and report the death of his parents to the police. At Montargis, at a town like that, there would be a bus to Pithiviers, perhaps even all the way to Chartres.

All night these matters rolled round in his mind, in the intervals of cold, uneasy slumber. He did not sleep well. Dawn came at about four, a thin grey light that stole into the loft, pointing the cobwebs strung between the rafters. He dozed and slept again; at about six he got up and went down the ladder and sluiced his face under the pump. The growth of thin stubble on his chin offended him, but he shrank from trying to shave beneath the pump. In Montargis there would be a hotel; he would wait till then.

The women were already busy about the work of the farm. He spoke to the older one, and asked if she would make some coffee for the children. Three francs, for the four of them, she said. He reassured her on that point, and went to get the children up.

He found them already running about; they had seen him go downstairs. He sent them down to wash their faces at the pump. The little boy in grey hung back. From the ladder Rose called to him, but he would not go.

Howard, folding up the blankets, glanced at him. 'Go on and wash your face,' he said in French. 'Rose is calling you.'

The little boy put his right hand on his stomach and bowed to him. 'Monsieur,' he whispered.

The old man stood looking at him nonplussed. It was the first time he had heard him speak. The child stood looking up at him imploringly, his hand still on his stomach.

'What's the matter, old boy?' Howard said in French. Silence. He dropped stiffly down upon one knee, till their heads were level. 'What is it?'

He whispered: '*J'ai perdu le sifflet.*'

The old man got up and gave it to him. 'Here it is,' he said. 'Quite safe. Now go on down and let Rose wash your face.' He watched him thoughtfully as he clambered backwards down the steps. 'Rose, wash his face for him.'

He gave the children their coffee in the kitchen of the farm with the remainder of the bread, attended to their more personal requirements, paid the old lady twenty francs for food and lodging. At about quarter past seven he led them one by one past the *chien méchant* and out on to the road again, pushing the pram before him.

High overhead a few aeroplanes passed on a pale blue, cloudless sky; he could not tell if they were French or German. It was another glorious summer morning. On the road the military lorries were thicker than ever, and once or twice in the first hour a team of guns passed by them, drawn by tired, sweating horses flogged westwards by dirty, unshaven men in horizon blue. That day there did not seem to be so many refugees upon the road. The cyclists and the walkers and the families in decrepit, overloaded pony-carts were just as numerous, but there were few private cars in evidence upon the road. For the first hour Howard walked continually looking backwards for a bus, but no bus came.

The children were very merry. They ran about and chattered to each other and to Howard, playing little games that now and then threatened their lives under the wheels of dusty lorries driven by tired men, and which had then to be checked. As the day grew warmer he let them take off their coats and jerseys and put them in the pram. Rose went barefoot as a matter of course; as a concession to the English children presently Howard let them take off stockings, though he made them keep their shoes on. He took off Pierre's stockings too.

The little boy seemed a trifle more natural, though he was still white and dumb. He had the whistle clutched tight in his hand and it still worked; now and again Sheila tried to get it away from him, but Howard had his eye upon her and put a stop to that.

'If you don't stop bothering him for it,' he said, 'you'll have to put your stockings on again.' He frowned at her; she eyed him covertly, and decided that he meant it.

From time to time Rose bent towards the little boy in

grey. '*Siffle*, Pierre,' she would say. '*Siffle pour* Rose.' At that he would put the whistle to his lips and blow a little thin note. 'Ah, *c'est chic, ca.*' She jollied him along all morning, smiling shyly up at Howard every now and then.

They went very slowly, making not more than a mile and a half in each hour. It was no good hurrying the children, Howard thought. They would reach Montargis by evening, but only if the children took their own pace.

At about ten in the morning firing broke out to the north of them. It was very heavy firing, as of guns and howitzers; it puzzled the old man. It was distant, possibly ten miles away or more, but definitely to the north, between them and Paris. He was worried and perplexed. Surely it could not be that the Germans were surrounding Paris to the south? Was that the reason that the train had stopped at Joigny?

They reached a tiny hamlet at about ten o'clock, a place that seemed to be called La Croix. There was one small *estaminet* which sold a few poor groceries in a side room that was a little shop. The children had been walking for three hours and were beginning to tire; it was high time they had a rest. He led them in and bought them two long orange drinks between the four of them.

There were other refugees there, sitting glum and silent. One old man said presently, to no one in particular: '*On dit que les Boches ont pris Paris.*'

The wizened old woman of the house said that it was true. It had said so on the radio. A soldier had told her.

Howard listened, shaken to the core. It was incredible that such a thing could happen. Silence fell upon the room again; it seemed that no one had any more to say. Only the children wriggled on their chairs and discussed their drink. A dog sat in the middle of the floor scratching industriously, snapping now and then at flies.

The old man left them and went through into the shop. He had hoped to find some oranges, but no oranges were left, and no fresh bread. He explained his need to the woman, and examined the little stock of food she had; he bought from her half a dozen thick, hard biscuits each nine or ten inches in diameter and grey in colour, rather like dog-biscuits. He also bought some butter and a long, brown doubtful-looking sausage. For his own weariness of the flesh, he bought a bottle of cheap brandy. That, with four bottles of the orange drink, completed his purchases. As he was turning away, however, he saw a single box of chocolate bars, and bought a dozen for the children.

Their rest finished, he led them out upon the road again. To encourage them upon the way he broke one of the chocolate bars accurately into four pieces and gave it to them. Three of the children took their portion avidly. The fourth shook his head dumbly and refused.

'Merci, monsieur,' he whispered.

The old man said gently in French: 'Don't you like chocolate, Pierre? It's so good.'

The child shook his head.

'Try a little bit.' The other children looked on curiously.

The little boy whispered: 'Merci, monsieur. Maman dit que non. Seulement après déjeuner.'

For a moment the old man's mind went back to the torn bodies left behind them by the roadside covered roughly with a rug; he forced his mind away from that. 'All right,' he said in French, 'we'll keep it, and you shall have it after déjeuner.' He put the morsel carefully in a corner of the pram seat, the little boy in grey watched with grave interest. 'It will be quite safe there.'

Pierre trotted on beside him, quite content.

The two younger children tired again before long; in four

hours they had walked six miles, and it was now very hot. He put them both into the pram and pushed them down the road, the other two walking by his side. Mysteriously now the lorry traffic was all gone; there was nothing on the road but refugees.

The road was full of refugees. Farm carts, drawn by great Flemish horses, lumbered down the middle of the road at walking pace, loaded with furniture and bedding and sacks of food and people. Between them and around them seethed the motor traffic; big cars and little cars, occasional ambulances and motor-bicycles, all going to the west. There were innumerable cyclists and long trails of people pushing hand-carts and perambulators in the torrid July heat. All were choked with dust, all sweating and distressed, all pressing on to Montargis. From time to time an aeroplane flew near the road; then there was panic and an accident or two. But no bombs were dropped that day, nor was the road to Montargis machine-gunned.

The heat was intense. At about a quarter to twelve they came to a place where a little stream ran beside the road, and here there was another block of many traffic blocks caused by the drivers of the farm wagons who stopped to water their horses. Howard decided to make a halt; he pushed the perambulator a little way over the field away from the road to where a little sandy spit ran out into the stream beneath the trees.

'We'll stop here for *déjeuner*,' he said to the children. 'Go and wash your hands and faces in the water.' He took the food and sat down in the shade; he was very tired, but there was still five miles or more to Montargis. Surely there would be a motor-bus there?

Ronnie said: 'May I paddle, Mr Howard?'

He roused himself. 'Bathe if you want to,' he said. 'It's hot enough.'

'May I really bathe?'

Sheila echoed: 'May I really bathe, too?'

He got up from the grass. 'I don't see why not,' he said slowly. 'Take your things off and have a bathe before *déjeuner*, if you want to.'

The English children needed no further encouragement. Ronnie was out of his few clothes and splashing in the water in a few seconds; Sheila got into a tangle with her Liberty bodice and had to be helped. Howard watched them for a minute, amused. Then he turned to Rose. 'Would you like to go in, too?' he said in French.

She shook her head in scandalised amazement. 'It is not nice, that, monsieur. Not at all.'

He glanced at the little naked bodies gleaming in the sun. 'No,' he said reflectively, 'I suppose it's not. Still, they may as well go on now they've started.' He turned to Pierre. 'Would you like to bathe, Pierre?'

The little boy in grey stared round-eyed at the English children. '*Non, merci, monsieur,*' he said.

Howard said: 'Wouldn't you like to take your shoes off and have a paddle, then? In the water?' The child looked doubtfully at him, and then at Rose. 'It's nice in the water.' He turned to Rose. 'Take him and let him put his feet in the water, Rose.'

She took the little boy's shoes and socks off and they went down and paddled at the very edge of the water. Howard went back to the shade of the trees and sat down again where he could see the children. Presently Sheila splashed a little water at the paddlers; he heard *la petite* Rose scolding. He saw the little boy in grey, standing in an inch of water, stoop and put his hand in and splash a little back. And then, among the chatter, he heard a shrill little sound that was quite new to him.

It was Pierre laughing.

Behind his back he heard a man say:

'God love a duck! Look at them bleeding kids – just like Brighton.'

Another said: 'Never mind about the muckin' kids. Look at the mud they've stirred up. We can't put that stuff in the radiator. Better go on up-stream a bit. And get a move on or we'll be here all the muckin' night.'

Howard swung round and there, before him in the field, were two men, dirty and unshaven, in British Royal Air Force uniform. One was a corporal and one a driver.

He started up. 'I'm English,' he burst out. 'Have you got a car?'

The corporal stared at him, amazed. 'And who the muckin' hell might you be?'

'I'm English. These children are English, two of them. We're trying to get through to Chartres.'

'Chartres?' The corporal was puzzled.

'Chartres, 'e means,' the driver said. 'I see that on the map.'

Howard said: 'You've got a car?'

'Workshop lorry,' said the corporal. He swung round on the driver. 'Get the muckin' water and start filling up, Bert.' The driver went off up-stream swinging his can.

The old man said: 'Can you give us a lift?'

'What, you and all them kids? I dunno about that, mate. How far do you want to go?'

'I'm trying to get back to England.'

'You ain't the only one.'

'I only want a lift to Chartres. They say that trains are running from there to St Malo.'

'You don't want to believe all these Froggies say. Tried to tell us it was all right goin' through a place called Susan yesterday, and when we got there it was full of muckin' Jerries! All loosing off their hipes at Bert and me like we was Aunt Sally! Ever drive a ten-ton Leyland, mate?'

The old man shook his head.

'Well, she don't handle like an Austin Seven. Bert stuck 'is foot down and I got the old Bren going over the windshield and we went round the roundabout like it was the banking at Brooklands, and out the way we come, and all we got was two bullets in the motor generator what makes the juice for lighting and that, and a little chip out of the aft leg of the Herbert, what won't make any odds if the officer don't notice it. But fancy saying we could go through there! Susan the name was, or something of that.'

The old man blinked at him. 'Where are you making for?'

The corporal said: 'Place called Brest. Not the kind of name I'd like to call a town, myself, but that's the way these Froggies are. Officer said to go there if we got cut off, and we'd get the lorry shipped back home from there.'

Howard said: 'Take us with you.'

The other looked uncertainly at the children. 'I dunno what to say. I dunno if there'd be room. Them kids ain't English.'

'Two of them are. They're speaking French now, but that's because they've been brought up in France.'

The driver passed them with his dripping can, going towards the road.

'What are the other two?'

'They're French.'

'I ain't taking no Froggie kids along,' the corporal said. 'I ain't got no room, for one thing, and they're just as well left in their own place, to my way of thinking. I don't mind obliging you and the two English ones.'

Howard said: 'You don't understand. The two French

ones are in my care.' He explained the situation to the man.

'It's no good, mate,' he said. 'I ain't got room for all of you.'

Howard said slowly: 'I see . . .' He stared for a moment absently at the traffic on the road. 'If it's a matter of room,' he said, 'will you take the four children through to Brest with you? They won't take up much room. I'll give you a letter for the RTO at Brest, and a letter to my solicitor in England. And I can give you money for anything they'll want.'

The other wrinkled his brows. 'Leaving you here?'

'I'll be all right. In fact, I'll get along quicker without them.'

'You mean take them two Froggie kids along 'stead of you? Is that what you're getting at?

'I'll be all right. I know France very well.'

'Don't talk so bloody soft. What 'ld I do with four muckin' kids and only Bert along o' me?' He swung round on his heel. 'Come on, then. Get them kids dressed toot and sweet – I ain't going to wait all night. And if I finds them messing with the Herbert I'll tan their little bottoms for them, straight I will.'

He swung off back towards his lorry. Howard hurried down to the sand pit and called the children to him. 'Come on and get your clothes on, quickly,' he said. 'We're going in a motor-lorry.'

Ronnie faced him, stark naked. 'Really? What sort is it? May I sit by the driver, Mr Howard?'

Sheila, similarly nude, echoed: 'May I sit by the driver too?'

'Come on and get your clothes on,' he repeated. He turned to Rose and said in French: 'Put your stockings on, Rose, and help Pierre. We've got to be very quick.'

He hurried the children all he could, but they were wet and the clothes stuck to them; he had no towel. Before he was finished the two Air Force men were back with him, worrying with their urgency to start. At last he had the children ready. 'Will you be able to take my perambulator?' he asked, a little timidly.

The corporal said: 'We can't take that muckin' thing, mate. It's not worth a dollar.'

The old man said: 'I know it's not. But if we have to walk again, it's all I've got to put the little ones in.'

The driver chipped in: 'Let 'im take it on the roof. It'll ride there all right, corp. We'll all be walking if we don't get hold of juice.'

'My muckin' Christ,' the corporal said. 'Call this a workshop lorry! Perishing Christmas tree, I call it. All right, stick it on the roof.'

He hustled them towards the road. The lorry stood gigantic by the roadside, the traffic eddying round it. Inside it was stuffed full of machinery. An enormous Herbert lathe stood in the middle. A grinding-wheel and valve-facing machine stood at one end, a little filing and sawing machine at the other. Beneath the lathe a motor-generator set was housed; above it was a long electric switchboard. The men's kitbags occupied what little room there was.

Howard hastily removed their lunch from the pram, and watched it heaved up on the roof of the van. Then he helped the children up among the machinery. The corporal refused point-blank to let them ride beside the driver. 'I got the Bren there, see?' he said. 'I don't want no perishing kids around if we runs into Jerries.'

Howard said: 'I see that.' He consoled Ronnie and climbed in himself into the lorry. The corporal saw them settled, then went round and got up by the driver; with a low purr and a lurch the lorry moved out into the traffic stream.

It was half an hour later that the old man realised that they had left Sheila's pants beside the stream in their hurry.

They settled down to the journey. The interior of the van was awkward and uncomfortable for Howard, with no place to sit down and rest; he had to stoop, half kneeling, on a kitbag. The children being smaller, were more comfortable. The old man got out their *déjeuner* and gave them food in moderation, with a little of the orange drink; on his advice Rose ate very little, and remained well. He had rescued Pierre's chocolate from the perambulator and gave it to him, as a matter of course, when they had finished eating. The little boy received it solemnly and put it into his mouth; the old man watched him with grave amusement.

Rose said: 'It is good, that, Pierre.' She bent down and smiled at him.

He nodded gravely. 'Very good,' he whispered.

Very soon they came to Montargis. Through a little trap-door in the partition between the workshop and the driver's seat the corporal said to Howard: 'Ever been here before, mate?'

The old man said: 'I've only passed it in the train, a great many years ago.'

'You don't know where the muckin' petrol dump would be? We got to get some juice from somewhere.'

Howard shook his head. 'I'm afraid I don't. I'll ask someone for you, if you like.'

'Christ. Do you speak French that good?'

The driver said: 'They all speak it, corp. Even the bloody kids.'

The corporal turned back to Howard. 'Just keep them kids down close along the floor, mate, case we find the Jerries like in that place Susan.'

The old man was startled. 'I don't think there are any Germans so far west as this,' he said. But he made the children lie down on the floor, which they took as a fine joke. So, with the little squeals of laughter from the body of the lorry, they rolled into Montargis and pulled up at the crossroads in the middle of the town.

At the corporal's request the old man got down and asked the way to the military petrol dump. A baker directed him to the north of the town; he got up into the driver's compartment and directed them through the town. They found the French transport park without great difficulty, and Howard went with the corporal to speak to the officer in charge, a lieutenant. They got a brusque refusal. The town was being evacuated, they were told. If they had no petrol they must leave their lorry and go south.

The corporal swore luridly, so luridly that Howard was quite glad that the English children, who might possibly have understood, were in the lorry.

'I got to get this muckin' lot to Brest,' he said. 'I don't leave it here and hop it, like he said.' He truned to Howard, suddenly earnest. 'Look, mate,' he said. 'Maybe you better beat it with the kids. You don't want to get mixed up with the bloody Jerries.'

The old man said: 'If there's no petrol, you may as well come with us.'

The Air Force man said: 'You don't savvy, mate. I *got* to get this lot to Brest. That big Herbert. You don't know lathes, maybe, but that's a treat. Straight it is. Machine tools is wanted back home. I *got* to get that Herbert home – I *got* to Let the Jerries have it for the taking, I suppose! Not bloody likely.'

He ran his eye around the park. It was filled with decrepit, dirty French lorries; rapidly the few remaining soldiers were leaving. The lieutenant that had refused them drove out in a little Citroën car. 'I bet there's juice somewhere about,' the corporal muttered.

He swung round and hailed the driver. 'Hey, Bert,' he said: 'Come on along.'

The men went ferreting about among the cars. They found no dump or store of petrol, but presently Howard saw them working at the deserted lorries, emptying the tanks into a *bidon*. Gleaning a gallon here and a gallon there, they collected in all about eight gallons and transferred it to the enormous tank of the Leyland. That was all that they could find. 'It ain't much,' said the corporal. 'Forty miles, maybe. Still, that's better 'n a sock in the jaw. Let's see the bloody map, Bert.'

The bloody map showed them Pithiviers, twenty-five miles farther on. 'Let's get goin'.' They moved out on the westward road again.

It was terribly hot. The van body of the lorry had sides made of wood, which folded outwards to enlarge the floor space when the lathe was in use. Little light entered round these wooden sides; it was dim and stuffy and very smelly in amongst the machinery. The children did not seem to suffer much, but it was a trying journey for the old man. In a short time he had a splitting headache, and was aching in every limb from the cramped positions he was constrained to take up.

The road was ominously clear to Pithiviers, and they made good speed. From time to time an aeroplane flew low above the road, and once there was a sharp burst of machine-gun fire very near at hand. Howard leaned over to the little window at the driver's elbow. 'Jerry bomber,' said the corporal. One o' them Stukas, as they call them.'

'Was he firing at us?'

'Aye. Miles off, he was.' The corporal did not seem especially perturbed.

In an hour they were near Pithiviers, five and twenty miles from Montargis. They drew up by the roadside half a mile from the town and held a consultation. The road stretched before them to the houses with no soul in sight. There was no movement in the town. It seemed to be deserted in the blazing sunlight of the afternoon.

They stared at it, irresolute. 'I dunno as I fancy it,' the corporal said. 'It don't look right to me.'

The driver said: Bloody funny nobody's about. You don't think its full of Jerries, corp? Hiding, like?'

'I dunno . . .'

Howard, leaning forward with his face to the trap in the partition, said over their shoulders: 'I don't mind walking in ahead to have a look, if you wait here.'

'Walk in ahead of us?'

'I don't see that there'd be much risk in that. With all these refugees about I can't see that there'd be much risk in it. I'd rather do that than drive in with you if there's any chance of being fired on.'

'Something in what he says,' the driver said. 'If the Jerries *are* there, we mightn't find another roundabout this time.'

They discussed it for a minute or two. There was no road alternative to going through the town that did not mean a ten-mile journey back towards Montargis. 'An' that's not so bloody funny, either,' said the corporal. 'Meet the Jerries coming up behind us, like as not.'

He hesitated, irresolute. 'Okay,' he said at last. 'Nip in and have a look, mate. Give us the wire if it's all okey-doke. Wave something if it's all right to come on.'

The old man said: 'I'll have to take the children with me.'

'My muckin' Christ! I don't want to sit here all the bloody day, mate.'

The old man said: 'I'm not going to be separated from the children.' He paused. 'You see, they're in my charge. Just like your lathe.'

The driver burst out laughing. 'That's a good one, corp! Just like your muckin' lathe,' he said.

The corporal said: 'Well, put a jerk in it, anyway.'

The old man got down from the lorry and lifted the children one by one down into the hot sunlight on the dusty, deserted road. He started off with them down the road towards the town, leading the two little ones by the hand, thinking uneasily that if he were to become separated from the lorry he would inevitably lose his perambulator. He made all speed possible, but it was twenty minutes before he led them into the town.

There were no Germans to be seen. The town was virtually deserted; only one or two very old women peered at him from behind curtains or around the half-closed doors of shops. In the gutter of the road that led towards the north a tattered, dirty child that might have been of either sex in its short smock, was chewing something horrible. A few yards up the road a dead horse had been dragged half up on to the pavement and left there, distended and stinking. A dog was tearing at it.

It was a beastly, sordid little town, the old man felt. He caught one of the old women at a door. 'Are the Germans here?' he said.

'They are coming from the north,' she quavered. 'They will ravish everyone, and shoot us.'

The old man felt instinctively that this was nonsense. 'Have you seen any Germans in the town yet?'

'There is one there.'

He looked round, startled. 'Where?'

'There.' She pointed a trembling, withered hand at the child in the gutter.

'There?' The woman must be mad, distraught with terror of the invaders.

'It speaks only German. It is the child of spies.' She caught his arm with senile urgency. 'Throw a stone and chase it away. It will bring the Germans to this house if it stays there.'

Howard shook her off. 'Are any German soldiers here yet?'

She did not answer, but shouted a shrill scream of dirty imprecations at the child in the gutter. The child, a little boy, Howard thought, lifted his head and looked at her with infantile disdain. Then he resumed his disgusting meal.

There was nothing more to be learned from the old hag; it was now clear to him there were no Germans in the town. He turned away; as he did so there was a sharp crack, and a fair-sized stone rolled down the pavement near the German spy. The child slunk off fifty yards down the street and squatted down again upon the kerb.

The old man was very angry, but he had other things to do. He said to Rose: 'Look after the children for a minute, Rose. Don't let them go away or speak to anyone.'

He hurried back along the road that they had entered the town by. He had to go a couple of hundred yards before he came in sight of the lorry, parked by the roadside half a mile away. He waved his hat at it, and saw it move towards him; then he turned and walked back to where he had left the children.

It overtook him near the cross-roads in the middle of the town. The corporal leaned down from the cab. 'Any juice here, do you think?' The old man looked at him uncomprehending. 'Petrol, mate.'

'Oh – I don't know. I wouldn't hang about here very long.'

'That's right,' the driver muttered. 'Let's get on out of it. It don't look so good to me.'

'We got to get juice.'

'We got close on five gallons left. Get us to Angerville.'

'Okay,' the corporal said to Howard. 'Get the kids into the back and we'll 'op it.'

Howard looked round for his children. They were not where he had left them; he looked round, and they were up the road with the German spy, who was crying miserably.

'Rose,' he shouted. 'Come on. Bring the children.'

She called in a thin, piping voice: '*Il est blessé.*'

'Come on,' he cried. The children looked at him, but did not stir. He hurried over to them. 'Why don't you come when I call you?'

Rose faced the old man, her little face crimson with anger. 'Somebody threw a stone at him and hit him. I saw them do it. It is not right, that.'

True enough, a sticky stream of blood was running down the back of the child's neck into his filthy clothes. A sudden loathing for the town enveloped the old man. He took his handkerchief and mopped at the wound.

La petite Rose said: 'It is not right to throw a stone at him, and a big woman, too, m'sieur. This is a bad, dirty place to do a thing like that.'

Ronnie said: 'He's coming with us, Mr Howard. He can sit on the other end of Bert's kitbag by the 'lectric motor.'

The old man said: 'He belongs here. We can't take him away with us.' But in his mind came the thought that it might be kind to do so.

'He doesn't belong here,' said Rose. 'Two days only he has been here. The woman said so.'

There was a hurried, heavy step behind them. 'For Christ's sake,' said the corporal.

Howard turned to him. 'They're throwing stones at this child,' he said. He showed the man the cut upon his neck.

'Who's throwing stones?'

'All the people in the village. They think he's a German spy.'

'Who – 'im?' The corporal stared. 'He ain't more'n seven years old!'

'I saw the woman do it,' said Ronnie. 'That house there. She threw a stone and did that.'

'My muckin' aunt,' the corporal said. He turned to Howard. 'Anyway, we got to beat it.'

'I know.' The old man hesitated. 'What'll we do? Leave him here in this disgusting place? Or bring him along with us?'

'Bring him along, mate, if you feel like it. I ain't worried over the amount of spying that he'll do.'

The old man bent and spoke to the child. 'Would you like to come with us?' he said in French.

The little boy said something in another language.

Howard said: *'Sprechen sie Deutsch?'* That was the limit of the German that he could recall at the moment, but it drew no response.

He straightened up, heavy with new responsibility. 'We'll take him with us,' he said quietly. 'If we leave him here they'll probably end by killing him.'

'If we don't get a move on,' said the corporal, 'the bloody Jerries will be here and kill the lot of us.'

Howard picked up the spy, who suffered that in silence; they hurried to the lorry. The child smelt and was plainly verminous; the old man turned his face away in nausea. Perhaps in Angerville there would be nuns who would take charge of him. They might take Pierre, too, though Pierre was so little bother that the old man didn't mind about him much.

They put the children in the workshop; Howard got in with them and the corporal got into the front seat by the driver. The big truck moved across the road from Paris and out upon the road to Angerville, seventeen miles away.

'If we don't get some juice at Angerville,' the driver said, 'we'll be bloody well sunk.'

In the van, crouched down beside the lathe with the children huddled round him, the old man pulled out a sticky bundle of his chocolate. He broke off five pieces for the children; as soon as the German spy realised what it was he stretched out a filthy paw and said something unintelligible. He ate it greedily and stretched out his hand for more.

'You wait a bit.' The old man gave the chocolate to the other children. Pierre whispered: '*Merci, monsieur.*'

La petite Rose leaned down to him. 'After supper, Pierre?' she said. 'Shall monsieur keep it for you to have after supper?'

The little boy whispered: 'Only on Sunday. On Sunday I may have chocolate after supper. Is today Sunday?'

The old man said: 'I'm not quite sure what day it is. But I don't think your mother will mind if you have chocolate after supper tonight. I'll put it away and you can have it then.'

He rummaged round and produced one of the thick, hard biscuits that he had bought in the morning, and with some difficulty broke it in two; he offered one half to the dirty little boy in the smock. The child took it and ate it ravenously.

Rose scolded at him in French: 'Is that the way to eat? A little pig would eat more delicately – yes, truly, I say – a little pig. You should thank monsieur, too.'

The child stared at her, not understanding why she was scolding him.

She said: 'Have you not been taught how to behave? You should say like this' – she swung round and bowed to Howard – '*Je vous remercie, monsieur.*'

Her words passed him by, but the pantomime was evident. He looked confused. '*Dank, Mijnheer,*' he said awkwardly. '*Dank u wel.*'

Howard stared at him, perplexed. It was a northern language, but not German. It might, he thought, be Flemish or Walloon, or even Dutch. In any case, it mattered very little; he himself knew no word of any of those languages.

They drove on at a good pace through the hot afternoon. The hatch to the driver's compartment was open; from time to time the old man leaned forward and looked through between the two men at the road ahead of them. It was suspiciously clear. They passed only a very few refugees, and very occasionally a farm cart going on its ordinary business. There were no soldiers to be seen, and of the seething refugee traffic between Joigny and Montargis there was no sign at all. The whole countryside seemed empty, dead.

Three miles from Angerville the corporal turned and spoke to Howard through the hatch. 'Getting near that next town now,' he said. 'We got to get some juice there, or we're done.'

The old man said: 'If you see anyone likely on the road I'll ask them where the depot is.'

'Okay.'

In a few minutes they came to a farm. A car stood outside it, and a man was carrying sacks of grain or fodder from the car into the farm. 'Stop here,' the old man said, 'I'll ask that chap.'

They drew up by the roadside, immediately switching off the engine to save petrol. 'Only about a gallon left now,' said the driver. 'We run it bloody fine, an' no mistake.'

Howard got down and walked back to the farm. The man,

a grey-beard of about fifty without a collar, came out towards the car. 'We want petrol,' said Howard. 'There is, without doubt, a depot for military transport in Angerville?'

The man stared at him. 'There are Germans in Angerville.'

There was a momentary silence. The old Englishman stared across the farmyard at the lean pig rooting on the midden, at the scraggy fowls scratching in the dust. So it was closing in on him.

'How long have they been there?' he asked quietly.

'Since early morning. They have come from the north.'

There was no more to be said about that. 'Have you petrol? I will buy any that you have, at your own price.'

The peasant's eyes glowed. 'A hundred francs a litre.'

'How much have you got?'

The man looked at the gauge upon the battered dashboard of his car. 'Seven litres. Seven hundred francs.'

Less than a gallon and a half of petrol would not take the ten-ton Leyland very far. Howard went back to the corporal.

'Not very good news, I'm afraid,' he said. 'The Germans are in Angerville.'

There was a pause. 'Bloody 'ell,' the corporal said at last. He said it very quietly, as if he were suddenly tired. 'How many are there there?'

Howard called back the enquiry to the peasant. 'A regiment,' he said. 'I suppose he means about a thousand men.'

'Come down from the north, like,' said the driver.

There was nothing much more to be said. The old man told them about the petrol. 'That's not much good,' the corporal said. 'With what we've got, that wouldn't take us more'n ten miles.' He turned to the driver. 'Let's 'ave the muckin' map.'

Together they pored over the sheet; the old man got up into the cab and studied it with them. There was no side road between them and the town; behind them there was no road leading to the south for nearly seven miles. 'That's right,' the driver said. 'I didn't see no road on that side when we came along.'

The corporal said quietly: 'An' if we did go back, we'd meet the Jerries coming along after us from that other muckin' place. Where he picked up the nipper what they told him was a spy.'

'That's right,' the driver said.

The corporal said: 'Got a fag?'

The driver produced a cigarette; the corporal lit it and blew a long cloud. 'Well,' he said presently, 'this puts the lid on it.'

The other two were silent.

'I wanted to get home with that big Herbert,' the corporal said. 'I wanted to get that through okay, as much as I ever wanted anything in all my life.' He turned to Howard: 'Straight, I did. But I ain't going to.'

The old man said gently: 'I am very sorry.'

The other shook himself. 'You can't always do them things you want to most.' He stirred. 'Well, this won't buy baby a new frock.'

He got down from the cab on to the ground. 'What are you going to do?' asked Howard.

'I'll show you what I'm going to do.' He led the old man to the side of the great lorry, about half-way down its length. There was a little handle sticking out through the side chassis member, painted bright red. 'I'm going to pull that tit, and run like bloody 'ell.'

'Demolition,' said the driver at his elbow. 'Pull that out an' up she goes.'

The corporal said: 'Come on, now. Get them muckin'

kids out of the back. I'm sorry we can't take you any farther, mate, but that's the way it is.'

Howard said: 'What will you do, yourselves?'

The corporal said: 'Mugger off cross-country to the south an' hope to keep in front of the Jerries.' He hesitated. 'You'll be all right,' he said, a little awkwardly. 'They won't do nothin' to you, with all them kids.'

The old man said: 'We'll be all right. Don't worry about us. You've got to get back home to fight again.'

'We got to dodge the muckin' Jerries first.'

Together they got the children down on to the road; then they lifted the pram from the top of the van. Howard collected his few possessions and stowed them in the pram, took the corporal's address in England, and gave his own.

There was nothing then to wait for.

'So long, mate,' said the corporal. 'See you one day.'

The old man said: 'So long.'

He gathered the children round him and set off with them slowly down the road in the direction of Angerville. There was a minor squabble as to who should push the pram, which finished up by Sheila pushing it with Ronnie to assist and advise. Rose walked beside them leading Pierre by the hand; the dirty little stranger in his queer frock followed along behind. Howard thought ruefully that somehow, somewhere, he must get him washed. Not only was he verminous and filthy, but the back of his neck and his clothes were clotted with dried blood from the cut.

They went slowly, as they always did. From time to time Howard glanced back over his shoulder; the men by the lorry seemed to be sorting out their personal belongings. Then one of them, the driver, started off across the field towards the south, carrying a small bundle. The other bent to some task at the lorry.

Then he was up and running from the road towards the driver. He ran clumsily, stumbling; when he had gone about two hundred yards there was a sharp, crackling explosion.

A sheet of flame shot outwards from the lorry. Parts of it sailed up into the air and fell upon the road and into the fields; then it sunk lower on the road. A little tongue of fire appeared, and it was in flames.

Ronnie said: 'Coo, Mr Howard. Did it blow up?'

Sheila echoed: 'Did it blow up itself, Mr Howard?'

'Yes,' he said heavily, 'that's what happened.' A column of thick black smoke rose from it on the road. He turned away. 'Don't bother about it any more.'

Two miles ahead of him he saw the roofs of Angerville. The net was practically closed upon him now. With a heavy heart he led the children down the road towards the town.

6

I broke into his story and said, a little breathlessly: 'This one's not far off.'

We sat tense in our chairs before the fire, listening to the rising whine of the bomb. It burst somewhere very near, and in the rumble of the falling debris we heard another falling, closer still. We sat absolutely motionless as the club rocked to the explosion and the glass crashed from the windows, and the whine of the third bomb grew shrill. It burst upon the other side of us.

'Straddled,' said old Howard, breaking the tension. 'That's all right.'

The fourth bomb of the stick fell farther away; then there was a pause, but for a burst of machine-gun fire. I got up from my chair and walked out to the corridor. It was in darkness. A window leading out on to a little balcony had been blown open. I went out and looked round.

Over towards the city the sky was a deep, cherry red with the glow of the fires. Around us there was a bright, yellow light from three parachute-flares suspended in the sky; Bren guns and Lewis guns were rattling away at these things in an attempt to shoot them down. Close at hand, down the street, another fire was getting under way.

I turned, and Howard was at my side. 'Pretty hot tonight,' he said.

I nodded. 'Would you like to go down into the shelter?'

'Are you going?'

'I don't believe it's any safer there than here,' I said.

We went down to the hall to see if there was anything we could do to help. But there was nothing to be done, and presently we went up to our chairs again beside the fire and poured another glass of the Marsala. I said: 'Go on with your story.'

He said diffidently: 'I hope I'm not boring you with all this?'

Angerville is a little town upon the Paris–Orleans road. It was about five o'clock when Howard started to walk towards it with the children, a hot, dusty afternoon.

He told me that that was one of the most difficult moments of his life. Since he had left Cidoton he had been travelling towards England; as he had gone on fear had grown upon him. Up to the last it had seemed incredible that he should not get through, hard though the way might be. But now he realised that he would not get through. The Germans were between him and the sea. In marching on to Angerville he was marching to disaster, to internment, probably to his death.

That did not worry him so much. He was old and tired; if an end came now he would be missing nothing very much. A few more days of fishing, a few more summers pottering in his garden. But the children – they were another matter. Somehow he must make them secure. Rose and Pierre might be turned over to the French police; sooner or later they would be returned to their relations. But Sheila and Ronnie – what arrangements could he possibly make for them? What would become of them? And what about the dirty little boy who now was with them, who had been stoned by old women mad with terror and blind hate? What would become of him?

The old man suffered a good deal.

There was nothing to be done but to walk straight into Angerville. The Germans were behind them, to the north, to the east, and to the west. He felt that it was hopeless to attempt a dash across the country to the south as the Air Force men had done; he could not possibly out-distance the advance of the invader. Better to go ahead and meet what lay before him bravely, conserving his strength that he might help the children best.

Ronnie said: 'Listen to the band.'

They were about half a mile from the town. Rose exclaimed with pleasure. '*Ecoute*, Pierre,' she said, bending down to him. '*Ecoute!*'

'Eh,' said Howard, waking from his reverie. 'What's that?'

Ronnie said: 'There's a band playing in the town. May we go and listen to it?' But his ears were keener than the old man's, and Howard could hear nothing.

Presently, as they walked into the town, he picked out the strains of Liebestraum.

On the way into the town they passed a train of very dirty lorries halted by the road, drawing in turn up to a garage and filling their tanks at the pump. The soldiers moving round them appeared strange at first; with a shock the old man realised that he was seeing what he had expected for the last hour to see; the men were German soldiers. They wore field-grey uniforms with open collars and patch pockets, with a winged eagle broidered on the right breast. Some of them were bare-headed; others wore the characteristic German steel helmet. They had sad, tired, expressionless faces; they moved about their work like so many machines.

Sheila said: 'Are those Swiss soldiers, Mr Howard?'

'No,' he said, 'they're not Swiss.'

Ronnie said: 'They wear the same kind of hat.'

Rose said: 'What are they?'

He gathered them around him. 'Look,' he said in French, 'you mustn't be afraid. They are German, but they won't hurt you.'

They were passing a little group of them. From the crowd an *Unterfeldwebel* came up to them; he wore long black boots and breeches stained with oil. 'That is the proper spirit,' he said in harsh, guttural French. 'We Germans are your friends. We bring you peace. Very soon you will be able to go home again.'

The children stared at him, as if they did not understand what he had said. Very likely this was so, because his French was very bad.

Howard said in French: 'It will be good when we have peace again.' There was no point in giving up before he was found out.

The man smiled, a set, expressionless grin. 'How far have you come?'

'From Pithiviers.'

'Have you walked so far?'

'No. We got a lift in a lorry which broke down a few miles back.'

The German said: 'So. Then you will want supper. In the *Place* there is a soup-kitchen which you may go to.'

Howard said: '*Je vous remercie.*' There was nothing else to say.

The man was pleased. He ran his eye over them and frowned at the little boy in the smock. He stepped up and took him by the head, not ungently, and examined the wound upon his neck. Then he looked at his own hands, and wiped them with disgust, having handled the child's head.

'So!' he said. 'By the church there is a field hospital. Take him to the *Sanitätsunteroffizier*.' He dismissed them curtly and turned back to his men.

One or two of the men looked at them woodenly, listlessly, but no one else spoke to them. They went on to the centre of the town. At the cross-roads in the middle, where the road to Orleans turned off to the left and the road to Paris to the right, there was a market square before a large grey church. In the centre of the square the band was playing.

It was a band of German soldiers. They stood there, about twenty of them, playing doggedly, methodically; doing their duty for their Führer. They wore soft field caps and silver tassels on their shoulders. A *Feldwebel* conducted them. He stood above them on a little rostrum, the baton held lovingly between his finger-tips. He was a heavy, middle-aged man; as he waved he turned from side to side and smile benignly on his audience. Behind the band a row of tanks and armoured cars were parked.

The audience was mostly French. A few grey-faced, listless German soldiers stood around, seemingly tired to death; the remainder of the audience were men and women of the town. They stood round gaping curiously at the intruder, peering at the tanks and furtively studying the uniforms and accoutrements of the men.

Ronnie said in English, 'There's the band, Mr Howard. May we go and listen to it?'

The old man looked quickly round. Nobody seemed to have heard him. 'Not now,' he said in French. 'We must go with this little boy to have his neck dressed.'

He led the children away from the crowd. 'Try not to speak English while we're here,' he said quietly to Ronnie.

'Why not, Mr Howard?'

Sheila said: 'May I speak English, Mr Howard?'

133

'No,' he said. 'The Germans don't like to hear people speaking English.'

The little girl said in English: 'Would the Germans mind if Rose spoke English?'

A passing Frenchwoman looked at them curiously. The old man beat down his irritation; they were only children. He said in French: 'If you speak English I'll find a little frog to put into your mouth.'

Rose said: 'Oo – to hear what monsieur has said! A little frog! It would be horrible, that.'

In mixed laughter and apprehension they went on talking in French.

The field hospital was on the far side of the church. As they went towards it every German soldier that they passed smiled at them mechanically, a set, expressionless grin. When the first one did it the children stopped to stare, and had to be herded on. After the first half-dozen they got used to it.

One of the men said: *'Bonjour, mes enfants.'*

Howard muttered quietly. *'Bonjour, m'sieur,'* and passed on. It was only a few steps to the hospital tent; the net was very close around him now.

The hospital consisted of a large marquee extending from a lorry. At the entrance a lance-corporal of the medical service, a *Sanitätsgefreiter*, stood idle and bored, picking his teeth.

Howard said to Rose: 'Stay here and keep the children with you.' He led the little boy up to the tent. He said to the man in French: 'The little boy is wounded. A little piece of plaster or a bandage, perhaps?'

The man smiled, that same fixed, mirthless smile. He examined the child deftly. *'So!'* he said. *'Kommen Sie – entrez.'*

The old man followed with the child into the tent. A

dresser was tending a German soldier with a burnt hand; apart from them the only other occupant was a doctor wearing a white overall. His rank was not apparent. The orderly led the child to him and showed him the wound.

The doctor nodded briefly. Then he turned the child's head to the light and looked at it, expressionless. Then he opened the child's soiled clothes and looked at his chest. Then, rather ostentatiously, he rinsed his hands.

He crossed the tent to Howard. 'You will come again,' he said in thick French. 'In one hour,' he held up one finger. 'One hour.' Fearing that he had not made himself understood he pulled out his watch and pointed to the hands. 'Six hours.'

'*Bien compris*,' said the old man. '*A six heures.*' He left the tent, wondering what dark trouble lay in store for him. It could not take an hour to put a dressing on a little cut.

Still there was nothing he could do. He did not dare even to enter into any long conversation with the German; sooner or later his British accent must betray him. He went back to the children and led them away from the tent.

Earlier in the day – how long ago it seemed! – Sheila had suffered a sartorial disaster, in that she had lost her knickers. It had not worried her or any of the children, but it had weighed on Howard's mind. Now was the time to rectify that omission. To ease Ronnie's longings they went and had a look at the German tanks in the *Place*; then, ten minutes later, he led them to a draper's shop not far from the field hospital.

He pushed open the door of the shop, and a German soldier was at the counter. It was too late to draw back, and to do so would have raised suspicion; he stood aside and waited till the German had finished his purchases. Then, as he stood there in the background, he saw that the German was the orderly from the hospital.

A little bundle of clothes lay upon the counter before him, a yellow jersey, a pair of brown children's shorts, socks, and a vest. 'Cinquante quatre, quatre vingt dix,' said the stout old woman at the counter.

The German did not understand her rapid way of speech. She repeated it several times; then he pushed a little pad of paper towards her, and she wrote the sum upon the pad for him. He took it and studied it. Then he wrote his own name and the unit carefully beneath. He tore off the sheet and gave it to her.

'You will be paid later,' he said, in difficult French. He gathered up the garments.

She protested. 'I cannot let you take away the clothes unless I have the money. My husband – he would be very much annoyed. He would be furious. Truly, monsieur – that is not possible at all.'

The German said stolidly: 'It is good. You will be paid. That is a good requisition.'

She said angrily: 'It is not good at all, that. It is necessary that you should pay with money.'

The man said: 'That is money, good German money. If you do not believe it, I will call the Military Police. As for your husband, he had better take our German money and be thankful. Perhaps he is a Jew? We have a way with Jews.'

The woman stared at him, dumb. There was a momentary silence in the shop; then the hospital orderly gathered up his purchases and swaggered out. The woman remained staring after him, uncertainly fingering the piece of paper.

Howard went forward and distracted her. She roused herself and showed him children's pants. With much advice from Rose upon the colour and design he chose a pair for Sheila, paid three francs fifty for them, and put them on her in the shop.

The woman stood fingering the money. 'You are not German, monsieur?' she said heavily. She glanced down at the money in her hand.

He shook his head.

'I thought perhaps you were. Flemish?'

It would never do to admit his nationality, but at any moment one of the children might betray him. He moved towards the door. 'Norwegian,' he said at random. 'My country has also suffered.'

'I thought you were not French,' she said. 'I do not know what will become of us.'

He left the shop and went a little way up the Paris road, hoping to avoid the people. German soldiers were still pouring into the town. He walked about for a time in the increasing crowd, tense and fearful of betrayal every moment. At last it was six o'clock; he went back to the hospital.

He left the children by the church. 'Keep them beside you,' he said to Rose. 'I shall only be at the hospital a little while. Stay here till I come back.'

He went into the tent, tired and worn with apprehension. The orderly saw him coming. 'Wait here,' he said. 'I will tell the Herr Oberstabsarzt.'

The man vanished into the tent. The old man stood waiting at the entrance patiently. The warm sun was pleasant now, in the cool of the evening. It would have been pleasant to stay free, to get back to England. But he was tired now, very, very tired. If only he could see the children right, then he could rest.

There was a movement in the tent, and the doctor was there, leading a child by the hand. It was a strange, new child, sucking a sweet. It was spotlessly clean, with short cropped hair trimmed close to its head with clippers. It was a little boy. He wore a yellow jersey and a pair of brown shorts, socks, and new shoes. The clothes were all brand new, and all seemed vaguely familiar to the old man. The little boy smelt very strong of yellow soap and disinfectant.

He wore a clean white dressing on his neck. He smiled at the old man.

Howard stared at him, dumbfounded. The doctor said genially; 'So! My orderly has given him a bath. That is better?'

The old man said: 'It is wonderful, Herr Doktor. And the clothes, too. And the dressing on his neck. I do not know how to thank you.'

The doctor swelled visibly. 'It is not me that you must thank, my friend,' he said with heavy geniality. 'It is Germany! We Germans have come to bring you peace, and cleanliness, and the ordered life that is true happiness. There will be no more war, no more wandering for you now. We Germans are your friends.'

'Indeed,' the old man said faintly, 'we realise that, Herr Doktor.'

'So,' said the man, 'what Germany has done for this boy, she will do for France, for all Europe. A new Order has begun.'

There was rather an awkward silence. Howard was about to say something suitable, but the yellow jersey caught his eye, and the image of the woman in the shop came into his mind and drove the words from his head. He stood hesitant for a minute.

The doctor gave the child a little push towards him. 'What Germany has done for this one little Dutchman she will do for all the children of the world,' he said. 'Take him away. You are his father?'

Fear lent speed to the old man's thoughts. A half-truth was best. 'He is not mine,' he said. 'He was lost and quite alone in Pithiviers. I shall take him to the convent.'

The man nodded, satisfied with that. 'I thought you might be Dutch yourself,' he said. 'You do not speak like these French.'

It would not do to say he was Norwegian again; it was too near to Germany. 'I am from the south,' he said. 'From Toulouse. But I am staying with my son in Montmirail. Then we got separated in Montargis; I do not know what has become of him. The children I was with are my grandchildren. They are now in the *Place*. They have been very good children, m'sieur, but it will be good when we can go home.'

He rambled on, getting into the stride of his tale, easily falling into the garrulity of an old man. The doctor turned away rudely. 'Well, take your brat,' he said. 'You can go home now. There will be no more fighting.'

He went back into the tent.

The old man took the little boy by the hand and led him round the church, passing on the other side of the shop that had sold children's clothes. He found Rose standing more or less where he had left her, with Sheila and Pierre. There was no sign of Ronnie.

He said anxiously to her: 'Rose, what has become of Ronnie? Where is he?'

She said: 'M'sieur, he has been so naughty. He wanted to see the tanks, but I told him it was wrong that he should go. I told him, m'sieur, that he was a very, very naughty little boy and that you would be very cross with him, m'sieur. But he ran off, all alone.'

Sheila piped up, loud and clear, in English: 'May I go and see the tanks, too, Mr Howard?'

Mechanically, he said in French: 'Not this evening. I told you that you were all to stay here.'

He looked around, irresolute. He did not know whether to leave the children where they were and go and look for Ronnie, or to take them with him. Either course might bring the other children into danger. If he left them they might get into further trouble. He took hold of the pram and pushed it ahead of him. 'Come this way,' he said.

Pierre edged up to him and whispered: 'May I push?'

It was the first time that the old man had heard the little boy volunteer a remark. He surrendered the handle of the pram. 'Of course,' he said. 'Rose, help him push.'

He walked beside them towards the parked tanks and lorries, anxiously scanning the crowd. There were German soldiers all about the transport, grey, weary men, consciously endeavouring to fraternise with a suspicious population. Some of them were cleaning up their clothes, some tending their machines. Others had little phrase books in their hands, and these were trying to make conversation with the crowd. The French peasants seemed sullen and uncommunicative.

Sheila said suddenly: 'There's Ronnie, over there!'

The old man turned, but could not see him. 'Where is he?'

Rose said: 'I see him – oh, m'sieur, what a naughty little boy. There, m'sieur, right inside the tank, there – with the German soldiers!'

A cold fear entered Howard's heart. His eyesight for long distances was not too good. He screwed his eyes up and peered in the direction Rose was pointing. True enough, there he was. Howard could see his little head just sticking out of a steel hatch at the top of the gun-turret as he chattered eagerly to the German soldier with him. The man seemed to be holding Ronnie in his arms, lifting him up to show him how the captain conned his tank. It was a pretty little picture of fraternisation.

The old man thought very quickly. He knew that Ronnie would most probably be talking French; there would be nothing to impel him to break into English. But he knew also that he himself must not go near the little boy nor must his sister; in his excited state he would at once break out in English to tell them all about the tank. Yet, he must be got away immediately, while he was still thinking of nothing but the tank. Once he began to think of other things, of their journey, or of Howard himself, he would inevitably betray them all in boyish chatter. Within five minutes of him losing interest in the tank the Germans would be told that he was English, that an old Englishman was strolling round the town.

Sheila plucked his sleeve. 'I want my supper,' she said. 'May I have my supper now? Please, Mr Howard, may I have my supper now?'

'In a minute,' he said absently. 'We'll all go and have our supper in a minute.' But that was an idea. If Sheila was hungry, Ronnie would be hungry too – unless the Germans had given him sweets. He must risk that. There was that soup kitchen that the German at the entrance to the town had spoken of; Howard could see the field-cookers a hundred yards down the *Place*.

He showed them to Rose. 'I am taking the little children down there, where the smoke is, for our supper,' he said casually. 'Go and fetch Ronnie, and bring him to us there. Are you hungry?'

'*Oui, m'sieur.*' She said that she was very hungry indeed.

'We shall have a fine hot supper, with hot soup and bread,' the old man said, drawing on his imagination. 'Go and tell Ronnie and bring him along with you. I will walk on with the little ones.'

He sent her off, and watched her running through the

crowd, her bare legs twinkling. He steered the other children rather away from the tank; it would not do for Ronnie to be able to hail him. He saw the little girl come to the tank and speak urgently to the Germans; then she was lost to sight.

The old man sent up an urgent, personal prayer for the success of her unwitting errand, as he helped Pierre push the pram towards the field-cookers. There was nothing now that he could do. Their future lay in the small hands of two children, and in the hands of God.

There was a trestle table, with benches. He parked the pram and sat Pierre and Sheila and the nameless little Dutch boy at the table. Soup was dispensed in thick bowls, with a hunk of bread; he went and drew four bowls for the lot of them and brought them to the table.

He turned and Rose was at his elbow with Ronnie. The little boy was flushed and ecstatic. 'They took me right inside!' he said in English.

The old man said gently in French: 'If you tell us in French, then Pierre can understand too.' He did not think that anyone had noticed. But the town was terribly dangerous for them; at any moment the children might break into English and betray them.

Ronnie said in French: 'There was a great big gun, and two little guns, m'sieur, and you steer with two handles and it goes seventy kilos an hour!'

Howard said: 'Come on and eat your supper.' He gave him a bowl of soup and a piece of bread.

Sheila said enviously. 'Did you go for a ride, Ronnie?'

The adventurer hesitated. 'Not exactly,' he said. 'But they said I might go with them for a ride tomorrow or one day. They did speak funnily. I could hardly understand what they wanted to say. May I go for a ride with them tomorrow, m'sieur? They say I might.'

The old man said: 'We'll have to see about that. We may not be here tomorrow.'

Sheila said: 'Why did they talk funny, Ronnie?'

Rose said suddenly: 'They are dirty Germans, who come here to murder people.'

The old man coughed loudly. 'Go on and eat your supper,' he said, 'all of you. That's enough talking for the present.' More than enough, he thought; if the German dishing out the soup had overheard they would all have been in trouble.

Angerville was no place for them; at all costs he must get the children out. It was only a matter of an hour or two before exposure came. He meditated for a moment; there were still some hours of daylight. The children were tired, he knew, yet it would be better to move on, out of the town.

Chartres was the next town on his list; Chartres, where he was to have taken train for St Malo. He could not get to Chartres that night; it was the best part of thirty miles farther to the west. There was little hope now that he would escape the territory occupied by Germans, yet for want of an alternative he would carry on to Chartres. Indeed, it never really occurred to him to do otherwise.

The children were very slow eaters. It was nearly an hour before Pierre and Sheila, the two smallest, had finished their meal. The old man waited, with the patience of old age. It would do no good to hurry them. When they had finished he wiped their mouths, thanked the German cook politely, collected the pram, and led them out on to the road to Chartres.

The children walked very slowly, languidly. It was after eight o'clock, long past their ordinary bed-time; moreover, they had eaten a full meal. The sun was still warm, though it was dropping towards the horizon; manifestly, they could not go very far. Yet he kept them at it, anxious to get as far as possible from the town.

The problem of the little Dutch boy engaged his attention. He had not left him with the Sisters, as he had been minded to; it had not seemed practical when he was in the town to search out a convent. Nor had he yet got rid of Pierre, as he had promised himself that he would do. Pierre was no trouble, but this new little boy was quite a serious responsibility. He could not speak one word of any language that they spoke. Howard did not even know his name. Perhaps it would be marked upon his clothes.

Then, with a shock of dismay, the old man realised that the clothes were gone for ever. They had been taken by the Germans when the little chap had been de-loused; by this time they were probably burnt. It might well be that his identity was lost now till the war was over, and enquiries could be made. It might be lost for ever.

The thought distressed old Howard very much. It was one thing to hand over to the Sisters a child who could be traced; it seemed to him to be a different matter altogether when the little boy was practically untraceable. As he walked along the old man revolved this new trouble in his mind. The only link now with his past lay in the fact that he had been found abandoned in Pithiviers upon a certain day in June – lay in the evidence which Howard alone could give. With that evidence, it might one day be possible to find his parents or his relatives. If now he were abandoned to a convent, that evidence might well be lost.

They walked on down the dusty road.

Sheila said fretfully: 'My feet hurt.'

She was obviously tired out. He picked her up and put her in the pram, and put Pierre in with her. To Pierre he gave the chocolate that had been promised to him earlier in the day, and then all the other children had to have a piece of chocolate too. That refreshed them and made them cheerful for a while, and the old man pushed the pram wearily ahead. It was essential that they should stop soon for the night.

He stopped at the next farm, left the pram with the children in the road, and went into the court-yard to see if it was possible for them to find a bed. There was a strange stillness in the place. No dog sprang out to bark at him. He called out, and stood expectant in the evening light, but no one answered him. He tried the door to the farmhouse, and it was locked. He went into the cowhouse, but no animals were there. Two hens scratched upon the midden; otherwise there was no sign of life.

The place was deserted.

As on the previous night, they slept in the hay loft. There were no blankets to be had this time, but Howard, searching round for some sort of coverlet, discovered a large, sail-like cover, used possibly to thatch a rick. He dragged this into the loft and arranged it double on the hay, laying the children down between its folds. He had expected trouble with them, excitement and fretfulness, but they were too tired for that. All five of them were glad to lie down and rest; in a short time they were all asleep.

Howard lay resting on the hay near them, tired to death. In the last hour he had taken several nips of brandy for the weariness and weakness that he was enduring; now as he lay upon the hay in the deserted farm fatigue came soaking out of him in great waves. He felt that they were in a desperate position. There could be no hope now of getting through to England, as he once had hoped. The German front was far ahead of them; by now it might have reached to Brittany itself. All France was overrun.

Exposure might come at any time, must come before so very long. It was inevitable. His own French, though good enough, was spoken with an English accent, as he knew well. The only hope of escaping detection would be to hide for a while until some plan presented itself, to lie up with the children in the house of some French citizen. But he knew no one in this part of France that he could go to.

And any way, no family would take them in. If he did know anybody, it would hardly be fair to plant himself on them.

He lay musing bitterly on the future, only half-awake.

It was not quite correct to say that he knew nobody. He did know, very slightly, one family at Chartres. They were people called Rouget – no, Rougand – Rougeron; that was it, Rougeron. They came from Chartres. He had met them at Cidoton eighteen months before, when he had been there with John for the ski-ing. The father was a colonel in the army; Howard wondered vaguely what had become of him. The mother had been typically fat and French, pleasant enough in a very quiet way. The daughter had ski'd well; closing his eyes in the doze of oncoming sleep the old man could see her flying down the slopes behind John, in a flurry of snow. She had had fair hair which she wore short and rather elaborately dressed, in the French style.

He had seen a good deal of the father. They had played draughts together in the evening over a Pernod, and had pondered together whether war would come. The old man began to consider Rougeron seriously. If by some freak of chance he should be in Chartres, there might yet be hope for them. He thought that Rougeron might help.

At any rate, they would get good advice from him. Howard became aware at this point of how much, how very much he wanted to talk to some adult, to discuss their difficulties and make plans. The more he thought of Rougeron, the more he yearned to talk to someone of that sort, frankly and without reserve.

Chartres was not far away, not much more than twenty-five miles. With luck they might get there tomorrow. Probably, Rougeron would be away from home, but – it was worth trying.

Presently he slept.

He woke several times in the night, gasping and breathless, with a very tired heart. Each time he sat upright for half an hour and drank a little brandy, presently slipping down again to an uneasy doze. The children also slept uneasily, but did not wake. At five o'clock the old man woke for good, and sitting up against a heap of hay, resigned himself to wait till it was time to wake the children.

He would go to Chartres, and look up Rougeron. The bad night that he had suffered was a warning; it might well be that his strength was giving out. If that should happen, he must get the children safe with someone else. With Rougeron, if he were there, the children would be safe; Howard could leave money for their keep, English money it was true, but probably negotiable. Rougeron might give him a bed, and let him rest a little till this deathly feeling of fatigue went away.

Pierre woke at about half-past six, and lay awake with him. 'You must stay quiet,' the old man said. 'It's not time to get up yet. Go to sleep again.'

At seven o'clock Sheila woke up, wriggled about, and climbed out of her bed. Her movements woke the other children. Howard got up stiffly and got them all up. He herded them before him down the ladder to the farmyard, and one by one made them sluice their faces beneath the pump.

There was a step behind him, and he turned to meet a formidable woman, who was the farmer's wife. She demanded crossly what he was doing there.

He said mildly: 'I have slept in your hay, madame, with

these children. A thousand pardons, but there was no other place where we could go.'

She rated him soundly for a few minutes. Then she said: 'Who are you? You are not a Frenchman. No doubt, you are English, and these children also?'

He said: 'These children are of all nationalities, madame. Two are French and two are Swiss, from Geneva. One is Dutch.' He smiled: 'I assure you, we are a little mixed.'

She eyed him keenly. 'But you,' she said, 'you are English.'

He said: 'If I were English, madame, what of that?'

'They are saying in Angerville that the English have betrayed us, that they have run away, from Dunkirk.'

He felt himself to be in peril. This woman was quite capable of giving them all up to the Germans.

He faced her boldly and looked her in the eyes. 'Do you believe that England has abandoned France?' he asked. 'Or do you think that is a German lie?'

She hesitated. 'These filthy politics,' she said at last. 'I only know that this farm is ruined. I do not know how we shall live.'

He said simply: 'By Grace of God, madame.'

She was silent for a minute. Then she said: 'You *are* English, aren't you?'

He nodded without speaking.

She said: 'You had better go away, before anybody sees you.'

He turned and called the children to him, and walked over to the pram. Then, pushing it in front of him, he went towards the gate.

She called after him: 'Where are you going to?'

He stopped and said: 'To Chartres.' And then he could have bitten out his tongue for his indiscretion.

She said: 'By the tram?'

He repeated uncertainly: 'The tram?'

'It passes at ten minutes past eight. There is still half an hour.'

He had forgotten the light railway, running by the road. Hope of a lift to Chartres surged up in him. 'Is it still running, madame?'

'Why not? These Germans say that they have brought us Peace. Well then, the tram will run.'

He thanked her and went out on to the road. A quarter of a mile farther on he came to a place where the track crossed the road; here he waited, and fed the children on the biscuits he had bought the day before, with a little of the chocolate. Presently, a little puff of steam announced the little narrow-gauge train, the so-called tram.

Three hours later they walked out into the streets of Chartres, still pushing the pram. It was as easy as that; a completely uneventful journey.

Chartres, like Angerville, was full of Germans. They swarmed everywhere, particularly in the luxury shops, buying with paper money silk stockings, underclothes, and all sorts of imported food. The whole town seemed to be on holiday. The troops were clean and well disciplined; all day Howard saw nothing in their behaviour to complain of, apart from their very presence. They were constrained in their behaviour, scrupulously correct, uncertain, doubtful of their welcome. But in the shops there was no doubt about it; they were spending genuine French paper money and spending it like water. If there were any doubts in Chartres, they stayed behind the locked doors of the banks.

In a telephone-booth the old man found the name of Rougeron in the directory; they lived in an apartment in the Rue Vaugiraud. He did not ring up, feeling the matter to be a little difficult for the telephone. Instead, he asked the way, and walked round to the place, still pushing the pram, the children trailing after him.

Rue Vaugiraud was a narrow street of tall, grey shuttered houses. He rang the bell of the house, and the door opened silently before him, disclosing the common staircase. Rougeron lived on the second floor. He went upstairs slowly, for he was rather short of breath, the children following him. He rang the bell of the apartment.

There was the sound of women's voices from behind the door. There was a step and the door opened before him. It was the daughter; the one that he remembered eighteen months before at Cidoton.

She said: 'What is it?'

In the passage it was a little dark. 'Mademoiselle,' he said, 'I have come to see your father, monsieur le colonel. I do not know if you will remember me; we have met before. At Cidoton.'

She did not answer for a moment. The old man blinked his eyes; in his fatigue it seemed to him that she was holding tight on to the door. He recognised her very well. She wore her hair in the same close curled French manner; she wore a grey cloth skirt and a dark blue jumper, with a black scarf at the neck.

She said at last. 'My father is away from home. I – I remember you very well, monsieur.'

He said easily in French: 'It is very charming of you to say so, mademoiselle. My name is Howard.'

'I know that.'

'Will monsieur le colonel be back today?'

She said: 'He has been gone for three months, Monsieur Howard. He was near Metz. That is the last we have heard.'

He had expected as much, but the disappointment was no less keen. He hesitated and then drew back.

'I am so sorry,' he said. 'I had hoped to see monsieur le colonel, as I was in Chartres. You have my sympathy, mademoiselle. I will not intrude any further upon your anxiety.'

She said: 'Is it – is it anything that I could discuss with you, Monsieur Howard?' He got a queer impression from her manner that she was pleading, trying to detain him at the door.

He could not burden a girl and her mother with his troubles; they had troubles of their own to face. 'It is nothing, mademoiselle,' he said. 'Merely a little personal matter that I wanted to talk over with your father.'

She drew herself up and faced him, looking him in the eyes. 'I understand that you wish to see my father, Monsieur Howard,' she said quietly. 'But he is away – we do not know where. And I . . . I am not a child. I know very well what you have come to talk about. We can talk of this together, you and I.'

She drew back from the door. 'Will you not come in and sit down?' she said.

7

He turned and motioned to the children. Then he glanced at the girl, and caught an expression of surprise, bewilderment, upon her face. 'There are rather a lot of us, I'm afraid,' he said apologetically.

She said: 'But . . . I do not understand, Monsieur Howard. Are these your children?'

He smiled. 'I'm looking after them. They aren't really mine.' He hesitated and then said: 'I am in a position of some difficulty, mademoiselle.'

'Oh . . .'

'I wished to talk it over with your father.' He wrinkled his brows in perplexity. 'Did you think that it was something different?'

She said, hastily: 'No, monsieur – not at all.' And then she swung round and called: 'Maman! Come quickly; here is Monsieur Howard, from Cidoton!'

The little woman that Howard remembered came bustling out; the old man greeted her ceremoniously. Then for a few minutes he stood with the children pressed close round him in the little salon of the flat, trying to make the two women understand his presence with them. It was not an easy task.

The mother gave it up. 'Well, here they are,' she said, content to let the why and wherefore pass. 'Have they had *déjeuner*? Are they hungry?'

The children smiled shyly. Howard said: 'Madame, they are always hungry. But do not derange yourself; we can get *déjeuner* in the town perhaps?'

She said that that was not to be thought of. 'Nicole, stay with m'sieur for a little, while I make arrangements.' She bustled off into the kitchen.

The girl turned to the old man. 'Will you sit down and rest a little,' she said. 'You seem to be very tired.' She turned to the children. 'And you, too, you sit down and stay quiet; *déjeuner* will be ready before long.'

The old man looked down at his hands, grimed with dirt. He had not washed properly, or shaved, since leaving Dijon. 'I am desolated that I should appear so dirty,' he said. 'Presently, perhaps I could wash?'

She smiled at him and he found comfort in her smile. 'It is not easy to keep clean in times like these,' she said. 'Tell me from the beginning, monsieur – how did you come to be in France at all?'

He lay back in the chair. It would be better to tell her the whole thing; indeed, he was aching to tell somebody, to talk over his position. 'You must understand, mademoiselle,' he began, 'that I was in great trouble early in the year. My only son was killed. He was in the Royal Air Force, you know. He was killed on a bombing raid.'

She said: 'I know, monsieur. I have the deepest sympathy for you.'

He hesitated, not quite sure if he had understood her correctly. Some idiom had probably misled him. He went on: 'It was intolerable to stay in England. I wanted a change of scene, to see new faces.'

He plunged into his story. He told her about the Cavanaghs at Cidoton. He told her of Sheila's illness, of their delay at Dijon. He told her about the chambermaid, about *la petite* Rose. He told her how they had become

153

stranded at Joigny, and touched lightly upon the horror of the Montargis road, because Pierre was with them in the room. He told her about the Royal Air Force men, and about the little Dutch boy they had found in Pithiviers. Then he sketched briefly how they had reached Chartres.

It took about a quarter of an hour to tell, in the slow, measured, easy tones of an old man. In the end she turned to him in wonder.

'So really, monsieur, none of these little ones have anything to do with you at all?'

'I suppose not,' he said, 'if you like to look at it that way.'

She pressed the point. 'But you could have left the two in Dijon for their parents to fetch from Geneva? You would have been able then, yourself, to have reached England in good time.'

He smiled slowly. 'I suppose so.'

She stared at him. 'We French people will never understand the English,' she said softly. And then she turned aside.

He was a little puzzled. 'I beg your pardon?'

She got to her feet. 'You will wish to wash,' she said. 'Come, I will show you. And then, I will see that the little ones also wash.'

She led him to an untidy bathroom; manifestly, they kept no servant in the flat. He looked around for a man's gear, hoping for a razor, but the colonel had been away too long. Howard contented himself with a wash, resolved at the first opportunity to see if he could get a shave.

The girl took the children to a bedroom, and washed them one by one quite thoroughly. Then it was time for *déjeuner*. By padding out the midday meal with rice, Madame Rougeron had produced a *risotto*; they sat down to it round the table in the salon and had the first civilised meal that Howard had eaten since Dijon.

And after lunch, sitting round the littered table over coffee, while the children played together in a corner of the salon, he discussed his future with them.

'I wanted to get back to England, of course,' he said. 'I still want to. But at the moment it seems difficult.'

Madame Rougeron said: 'There are no boats to England now, m'sieur. The Germans have stopped everything.'

He nodded. 'I was afraid so,' he said quietly. 'It would have been better if I had gone back to Switzerland.'

The girl shrugged her shoulders. 'It is always easy to be wise later,' she said. 'At the time, a week ago, we all thought that Switzerland would be invaded. I think so still. I do not think that Switzerland would be at all a good place for you to go.'

There was a silence.

Madame said: 'These other children, monsieur. The one called Pierre and the other little Dutchman. Would you have taken them to England?'

Sheila, bored with playing on the floor, came up and pulled his sleeve, distracting him. 'I want to go out for a walk, M'sieur Howard, may we go out for a walk and see some tanks?'

He put his arm round her absently. 'Not just now,' he said. 'Stay quiet for a little. We'll go out presently.' He turned to Madame Rougeron. 'I don't see that I can leave them, unless with their relations,' he said. 'I have been thinking about this a good deal. It might be very difficult to find their relations at this time.'

The mother said: 'That is very true.'

Pursuing his train of thought, he said: 'If I could get them to England, I think I'd send them over to America until the war is over. They would be quite safe there.' He explained. 'My daughter, who lives in the United States, has a big house on Long Island. She would make a home for them till the war ends, and then we could try and find their parents.'

The girl said: 'That would be Madame Costello?'

He turned to her faintly surprised. 'Yes, that is her married name. She has a little boy herself, about their age. She would be very good to them.'

'I am sure of that, m'sieur.'

For the moment the difficulty of getting them to England escaped him. He said: 'It's going to be practically impossible to find the little Dutchman's parents, I'm afraid. We don't even know his name.'

Beneath his arm, Sheila said: 'I know his name.'

He stared down at her. 'You do?' And then, remembering Pierre, he said, 'What do you think he's called?'

She said: 'Willem. Not William, just Willem.'

Howard said: 'Has he got another name?'

'I don't think so. Just Willem.'

Ronnie looked up from the floor. 'You are a story,' he said without heat. 'He has got another name, Mr Howard. He's called Eybe.' He explained. 'Just like I'm called Ronnie Cavanagh, so he's called Willem Eybe.'

'Oh . . .' said Sheila.

Madame said: 'But if he can't speak any French or English, how did you find that out?'

The children stared at her, uncomprehending, a little impatient of adult density. 'He *told* us,' they explained.

Howard said: 'Did he tell you anything more about himself?' There was a silence. 'Did he say who his daddy or his mummy were, or where he came from?'

The children stared at him, awkward and embarrassed. The old man said: 'Suppose you ask him where his daddy is?'

Sheila said: 'But we can't understand what he *says*.' The others stayed silent.

Howard said: 'Never mind, then.' He turned to the two women. 'They'll probably know all about him in a day or two,' he said. 'It takes a little time.'

The girl nodded. 'Perhaps we can find somebody who speaks Dutch.'

Her mother said: 'That might be dangerous. It is not a thing to be decided lightly, that. One must think of the Germans.'

She turned to Howard: 'So, monsieur,' she said, 'it is clear that you are in a difficulty. What is it that you want to do?'

He smiled slowly. 'I want to get to England with these children, madame,' he said. 'Only that.'

He thought for a minute. 'Also,' he said gently, 'I do not wish to get my friends into trouble.' He rose from his chair. 'It has been most kind of you to give us *déjeuner*,' he said. 'I am indeed sorry to have missed seeing monsieur le colonel. I hope very much that when we meet again you will be reunited.'

The girl sprang up. 'You must not go,' she said. 'It is not possible at all, that.' She swung round on her mother. 'We must devise something, Mother.'

The older woman shrugged her shoulders. 'It is impossible. The Germans are everywhere.'

The girl said: 'If father were here, he would devise something.'

There was a silence in the room, broken only by Ronnie and Rose chanting in a low tone their little song about the numerals. Faintly, from the town, came the air of a band playing in the main square.

Howard said: 'You must not put yourselves to inconvenience on our account. I assure you, we can get along very well.'

The girl said: 'But monsieur – your clothes alone – they are not in the French fashion. One would say at once that you are an Englishman, to look at you.'

He glanced down ruefully; it was very true. He had been proud of his taste in Harris tweeds, but now they were quite undeniably unsuitable for the occasion. 'I suppose so,' he said. 'It would be better if I got some French clothes, for a start.'

She said: 'My father would be glad to lend you an old suit, if he were here.' She turned to her mother. 'The brown suit, Mother.'

Madame shook her head. 'The grey is better. It is less conspicuous.' She turned to the old man. 'Sit down again,' she said quietly. 'Nicole is right. We must devise something. Perhaps it will be better if you stay here for the night.'

He sat down again. 'That would be too much trouble for you,' he said. 'But I should be grateful for the clothes.'

Sheila came up to him again, fretful. 'Can't we go out now and look at the tanks, Mr Howard?' she said in English, complaining, 'I do want to go out.'

'Presently,' he said. He turned to the two women, speaking in French. 'They want to go out.'

The girl got to her feet. 'I will take them for a walk,' she said. 'You stay here and rest.'

After a little demur he agreed to this; he was very tired. 'One thing,' he said. 'Perhaps while you are out it would be possible for me to borrow an old razor?'

The girl led him to the bathroom and produced all that he needed. 'Have no fear for the little ones,' she said. 'I will not let them get into trouble.'

He turned to her, razor in hand. 'You must be very careful not to speak English, mademoiselle,' he said. 'The two English children understand and speak French very well. Sometimes they speak English, but that is dangerous now. Speak to them in French all the time.'

She laughed up at him. 'Have no fear, *cher* Monsieur Howard,' she said. 'I do not know any English. Only a phrase or two.' She thought for a minute, and said carefully, in English, 'A little bit of what you fancy does you good.' And then, in French again, 'That is what one says about the *apéritif*?'

'Yes,' he said. He stared at her, puzzled again.

She did not notice. 'And to rebuke anybody,' she said, 'you "tear him off a strip". That is all I know of English, monsieur. The children will be safe with me.'

He said quietly, suddenly numb with an old pain: 'Who told you those phrases, mademoiselle? They are quite up to date.'

She turned away. 'I do not know,' she said awkwardly. 'It is possible that I have read them in a book.'

He went back with her to the salon and helped her to get the children ready to go out, and saw them off together down the stairs. Then he went back into the little flat; madame had disappeared, and he resorted to the bathroom for his shave. Then, in the corner of the settee in the salon he fell asleep, and slept uneasily for about two hours.

The children woke him as they came back into the flat. Ronnie rushed up to him. 'We saw bombers,' he said ecstatically. 'Real German ones, ever so big, and they showed me the bombs and they let me go and touch them, too!'

Sheila said: 'I went and touched them, too!'

Ronnie said: 'And we saw the bombers flying, and taking off and landing, and going out to bomb the ships upon the sea! It was *fun*, Mr Howard.'

He said, mildly: 'I hope you said "Thank you" very nicely to Mademoiselle Rougeron for taking you for such a lovely walk.'

They rushed up to her. 'Thank you *ever* so much, Mademoiselle Rougeron,' they said.

He turned to her. 'You've given them a very happy afternoon,' he said. 'Where did you take them to?'

She said: 'To the aerodrome, monsieur.' She hesitated. 'I would not have gone there if I had realised . . . But they do not understand, the little ones.'

'No,' he said. 'It's all great fun to them.'

He glanced at her. 'Were there many bombers there?'

'Sixty or seventy. More, perhaps.'

'And going out to bomb the ships of my country?' he said gently.

She inclined her head. 'I would not have taken them there,' she said again. 'I did not know.'

He smiled. 'Well,' he said, 'there's not much we can do to stop them, so it's no good worrying about it.'

Madame appeared again; it was nearly six o'clock. She had made soup for the children's supper and she had prepared a bed in her own room for the two little girls. The three little boys were to sleep in a bed which she had made up on the floor of the corridor; Howard had been given a bedroom to himself. He thanked her for the trouble she had taken.

'One must first get the little ones to bed,' she said. 'Then we will talk, and devise something.'

In an hour they were all fed, washed, and in bed, settling for the night. Howard sat down with the two women to a supper of a thick meat broth and bread and cheese, with a little red wine mixed with water. He helped them to clear the table, and accepted a curious, thin, dry, black cigar from a box left by his absent host.

Presently he said: 'I have been thinking quietly this afternoon, madame,' he said. 'I do not think I shall go back to Switzerland. I think it would be better to try and get into Spain.'

The woman said: 'It is a very long way to go.' They discussed the matter for a little time. The difficulties were obvious; when he had made the journey there was no sort of guarantee that he could ever get across the frontier.

The girl said: 'I also have been thinking, but in quite the opposite direction.' She turned to her mother. 'Jean Henri Guinevec,' she said, and she ran the two Christian names together to pronounce them Jenri.

Madame said placidly: 'Jean Henri may have gone already, *ma petite*.'

Howard said: 'Who is he?'

The girl said: 'He is a fisherman, of Le Conquet. In Finisterre. He has a very good boat. He is a great friend of my father, monsieur.'

They told him about this man. For thirty years it had been the colonel's habit to go to Brittany each summer. In that he had been unusual for a Frenchman. The sparse, rocky country, the stone cottages, and the wild coast attracted him, and the strong sea winds of the Atlantic refreshed him. Morgat, Le Conquet, Brest, Douarnenez, Audierne, Concarneau – these were his haunts, the places that he loved to visit in the summer. He used to dress the part. For going in the fishing-boats he had the local costume, faded rust and rose coloured sailcloth overalls and a large, floppy black Breton casque.

'He used to wear the sabots, too, when we were married first,' his wife said placidly. 'But then, when he got corns upon his feet, he had to give them up.'

His wife and daughter had gone with him, every year. They had stayed in some little *pension* and had gone for little, bored walks, while the colonel went out in the boats with the fishermen, or sat yarning with them in the café.

'It was not very gay,' the girl said. 'One year we went to Paris-Plage, but next year we went back to Brittany.'

She had come to know his fishermen friends through the years. 'Jenri would help us to help Monsieur Howard,' she said confidently. 'He has a fine big boat that could cross easily to England.'

Howard gave this serious attention. He knew a little of the Breton fishermen; when he had practised as a solicitor in Exeter there had been occasional legal cases that involved them, cases of fishing inside the three-mile limit. Sometimes, they came into Torbay for shelter in bad weather. Apart from their fishing peccadilloes they were popular in Devon; big burly men with boats as big and burly as they were themselves; fine seamen, speaking a language very similar to Gaelic, that a Welshman could sometimes understand.

They discussed this for some time; it certainly seemed more hopeful than any attempt to get back through Spain. 'It's a long way to go,' he said a little ruefully. It was; Brest is two hundred miles or so from Chartres. 'Perhaps I could go by train.' He would be going away from Paris.

They discussed it in all aspects. Obviously, it was impossible to find out how Guinevec was placed; the only thing to do would be to go there and find out. 'But if Jenri should have gone away,' the mother said, 'there are all the others. One or other of them will help you, when they know that you are friendly with my husband.' She spoke with simple faith.

The girl confirmed this: 'One or other of them will help.'

The old man said presently: 'It really is most kind of you to suggest this. If you would give me a few addresses, then – I would go tomorrow, with the children.' He hesitated. 'It will be better to go soon,' he said. 'Later, the Germans may become more vigilant.'

'That we can do,' said madame.

Presently, as it was getting late, she got up and went out of the room. After a few minutes the girl followed her; from the salon Howard could hear the mutter of their voices in the kitchen, talking in low tones. He could not hear what they were saying, nor did he try. He was deeply grateful for the help and encouragement that he had had from them. Since he had parted from the two Air Force men he had rather lost heart; now he felt again that there was a good prospect that he would get through to England. True, he had still to get to Brittany. That might be difficult in itself; he had no papers of identification other than a British passport, and none of the children had anything at all. If he were stopped and questioned by the Germans the game would be up, but so far he had not been stopped. So long as nobody became suspicious of him, he might be all right.

Nicole came back alone from the kitchen. 'Maman has gone to bed,' she said. 'She gets up so early in the morning. She has asked me to wish you a very good night on her behalf.'

He said something conventionally polite. 'I think I should be better in bed, myself,' he said. 'These last days have been tiring for a man as old as I am.'

She said: 'I know, monsieur.' She hesitated and then said a little awkwardly: 'I have been talking with my mother. We both think that it would be better that I should come with you to Brittany, Monsieur Howard.'

There was a momentary silence; the old man was taken by surprise. 'That is a very kind offer,' he said. 'Most generous of you, mademoiselle. But I do not think I should accept it.'

He smiled at her. 'You must understand,' he said, 'I may get into trouble with the Germans. I should not like to think that I had involved you in my difficulties.'

She said: 'I thought you might feel that, monsieur. But I assure you, I have discussed the matter with maman, and it is better that I should go with you. It is quite decided.'

He said: 'I cannot deny that you would be an enormous help to me, mademoiselle. But one does not decide a point like that all in one moment. One weighs it carefully and one sleeps upon it.'

It was growing dusk. In the half-light of the salon it seemed to him that her eyes were very bright, and that she was blinking a little. 'Do not refuse me, Monsieur Howard,' she said at last. 'I want so very much to help you.'

He was touched. 'I was only thinking of your safety, mademoiselle,' he said gently. 'You have done a very great deal for me already. Why should you do any more?'

She said: 'Because of our old friendship.'

He made one last effort to dissuade her. 'But mademoiselle,' he said, 'that friendship, which I value, was never more than a slight thing – a mere hotel acquaintance. You have already done more for me than I could have hoped for.'

She said: 'Perhaps you did not know, monsieur. Your son and I . . . John . . . we were good friends.' There was an awkward pause.

'So it is quite decided,' she said, turning away. 'We are quite of one mind, my mother and I. Now, monsieur, I will show you your room.'

She took him down the corridor and showed him the room. Her mother had been before her, and had laid out upon the bed a long, linen nightgown, the slumber-wear of Monsieur le Colonel. On the dressing-table she had put his cut-throat razor, and a strop, and his much-squeezed tube of shaving-paste, and a bottle of scent called FLEURS DE ALPES.

The girl looked round. 'I think that there is everything

you will want,' she said. 'If there is anything we have forgotten, I am close by. You will call?'

He said: 'Mademoiselle, I shall be most comfortable.'

'In the morning,' she said, 'do not hurry. There are arrangements to be made before we can start for Brittany, and one must make enquiries – on the quiet, you will understand, monsieur. That we can best do alone, my mother and I. So it will be better if you stay in bed, and rest.'

He said: 'Oh, but there are the children. I shall have to see to them.'

She smiled: 'In England, do the men look after children when there are two women in the house?'

'Er – well,' he said. 'I mean, I didn't want to bother you with them.'

She smiled again. 'Stay in bed,' she said. 'I will bring coffee to you at about eight o'clock.'

She went out and closed the door behind her; he remained for a time staring thoughtfully after her. She was, he thought, a very peculiar young woman. He could not understand her at all. At Cidoton, as he remembered her, she had been an athletic young creature, very shy and reserved, as most middle-class French girls are. He remembered her chiefly for the incongruity of her close-curled, carefully-tended head, her daintily-trimmed eyebrows and her carefully-manicured hands, in contrast with the terrific speed with which she took the steepest slopes when sliding on a pair of skis. John, who himself was a fine skier, had told his father that he had his work cut out to keep ahead of her upon a run. She took things straight that he made traverse upon and never seemed to come to any harm. But she had a poor eye for ground, and frequently ran slowly on a piece of flat while he went sailing on ahead of her.

165

That was, literally, about all the old man could remember of her. He turned from the door and began slowly to undress. She had changed very much, it seemed to him. It had been nice of her to tell him in her queer, French way that she had been good friends with John; his heart warmed to her for that. Both she and her mother were being infinitely kind to him, and this proposal that Nicole should come with him to Brittany was so kind as to verge on the quixotic. He could not refuse the offer; already he had come near to giving pain by doing so. He would not press a refusal any more; to have her help might make the whole difference to his success in getting the children to England.

He put on the long nightgown and got into bed; the soft mattress and the smooth sheets were infinitely soothing after two nights spent in haylofts. He had not slept properly in bed since leaving Cidoton.

She had changed very much, that girl. She still had the carefully-tended curly head; the trimmed eyebrows and the manicured hands were just the same. But her whole expression was different. She looked ten years older; the dark shadows beneath her eyes matched the black scarf she wore about her neck. Quite suddenly the thought came into his mind that she looked like a widow. She was a young, unmarried girl, but that was what she reminded him of, a young widow. He wondered if she had lost a fiancé in the war. He must ask her mother, delicately, before he left the flat; it would be as well to know in order that he might avoid any topic that was painful to her.

With all that, she seemed very odd to him. He did not understand her at all. But presently the tired limbs relaxed, his active mind moved more slowly, and he drifted into sleep.

He slept all through the night, an unusual feat for a man

of his age. He was still sleeping when she came in with his coffee and rolls on a tray at about a quarter past eight. He woke easily and sat up in bed, and thanked her.

She was fully dressed. Beyond her, in the corridor, the children stood, dressed and washed, peeping in at the door. Pierre ventured in a little way.

'Good morning, Pierre,' said the old man gravely. The little boy placed his hand upon his stomach and bowed to him from the waist. '*Bon jour*, M'sieur Howard.'

The girl laughed and ran her hand through his hair. 'It is a little boy *bien élevé*, this one,' she said. 'Not like the other ones that you have collected.'

He said a little anxiously: 'I do hope that they have not been a trouble to you, mademoiselle.'

She said: 'Children will never trouble me, monsieur.'

He thought again, a very odd young woman with a very odd way of expressing herself.

She told him that her mother was already out marketing in the town, and making certain enquiries. She would be back in half an hour or so; then they would make their plans.

The girl brought him the grey suit of her father's, rather worn and shabby, with a pair of old brown canvas shoes, a horrible violet shirt, a celluloid collar rather yellow with age, and an unpleasant tie. 'These clothes are not very chic,' she said apologetically. 'But it will be better for you to wear them, Monsieur Howard, because then you will appear like one of the little *bourgeoisie*. I assure you, we will keep your own clothes for you very carefully. My mother will put them in the cedar chest with the blankets, because of the moths, you understand.'

Three-quarters of an hour later he was up and dressed, and standing in the salon while the girl viewed him critically. 'You should not have shaved again so soon,' she said. 'It makes the wrong effect, that.'

He said that he was sorry. Then he took note of her appearance. 'You have made yourself look shabby to come with me, mademoiselle,' he said. 'That is a very kind thing to have done.'

She said: 'Marie, the servant, lent me this dress.'

She wore a very plain, black dress to her ankles, without adornment of any kind. Upon her feet she wore low-heeled, clumsy shoes and coarse black stockings.

Madame Rougeron came in and put down her basket on the table in the salon. 'There is a train for Rennes at noon,' she said unemotionally. 'There is a German soldier at the *guichet* who asks why you must travel, but they do not look at papers. They are very courteous and correct.' She paused. 'But there is another thing.'

She took from the pocket of her gown a folded handbill. 'A German soldier left this paper with the *concierge* this morning. There was one for each apartment.'

They spread it out upon the table. It was in French, and it read:

CITIZENS OF THE REPUBLIC!

The treacherous English, who have forced this unnecessary war upon us, have been driven into disorderly flight from our country. Now is the time to rise and root out these plutocratic warmongers wherever they may be hiding, before they have time to plot fresh trouble for France.

These scoundrels who are roaming the country and living in secret in our homes like disgusting parasites, will commit acts of sabotage and espionage and make trouble for all of us with the Germans, who are only anxious to build up a peaceful regime in our country. If these cowardly fugitives should commit such acts, the Germans will keep our fathers, our husbands, and our sons in long captivity. Help to bring back your men by driving out these pests!

It is your duty if you know of an Englishman in hiding to tell the gendarmerie, or tell the nearest German soldier. This is a simple thing that anyone can do, which will bring peace and freedom to our beloved land.

Severe penalties await those who shield these rats.

VIVE LA FRANCE!

Howard read it through quietly twice. Then he said: 'It seems that I am one of the rats, madame. After this, I think it would be better that I should go alone, with the children.'

She said that it was not to be thought of. And then she said, Nicole would never agree.

The girl said: 'That is very true. It would be impossible for you to go alone, as things are now. I do not think you would get very far before the Germans found that you were not a Frenchman, even in those clothes.' She flipped the paper with disgust. 'This is a German thing,' she said. 'You must not think that French people talk like this, Monsieur Howard.'

'It is very nearly the truth,' he said ruefully.

'It is an enormous lie,' she said.

She went out of the room. The old man, grasping the opportunity, turned to her mother. 'Your daughter has changed greatly since we were at Cidoton, madame,' he said.

The woman looked at him. 'She has suffered a great deal, monsieur.'

He said: 'I am most sorry to hear that. If you could tell me something about it – perhaps I could avoid hurting her in conversation.'

She stared at him. 'You do not know, then?'

'How should I know anything about her trouble, madame?' he said gently. 'It is something that has happened since we met at Cidoton.'

She hesitated for a minute. Then she said: 'She was in love with a young man. We did not arrange the affair and she tells me nothing.'

'All young people are like that,' he said, quietly. 'My son was the same. The young man is a prisoner in German hands, perhaps?'

Madame said: 'No, monsieur. He is dead.'

Nicole came bursting into the room, a little fibre case in her hand. 'This we will carry in your perambulator,' she said. 'Now, monsieur, I am ready to go.'

There was no time for any more conversation with Madame Rougeron, but Howard felt he had the gist of it; indeed, it was just what he had expected. It was hard on the girl, terribly hard; perhaps this journey, dangerous though it might be, would not be altogether a bad thing for her. It might distract her mind, serve as an anodyne.

There was a great bustle of getting under way. They all went downstairs; Madame Rougeron had many bundles of food, which they put in the perambulator. The children clustered round them and impeded them.

Ronnie said: 'Will we be going where there are tanks, Mr Howard?' He spoke in English. 'You said that I might go with the Germans for a ride.'

Howard said, in French: 'Not today. Try and talk French while Mademoiselle Rougeron is with us, Ronnie;

it is not very nice to say what other people cannot understand.'

Rose said: 'That is very true, m'sieur. Often I have told Ronnie that it was not polite to speak in English.'

Madame Rougeron said to her daughter in a low tone: 'It is clever that.' The girl nodded.

Pierre said suddenly: 'I do not speak English, m'sieur.'

'No, Pierre,' the old man said. 'You are always polite.'

Sheila said: 'Is Willem polite, too?' She spoke in French.

Nicole said: 'All of you are polite, all *trés bien élevés*. Now we are quite ready.' She turned and kissed her mother.

'Do not fret,' she said gently. 'Five days – perhaps a week, and I will be home again. Be happy for me, Maman.'

The old woman stood trembling, suddenly aged. '*Prenez bien garde*,' she said tremulously. 'These Germans – they are wicked, cruel people.'

The girl said gently: 'Be tranquil. I shall come to no harm.' She turned to Howard. '*En route, donc*, Monsieur Howard,' she said. 'It is time for us to go.'

They left the apartment and started down the street, Howard pushing the loaded pram and Nicole shepherding the children. She had produced a rather shabby black Homburg hat for the old man, and this, with his grey suit and brown canvas shoes, made him look very French. They went slowly for the sake of the children; the girl strolled beside him with a shawl over her shoulders.

Presently she said: 'Give me the pram, monsieur. That is more fitting for a woman to push, in the class that we represent.'

He surrendered it to her; they must play up to their disguise. 'When we come to the station,' she said, 'say nothing at all. I will do all the talking. Do you think you could behave as a much older man? As one who could hardly talk at all?'

He said: 'I would do my best. You want me to behave as a very old man indeed.'

She nodded. 'We have come from Arras,' she said. 'You are my uncle, you understand? Our house in Arras was destroyed by the British. You have a brother, my other uncle, who lives in Landerneau.'

'Landerneau,' he said. 'Where is that, mademoiselle?'

She said: 'It is a little country town twenty kilometres this side of Brest, monsieur. If we can get there we can then walk to the coast. And it is inland, forty kilometres from the sea. I think they may allow us to go there, when it would be impossible for us to travel directly to the coast.'

They approached the station. 'Stay with the children,' she said quietly. 'If anyone asks you anything, be very stupid.'

The approach to the station was crowded with German transport lorries; German officers and soldiers thronged around. It was clear that a considerable detachment of troops had just arrived by train; apart from them the station was crowded with refugees. Nicole pushed the pram through into the booking-hall, followed by Howard and the children. The old man, mindful of his part, walked with a shambling tread; his mouth hung open a little, and his head shook rhythmically.

Nicole shot a glance at him. 'It is good, that,' she said. 'Be careful you do not forget your rôle.'

She left the pram with him and pressed forward to the booking-office. A German *Feldwebel*, smart and efficient in his grey-green uniform, stopped her and asked a question. Howard, peering through the throng with sagging head and half-closed eyes, saw her launch out into a long, rambling peasant explanation.

She motioned towards him and the children. The *Feldwebel* glanced over them, shabby and inoffensive, their only luggage in an ancient pram. Then he cut short the torrent of her talk and motioned her to the booking-office. Another woman claimed his attention.

Nicole came back to Howard and the children with the tickets: 'Only as far as Rennes,' she said, in coarse peasant tones. 'That is as far as this train goes.'

The old man said: 'Eh?' and wagged his sagging head. She shouted in his ear. 'Only to Rennes.'

He mumbled thickly: 'We do not want to go to Rennes.'

She made a gesture of irritation and pushed him ahead of her to the barrier. A German soldier stood by the ticket-puncher; the old man checked and turned back to the girl in senile bewilderment. She said something cross and pushed him through.

Then she apologised to the ticket-puncher. 'He is my uncle,' she said. 'He is a good old man, but he is more trouble to me than all these children.'

The man said: 'Rennes. On the right,' and passed them through. The German stared at them indifferently; one set of refugees was very like another. So they passed through on to the platform and climbed into a very old compartment with hard wooden seats.

Ronnie said: 'Is this the train we're going to sleep in, M'sieur Howard?' He spoke in French, however.

Howard said: 'Not tonight. We shan't be in this train for very long.'

But he was wrong.

From Chartres to Rennes is about two hundred and sixty kilometres; it took them six hours. In the hot summer afternoon the train stopped at every station, and many times between. The body of the train was full of German soldiers travelling to the west; three coaches at the end were reserved for French civilians and they travelled in one of these. Sometimes the compartment was shared with other travellers for a few stations, but no one travelled with them continuously.

It was an anxious journey, full of fears and subterfuges. When there were other people with them in the carriage the old man lapsed into senility, and Nicole would explain their story once again, how they were travelling to Landerneau from their house in Arras, which had been destroyed by the British. At first there was difficulty with the children, who were by no means inclined to lend support to what they rightly knew to be a pack of lies. Each time the story was retold Nicole and Howard rode on a knife edge of suspense, their attention split between the listener and the necessity of preventing the children from breaking into the conversation. Presently the children lost interest, and became absorbed in running up and down the corridor, playing 'My great-aunt lives in Tours,' with all its animal repetitions, and looking out of the window. In any event, the peasants and small shopkeepers who travelled with them were too anxious to start talking and to tell the story of their own troubles to have room for much suspicion in their minds.

At long last, when the fierce heat of the day was dying down, they pulled into Rennes. There the train stopped and everyone got out; the German soldiers fell in in two ranks in orderly array upon the platform and were marched away, leaving a fatigue party to load their kits on to a lorry. There was a German officer by the ticket-collector. Howard put on his most senile air, and Nicole went straight up to the collector to consult him about trains to Landerneau.

Through half-closed eyes Howard watched her, the children clustered round him, dirty and fretful from their journey. He waited in an agony of apprehension; at any moment the officer might ask for papers. Then it would all be over. But finally he gave her a little pasteboard slip, shrugged his shoulders and dismissed her.

She came back to Howard. 'Mother of God!' she said crossly and rather loudly. 'Where is now the pram? Do I have to do everything?'

The pram was still in the baggage-car. The old man shambled towards it, but she pushed him aside and got into the car and pulled it down on to the ground herself. Then, in a little confused huddle, she shepherded them to the barrier.

'It is not five children that I have,' she said bitterly to the ticket-collector. 'It is six.' The man laughed, and the German officer smiled faintly. So they passed out into the town of Rennes.

She said quietly to him as they walked along: 'You are not angry, Monsieur Howard? It is better that I should pretend that I am cross. It is more natural so.'

He said: 'My dear, you have done wonderfully well.'

She said: 'Well, we have got half-way without suspicion. Tomorrow, at eight in the morning, a train leaves for Brest. We can go on that as far as Landerneau.'

She told him that the German officer had given them permission to go there. She produced the ticket he had given to her. 'We must sleep tonight in the refugee hostel,' she said. 'This ticket admits us. It will be better to go there, m'sieur, like all the others.'

He agreed. 'Where is it?' he enquired.

'In the Cinema du Monde,' she said. 'I have never slept in a cinema before.'

He said: 'Mademoiselle, I am deeply sorry that my difficulties should make you do so now.'

She smiled: '*Ne vous en faites pas*,' she said. 'Perhaps as it is under German management it will be clean. We French are not so good at things like that.'

175

They gave up their cards at the entrance, pushed their pram inside and looked around. The seats had all been removed, and around the walls were palliasses stacked, filled with old straw. There were not many people in the place; with the growing restrictions upon movements as the German took over control, the tide of refugees was less than it had been. An old Frenchwoman issued them with a palliasse and a blanket each and showed them a corner where they could make a little camp apart from the others. 'The little ones will sleep quiet there,' she said.

There was an issue of free soup at a table at the end of the hall, dispensed by a German cook, who showed a fixed, beaming smile of professional good humour.

An hour later the children were laid down to rest. Howard did not dare to leave them, and sat with his back against the wall, tired to death, but not yet ready for sleep. Nicole went out and came back presently with a packet of caporal cigarettes. 'I bought these for you,' she said. 'I did not dare to get your Players; it would not be safe, that.'

He was not a great smoker, but touched by her kindness he took one gratefully. She poured him out a little brandy in a mug and fetched a little water from the drinking fountain for him; the drink refreshed him and the cigarette was a comfort. She came and sat beside him, leaning up against the wall.

For a time they talked in low tones of their journey, about her plans for the next day. Then, fearing to be overheard, he changed the subject and asked about her father.

She had little more to tell him than he already knew. Her father had been commandant of a fort in the Maginot Line not very far from Metz; they had heard nothing of him since May.

The old man said: 'I am very, very sorry, mademoiselle.' He paused, and then he said, 'I know what that sort of anxiety means . . . very well. It blackens everything for a long time afterwards.'

She said quietly: 'Yes. Day after day you wait, and wait. And then the letter comes, or it may be the telegram, and you are afraid to open it to see what it says.' She was silent for a minute. 'And then at last you do open it.'

He nodded. He felt very close to her; they had shared the same experience. He had waited and waited just like that when John had been missing. For three days he had waited; then the telegram had come. It became clear to him that she had been through the same trouble; indeed, her mother had told him that she had. He was immensely sorry for her.

Quite suddenly, he felt that he would like to talk to her about John. He had not been able to talk about his son to anybody, not since it happened. He had feared sympathy, and had shunned intrusion. But this girl Nicole had known John. They had been ski-ing companions – friends, she had said.

He blew out a long cloud of smoke. 'I lost my son, you know,' he said with difficulty, staring straight ahead of him. 'He was killed flying – he was a squadron leader, in our Royal Air Force. He was shot down by three Messerschmitts on his way back from a bombing raid. Over Heligoland.'

There was a pause.

She turned towards him. 'I know that,' she said gently. 'They wrote to me from the squadron.'

8

The cinema was half-full of people, moving about and laying down their palliasses for the night. The air was full of the fumes of the cooking-stove at the far end, and the smoke of French cigarettes; in the dim light it seemed thick and heavy.

Howard glanced towards the girl. 'You knew my son as well as that, mademoiselle?' he said. 'I did not know.'

In turn, she felt the urge to talk. 'We used to write,' she said. She went on quickly, 'Ever since Cidoton we used to write, almost each week. And we met once, in Paris – just before the war. In June, that was.' She paused, and then said quietly, 'Almost a year ago today.'

The old man said: 'My dear, I never knew anything about this at all.'

'No,' she said. 'Nor did I tell my parents.'

There was a silence while he tried to collect his thoughts and readjust his outlook. 'You said they wrote to you,' he said at last. 'But how did they know your address?'

She shrugged her shoulders. 'He would have made arrangements,' she said. 'He was very kind, monsieur; very, very kind. And we were great friends . . .'

He said quietly: 'You must have thought me very different, mademoiselle. Very rude. But I assure you, I knew nothing about this. Nothing at all.'

There was a little pause.

'May I ask one question?' he said presently.

'But yes, Monsieur Howard.'

He stared ahead of him awkwardly. 'Your mother told me that you had had trouble,' he said. 'That there had been a young man – who was dead. No doubt, that was somebody else?'

'There was nobody else,' she said quietly. 'Nobody but John.'

She shook herself and sat up. 'See,' she said, 'one must put down a palliasse, or there will be no room left by the wall.' She got to her feet and stirred him, and began to pull down one of the sacks of straw from the pile. He joined her, reluctant and confused, and for a quarter of an hour they worked, making their beds.

'There,' she said at last, standing back to survey their work. 'It is the best that can be done.' She eyed him diffidently. 'Will it be possible for you to sleep so, Monsieur Howard?'

He said: 'My dear, of course it will.'

She laughed shortly. 'Then, let us try.'

Over the palliasses he stood looking at her, blanket in hand. 'May I ask one more question?'

She faced him: 'Yes, monsieur.'

'You have been very good to me,' he said quietly. 'I think I understand now. That was because of John?'

There was a long silence. She stood looking out across the room, motionless. 'No,' she said at last. 'That was because of the children.'

He said nothing, not quite understanding what she meant.

'One loses faith,' she said quietly. 'One thinks that everything is false and bad.'

He glanced at her, puzzled.

179

'I did not think there could be anyone so kind and brave as John,' she said. 'But I was wrong, monsieur. There was another one. There was his father.'

She turned away. 'So,' she said, 'we must sleep.' She spoke practically, almost coldly; it seemed to the old man that she had set up a barrier between them. He did not resent that; he understood the reason for her curtness. She did not want to be questioned any more. She did not want to talk.

He lay down on the palliasse, shifted the rough, straw-filled pillow and pulled the blanket round him. The girl settled down upon her own bed on the other side of the children.

Howard lay awake, his mind in a tumult. He felt that he had known that there had been something between this girl and John, yet that knowledge had not reached the surface of his mind. But looking back, there had been little hints all the time that he had been with them in the flat. Indeed, she had used John's very words about a cocktail when she had said in English that: 'A little bit of what you fancy does you good.' Thinking back, he remembered the little twinges of pain that he had suffered when she had said that and yet he had not realised.

How close had their friendship been, then? They had written freely to each other; on top of that it seemed that they had met in Paris just before the war. No breath of that had reached him previously. But thinking back, he could remember now that there had been a space of two week-ends in June when he had seen nothing of the boy; he had assumed that duties with the squadron had prevented him from coming over to see him, or even from ringing up. Was that the time? It must have been.

His mind turned to Nicole. He had thought her a very odd young woman previously; he did not think of her in quite the same way now. Dimly he began to realise a little of her difficulties with regard to John, and to himself. It seemed that she had told her mother little about John; she had nursed her grief in silence, dumb and inarticulate. Then he had turned up, quite suddenly, at the door one day. To her secret grief he added an acute embarrassment.

He turned over again. He must let her alone, let her talk if she wanted to, be silent if she chose. If he did that, perhaps she would open out as time went on. It had been of her own volition she had told him about John.

He lay awake for several hours, turning these matters over in his mind. Presently, after a long time, he slept.

He woke in the middle of the night, to the sound of wailing. He opened his eyes; the wailing came from one of the children. He sat up, but Nicole was before him; by the time he was fully awake she was out of her bed, crouching down by a red-faced, mournful little boy sitting up and crying bitterly.

It was Willem, crying as if his heart was going to break. The girl put her arm round him and spoke to him in soft, baby French. The old man rolled out of his blanket, got up stiffly and moved over to them.

'What is it?' he enquired. 'What is the matter?'

The girl said: 'I think he has had a nightmare – that is all. Presently he will sleep again.' She turned again to comfort him.

Howard felt singularly helpless. His way with the children had been to talk to them, to treat them as equals. That simply did not work at all, unless you knew the language, and he knew no word of any language that this little Dutch boy spoke. Left to himself he might have taken him upon his knee and talked to him as man to man; he could never have soothed him as this girl was soothing him.

He knelt down clumsily beside them. 'Do you think he

is unwell?' he asked. 'He has perhaps eaten something that upset him?'

She shook her head; already the sobs were dying down. 'I do not think so,' she said softly. 'Last night he did this, twice. It is bad dreams, I think. Only bad dreams.'

The old man's mind drifted back to the unpleasant town of Pithiviers; it would be natural, he thought, for bad dreams to haunt the child.

He wrinkled his forehead. 'You say that he did this twice last night, mademoiselle?' he said. 'I did not know.'

She said: 'You were tired and sleeping very well. Besides your door was shut. I went to him, but each time he very soon went to sleep again.' She bent over him. 'He is almost asleep again now,' she said softly.

There was a long, long silence. The old man stared around; the long, sloping floor was lit by one dim blue light over the door. Dark forms lay huddled upon palliasses here and there; two or three snorers disturbed the room; the air was thick and hot. From sleeping in his clothes he felt sticky and dirty. The pleasant, easy life that he had known in England seemed infinitely far away. This was his real life. He was a refugee, sleeping upon straw in a disused cinema with a German sentry at the door, his companion a French girl, a pack of foreign children in his care. And he was tired, tired, dead tired.

The girl raised her head. She said very softly: 'He is practically asleep, this one. In a minute I will lay him down.' She paused, and then she said, 'Go back to bed, Monsieur Howard. I shall not be long.'

He shook his head and stayed there watching her. Presently, the little boy was sound asleep; she laid him gently down upon his pillow and pulled the blanket round him. Then she got up. 'Now,' she said quietly, 'one can sleep again, until next time.'

He said: 'Good night, Nicole.'

She said: 'Good night. Do not get up if he should wake again. He is no trouble.'

He did not wake again in the two or three hours that were left of the night. By six o'clock the place was all astir; there was no chance of any further sleep. Howard got up and straightened out his clothes as well as he could; he felt dirty and unshaven.

The girl got the children up and, with Howard, helped them to dress. She, too, was feeling dirty and unkempt; her curly hair was draggled, and she had a headache. She would have given a great deal for a bath. But there was no bath in the place, nor even anywhere to wash.

Ronnie said: 'I don't like this place. May we sleep in a farm tomorrow?'

Rose said: 'He means tonight, m'sieur. He talks a great deal of nonsense, that one.'

Howard said: 'I'm not quite sure where we shall sleep tonight. We'll see when the time comes.'

Sheila, wriggling her shoulders in her Liberty bodice, said: 'I do *itch*.'

There was nothing to be done about that. To distract her mind Howard led her off with the other children to the end of the hall, where the German cook was dispensing mugs of coffee. With each mug went a large, unattractive hunk of bread. Howard left the children at a trestle table and went to draw their bread and coffee.

Nicole joined them as he brought it to the table and they all had breakfast together. The bread was hard and tasteless and the coffee bitter, acid stuff with little milk. The children did not like it, and were querulous; it needed all the tact of the old man and the girl to prevent their grumbles calling the attention of the German cook. There was some chocolate left of the provisions he had bought upon the road from Joigny;

he shared this out among them and this made a little relish to the meal.

Presently, they left the Cinema du Monde and, pushing the pram before them, made their way towards the railway station. The town was full of Germans parading down the streets, Germans driving lorries, Germans lounging at the doors of billets, Germans in the shops. They tried to get chocolate for the children at several shops, but the soldiers had swept the town clean of sweets of every kind. They bought a couple of long rolls of bread and a brown sausage of doubtful origin as provision for their journey. Fruit was unobtainable, but they bought a few lettuces.

At the railway station they passed the barrier without difficulty, surrendering their billeting pass to the German officer. They put the pram into the baggage-wagon on the train for Brest, and climbed up into a third-class carriage.

It was only when the train was well upon the way that Howard discovered that *la petite* Rose was nursing a very dirty black and white kitten.

Nicole was at first inclined to be sharp with her. 'We do not want a little cat,' she said to Rose. 'No, truly we do not want that cat or any other cat. You must put him out at the next station.'

The corners of the little girl's mouth drooped, and she clutched the kitten tighter. Howard said: 'I wouldn't do that. He might get lost.'

Ronnie said: '*She* might get lost, Mr Howard. Rose says it's a lady cat. How do you know it's a lady cat, Rose?'

Nicole expostulated: 'But Monsieur Howard, the little cat belongs to somebody else. It is not our cat, that one.'

He said placidly: 'It's our cat now.'

She opened her mouth to say something impetuous, thought better of it, and said nothing. Howard said: 'It is a very little thing, mademoiselle. It won't add to our difficulties, but it will give them a good deal of pleasure.'

Indeed, what he said was perfectly correct. The children were clustered round intent upon the kitten, which was washing its face upon Rose's lap. Willem turned to Nicole, beaming, and said something unintelligible to her. Then he turned back, watching the kitten again, entranced.

Nicole said, in a resigned tone: 'As you wish. In England, does one pick up cats and take them away like that?'

He smiled, 'No, mademoiselle,' he said. 'In England only the kind of person who sleeps on straw mattresses in cinemas does that sort of thing. The very lowest type of all.'

She laughed. 'Thieves and vagabonds,' she said. 'Yes, that is true.'

She turned to Rose. 'What is her name?' she asked.

The little girl said: 'Jo-Jo.'

The children clustered round, calling the kitten by its new name, trying to make it answer. The kitten sat unmoved, washing its face with a tiny paw. Nicole looked at it for a few moments.

Then she said: 'It is like the lions, in the Zoo de Vincennes. They also do like that.'

Howard had never been to the Paris zoo. He said: 'Have they many lions and tigers there?'

She shrugged her shoulders. 'They have some. I do not know how many – I have only been there once.' And then, to his surprise, she looked up at him with laughter in her eyes. 'I went there with John,' she said. 'Naturally, one would not remember how many lions and tigers there were in the zoo.'

He was startled; then he smiled a little to himself. 'Naturally,' he said drily. 'But did you never go there as a child?'

She shook her head. 'One does not go to see these places

except when one is showing the sights of Paris to a friend, you understand,' she said. 'That was the reason that John came to Paris, because he had never seen Paris. And I said that I would show him Paris. That was how it was.'

He nodded. 'Did he like the zoo?' he asked.

She said: 'It was a very happy day that. It was a French day.' She turned to him a little shyly. 'We had arranged a joke, you see – we should speak only in French one day and in English on the next day. On the English day we did not talk very much,' she said reminiscently. 'It was too difficult; we used to say that the English day ended after tea . . .'

Mildly surprised, he said: 'Did he speak French well?' Because that was most unlike John.

She laughed outright. 'No – not at all. He spoke French very, *very* badly. But that day, on the way out to Vincennes, the taxi-driver spoke English to John, because there are many tourists in Paris and some of the drivers can speak a little English. And John spoke to him in English. Because I had a new summer hat, with carnations, you understand – not a smart hat, but a little country thing with a wide brim. And John asked the taxi-driver to tell him what the French was for' – she hesitated for a moment, and then said – 'to tell me that I was looking very pretty. And the man laughed a lot and told him, so then John knew and he could say it to me himself. And he gave the driver twenty francs.'

The old man said: 'It was probably worth that, mademoiselle.'

She said: 'He wrote it down. And then, when he wanted me to laugh, he used to get out his little book and read it out to me.'

She turned and stared out of the window at the slowly-moving landscape. The old man did not pursue the subject;

indeed, he could think of nothing adequate to say. He got out his packet of caporal cigarettes and offered one to Nicole, but she refused.

'It is not in the part, that, monsieur,' she said quietly. 'Not in this dress.'

He nodded; lower middle-class Frenchwomen do not smoke cigarettes in public. He lit one himself, and blew a long cloud of the bitter smoke. It was hot already in the carriage, though they had the windows open. The smaller children, Pierre and Sheila, were already tired and inclined to be fretful.

All day the train ground slowly on in the hot sun. It was not crowded, and they seldom had anybody in the carriage with them, which was a relief. As on the previous day, the German troops travelling were confined strictly to their own part of the train. On all the station platforms they were much in evidence. At towns such as St Brieuc, the exit from the station appeared to be picketed by a couple of German soldiers; at the wayside halts they did not seem to worry about passengers leaving the station.

Nicole drew Howard's attention to this feature. 'It is good, that,' she said. 'At Landerneau it may be possible to go through without questioning. But if we are stopped, we have still a good story to tell.'

He said: 'Where are we going tonight, mademoiselle? I am entirely in your hands.'

She said. 'There is a farm, about five miles from Landerneau, to the south. Madame Guinevec, wife of Jean Henri – that was her home before she was married. I have been there with my father, at the time of the horse fair, the fête, at Landerneau.'

'I see,' he said. 'What is the name of the people at the farm?'

'Arvers,' she said. 'Aristide Arvers is the father of Marie.

They are in good circumstances, you understand, Aristide is a careful man, my father used to say. He breeds horses a little, too, for our army. Marie was Queen of Beauty at the Landerneau Fête one year. It was then that Jean Henri first met her.'

He said: 'She must have been a very pretty girl.'

'She was lovely,' Nicole said. 'That was when I was little – over ten years ago. She is still beautiful.'

The train ground on in the hot sunlight, stopping now and again at stations and frequently in between. They gave the children *déjeuner* of bread and sausage with a little lemonade. That kept them amused and occupied for a time, but they were restless and bored.

Ronnie said: 'I do wish we could go and bathe.'

Sheila echoed: 'May we bathe, Monsieur Howard?'

He said: 'We can't bathe, while we're in the train. Later on, perhaps. Run along out into the corridor; it's cooler there.'

He turned to Nicole. 'They're thinking of a time three days ago – or four was it? – just before we met the Air Force men. I let them have a bathe in a stream.'

'It was lovely,' said Ronnie. 'Ever so cool and nice.' He turned and ran with his sister out into the corridor followed by Willem.

Nicole said: 'The English are great swimmers, are they not, monsieur? Even the little ones think of nothing else.'

He had not thought about his country in that way: 'Are we?' he said. 'Is that how we appear?'

She shrugged her shoulders. 'I do not know so many English people,' she said frankly. 'But John – he liked more than anything for us to go bathing.'

He smiled. 'John was a very good swimmer,' he said reminiscently. 'He was very fond of it.'

She said: 'He was very, very naughty, Monsieur Howard.

He would not do any of the things that one should do when one visits Paris for the first time. I had prepared so carefully for his visit – yes, I had arranged for each day the things that we would do. On the first day of all I had planned to go to the Louvre, but imagine it – he was not interested. Not at all.'

The old man smiled again. 'He never was one for museums, much,' he said.

She said: 'That may be correct in England, monsieur, but in Paris one should see the things that Paris has to show. It was very embarrassing, I assure you. I had arranged that he should see the Louvre, and the Trocadéro, and for a contrast the Musée de l'Homme, and the museum at Cluny, and I had a list of galleries of modern art that I would show him. And he never saw any of it at all!'

'I'm sorry about that,' said Howard. There seemed nothing else to say. 'What did you do?'

She said: 'We went bathing several times, at the Piscine Molitor in Auteuil. It was very hot weather, sunny all the time. I could not get him into one museum – not one! He was very, very naughty.'

'I expect that was very pleasant, though,' he said.

She smiled. 'It was not what I had arranged,' she said. 'I had not even got a costume. We had to go together, John and I, to buy a bathing-costume. Never have I done a thing like that before. It was a good thing I had said that we would meet in Paris, not in Chartres. In France there are conventions, Monsieur Howard, you understand.'

'I know,' he said. 'John never worried much about those. Did he get you a nice bathing-dress?'

She smiled: 'It was very beautiful,' she said. 'An American one, very chic, in silver and green. It was so pretty that it was a pleasure to be seen in it.'

'Well,' he said. 'You couldn't have worn that in a museum.'

She stared at him, nonplussed. 'But no . . .' And then she laughed. 'It would be quite ridiculous, that.' She smiled again at the thought. 'Monsieur, you say absurd things, just the same as John.'

It was four o'clock when the train pulled into the little station of Landerneau. They tumbled out of the carriage with relief, Nicole lifting each child down on to the platform except Ronnie, who insisted on getting down himself. They fetched the pram from the baggage-car and put the remainder of their lunch in it, with the kitten.

There was no guard at the *guichet* and they passed through into the town.

Landerneau is a little town of six or seven thousand people, a sleepy little place upon a tidal river running to the Rade de Brest. It is built of grey stone, set in a rolling country dotted round with little woods; it reminded Howard of the Yorkshire wolds. The air, which had been hot and stuffy in the railway carriage, now seemed fresh and sweet, with a faint savour suggesting that the sea was not so very far away.

The town was sparsely held by Germans. Their lorries were parked in the square beneath the plane-trees by the river, but there were few of them to be seen. Those that were in evidence seemed ill at ease, anxious to placate the curiosity of a population which they knew to be pro-English. Their behaviour was most studiously correct. The few soldiers in the streets were grey faced and tired looking, wandering round in twos and threes and staring listlessly at the strange sights. One thing was very noticeable; they never seemed to laugh.

Unchallenged, Howard and Nicole walked through the town and out into the country beyond, upon the road that led towards the south. They went slowly for the sake of the children; the old man was accustomed now to the slow pace that they could manage. The road was empty and they straggled all over it. It led up on to the open wold.

Rose and Willem were allowed to take their shoes off and go barefoot, rather to the disapproval of Nicole. 'I do not think that that is in the part,' she said. 'The class which we represent would not do that.'

The old man said: 'There's nobody to see.'

She agreed that it did not matter much, and they went sauntering on, Willem pushing the pram with Pierre. Ahead of them three aircraft crossed the sky in steady, purposeful flight towards the west, flying at about two thousand feet.

The sight woke memories in Rose. 'M'sieur,' she cried. 'Three aeroplanes – look! Quick, let us get into the ditch!'

He calmed her. 'Never mind them,' he said equably. 'They aren't going to hurt us.'

She was only half-reassured. 'But they dropped bombs before and fired their guns!'

He said: 'These are different aeroplanes. These are good aeroplanes. They won't hurt us.'

Pierre said, suddenly and devastatingly, in his little piping voice: 'Can you tell good aeroplanes from bad aeroplanes, M'sieur Howard?'

With a sick heart the old man thought again of the shambles on the Montargis road. 'Why, yes,' he said gently. 'You remember the aeroplanes that mademoiselle took you to see at Chartres? The ones where they let you touch the bombs? They didn't hurt you, did they? Those were good aeroplanes. Those over there are the same sort. They won't hurt us.'

Ronnie, anxious to display expert technical knowledge,

endorsed these statements. 'Good aeroplanes are our own aeroplanes, aren't they, Mr Howard?'

'That's right,' the old man said.

Nicole drew him a little way aside. 'I don't know how you can think of such things to say,' she said in a low tone. 'But those are German aeroplanes.'

'I know that. But one has to say something.'

She stared at the three pencil-like shapes in the far distance. 'It was marvellous when aeroplanes were things of pleasure,' she said.

He nodded. 'Have you ever flown?' he asked.

She said: 'Twice, at a fête, just for a little way each time. And then the time I flew with John over Paris. It was wonderful, that . . .'

He was interested. 'You went with a pilot, I suppose. Or did he pilot the machine himself?'

She said: 'But he flew it himself, of course, m'sieur. It was just him and me.'

'How did he get hold of the aeroplane?' He knew that in a foreign country there were difficulties in aviation.

She said: 'He took me to dance, at the flying club, in the Rue François Premier. He had a friend – *un capitaine de l'Aéronautique* – that he had met in England when he had been with our Embassy in London. And this friend arranged everything for John.'

She said: '*Figurez-vous*, monsieur! I could not get him to one art gallery, not one! All his life he is used to spend in flying, and then he comes to Paris for a holiday and he wants to go to the aerodrome and fly!'

He smiled gently. 'He was like that . . . Did you enjoy yourself?'

She said: 'It was marvellous. It was a fine, sunny day with a fresh breeze, and we drove out to Orly, to the hangar of the flying club. And there, there was a beautiful aeroplane waiting for us, with the engine running.'

Her face clouded a little, and then she smiled. 'I do not know very much about flying,' she said frankly. 'It was very chic, with red leather seats and chromium steps to make it easy to get in. But John was so rude.'

The old man said: 'Rude?'

'He said it looked like a bed bug, monsieur, but not so that the mechanics could hear what he said. I told him that I was very cross to hear him say such a thing, when they had been so kind to lend it to us. He only laughed. And then, when we were flying over Paris at *grande vitesse*, a hundred and twenty kilometres an hour or more, he turned to me and said: "And what's more, it flies like one!" Imagine that! Our aeroplanes are very good, monsieur. Everybody in France says so.'

Howard smiled again. 'I hope you put him in his place,' he said.

She laughed outright; it was the first time that he had heard that happen. 'That was not possible, Monsieur Howard,' she said. 'Never could I put him in his place, as you say.'

He said: 'I'm sorry about that.' He paused, and then he said: 'I have never flown over Paris. Is it beautiful?'

She shrugged her shoulders. 'Beautiful? I do not think that anything is beautiful seen from the air, except the clouds. But that day was marvellous, because there were those big, fleecy clouds that John called cum . . . something.'

'Cumulus?'

She nodded. 'That was it. For more than an hour we played in them, flying around and over the top and in between the white cliffs in the deep gorges of the mist. And every now and then, far below, one would see Paris, the Concorde or perhaps the Etoile. Never shall I forget that day. And when we landed I was so sleepy that I went to sleep in the car on the way back to Paris, leaning up against John, with my head on his shoulder.'

They walked on in silence for a time. Pierre and Willem tired of pushing the pram and gave place to Rose, with Sheila trotting at her side. The kitten lay curled up in the pram, sound asleep.

Presently Nicole pointed ahead of them. 'That is the house – amongst those trees.'

The house that she pointed to lay about a mile ahead of them. It seemed to be a fairly large and prosperous farm, grouped round a modest country house standing among trees as shelter from the wind. About it rolled the open pasture of the wold, as far as could be seen.

In half an hour they were close up to it. A long row of stabling showed the interests of the owner; there were horses running in the paddocks near the farm. The farm buildings were better kept and laid out than the farms that Howard had had dealings with upon his journey; this was a cut above the usual run of things.

They went up to a house that stood beside the entrance, in the manner of a lodge; here Nicole enquired for M. Arvers. They were directed to the stables; leaving the children with the pram at the gate, they went forward together.

They met their man half-way.

Aristide Arvers was a small man of fifty-five or so, thin, with sharp features and a shrewd look. Howard decided at the first glance that this man was no fool. And the second thought that came into his mind was realisation that this man could well be the father of a beauty queen, of Miss Landerneau. The delicate features, sharpening by advancing age, might well be fascinating in a young girl.

He wore a shapeless black suit with a soiled scarf

wrapped around his neck in lieu of collar; a black hat was on his head.

Nicole said: 'Monsieur Arvers, do you remember me? You were so kind as to invite me here one day, with my father, Colonel Rougeron. You showed my father round your stables. After that you entertained us in your house. That was three years ago – do you remember?'

He nodded. 'I remember that very well, mademoiselle. M. le colonel was very interested in my horses for the army, being himself an artillery officer, if I remember right.' He hesitated. 'I hope you have good news of M. le colonel?'

She said: 'We have had no news for three months, when he was at Metz.'

'I am desolated, mademoiselle.'

She nodded, having nothing much to say to that. She said: 'If my father had been at home he would no doubt have come to see you himself. As he is not, I have come instead.'

His brows wrinkled slightly, but he bowed a little. 'That is an added pleasure,' he said perfunctorily.

'May we, perhaps, go to your office?'

'But certainly.'

He turned and led them to the house. There was a littered, dusty office, full of sad-looking account-books and files, with bits of broken harness thrown aside in corners. He closed the door behind them and gave them rickety chairs; there being no other seats, he leaned backwards against the edge of the desk.

'First,' said the girl, 'I wish to introduce you to Monsieur Howard. He is an Englishman.'

The horse-breeder raised his eyebrows a little, but bowed ceremonious. '*Enchanté,*' he said.

Nicole said: 'I will come directly to the point, Monsieur Arvers. Monsieur Howard is a very old friend of my family.

195

He is travelling with several children, and he is trying to return to England in spite of the Germans. My mother and I have talked about this, in the absence of my father, and it seemed to us that Jean Henri could help perhaps with one of his boats. Or, if that was impossible, Jean Henri might know some friend who would help. There is money enough to pay for any services.'

The man said nothing for a time. At last: 'The Germans are not to be trifled with,' he said.

Howard said: 'We appreciate that, monsieur. We do not wish that anyone should run into trouble upon our behalf. That is why mademoiselle has come to talk to you before going to your son-in-law.'

The other turned to him. 'You speak French better than most Englishmen.'

'I have had longer than most Englishmen to learn it.'

The Frenchman smiled. 'You are very anxious to return to England?'

The old man said: 'For myself, not so very anxious. I should be quite happy to live in France for a time. But I have children in my care you understand, English children that I have promised that I would escort to England.' He hesitated. 'And, as a matter of fact, there are three others now.'

'What are those other children? How many of you are there altogether? And where have you come from?'

It took nearly twenty minutes to elucidate the story. At last the Frenchman said: 'These other children, the little one called Pierre and the little Dutchman. What is going to become of them when they reach England?'

Howard said: 'I have a daughter, married, in America. She is in easy circumstances. She would make a home for those two in her house at Long Island till the war is over and we can trace their relations. They would be very happy there.'

The man stared at him keenly. 'In America? That I can well believe. You will send them over the Atlantic to your daughter? Will she be good to them – children that she has never seen? Unknown, foreign children?'

The old man said: 'My daughter has one child of her own, and now hopes for another. She is very fond of all children. They will be safe with her.'

Arvers got up suddenly from the desk. 'It is impossible,' he said. 'If Jean Henri should put his hand to this he would be in great danger. The Germans would shoot him, beyond all doubt. You have no right to suggest such a thing.' He paused, and then he said: 'I have my daughter to consider.'

There was a long, slow pause. At last the old man turned to Nicole. 'That's the end of that,' he said. He smiled at Arvers. 'I understand perfectly,' he said. 'In your place, thinking of my daughter, I should say the same.'

The Frenchman turned to the girl. 'I regret very much that I cannot help you in the way you want,' he said.

She shrugged her shoulders. '*Tant pis*,' she said. '*N'y pensez plus.*'

He looked uncomfortable. 'These children,' he said. 'Where are they now?'

They told him that they were waiting in the road, and he walked with them to the gate. It was getting towards evening. The children were playing at the edge of a pond, muddy and rather fractious. There were tear streaks around Sheila's face.

Arvers said awkwardly: 'Would it help you to stay here for the night? I do not think we have beds for so many, but something could perhaps be managed.'

Nicole said warmly: 'You are very kind, monsieur.'

They called the children and introduced them one by one to the horse-dealer; then they went towards the house.

The man called his wife as they approached the door; she came from the kitchen, a stolid peasant woman. He spoke to her, told her that the party were to stay with them for the night, introduced her formally to them. Nicole shepherded the children after her into the kitchen. Arvers turned to Howard.

'You will take a little glass of Pernod, perhaps?' he said.

A little glass of Pernod seemed to the old man to be a very good idea. They went into the salon because the kitchen was full of children. The salon was a stiff and formal room, with gilt-legged furniture upholstered in red plush. On the wall there was a very large oleograph of a white-robed little girl kneeling devoutly in a shaft of light. It was entitled: '*La Première Communion.*'

Arvers brought the Pernod, with glasses and water, and the two men settled down together. They talked about horses and about country matters. Arvers had been to England once, to Newmarket as a jockey when he was a very young man. They chatted pleasantly enough for a quarter of an hour.

Suddenly Arvers said: 'Your daughter, Monsieur Howard. She will surely find so many foreign children an encumbrance? Are you so certain that they will be welcome in her home?'

The old man said: 'They will be welcome, all right.'

'But how can you possibly know that? Your daughter may find it very inconvenient to have them.'

He shook his head. 'I don't think so. But if that should be so, then she would make arrangements for them for me. She would engage some kind woman to make a home for them, because that is my wish, that they should have a good home in America – away from all this.' He motioned with his hand. 'And there is no difficulty over money, you understand.'

The Frenchman sat silent for a little time, staring into his glass.

'This is a bad time for children, this filthy war,' he said at last. 'And now that France is defeated, it is going to be worse. You English now will starve us, as we starved Germany in 1918.'

Howard was silent.

'I shall not blame your country if you do that. But it will be bad for children here.'

'I am afraid it may be,' said the old man. 'That is why I want to get these children out of it. One must do what one can.'

Arvers shrugged his shoulders. 'There are no children in this house, thank God. Or – only one.' He paused. 'That was a hard case, if you like.'

Howard looked at him enquiringly. The Frenchman poured him out another Pernod. 'A friend in Paris asked me if I had work for a Pole,' he said. 'In December, that was – just at Christmas time. A Polish Jew who knew horses, who had escaped into Rumania and so by sea to Marseilles. Well, you will understand, the mobilisation had taken five of my eight men, and it was very difficult.'

Howard nodded. 'You took him on?'

'Assuredly. Simon Estreicher was his name, and he arrived one day with his son, a boy of ten. There had been a wife, but I will not distress you with that story. She had not escaped the Boche, you understand.'

The old man nodded.

'Well, this man Estreicher worked here till last week, and he worked well. He was quiet and gave no trouble, and the son worked in the stables too. Then last week the Germans came here and took him away.'

'Took him away?'

'Took him away to Germany, to their forced labour. He

was a Pole, you see, m'sieur, and a Jew as well. One could do nothing for him. Some filthy swine in town had told them about him, because they came straight here and asked for him. They put handcuffs on him and took him in a camion with several others.'

'Did they take the son as well?'

'They never asked for him, and he was in the paddock at the time, so I said nothing. One does not help the Germans in their work. But it was very hard on that young boy.'

Howard agreed with him. 'He is with you still, then?'

'Where else could he go? He is useful in the stables, too. But before long I suppose they will find out about him, and come back for him to take him away also.'

Nicole came to them presently, to call them to the kitchen for supper. She had already given the children a meal, and had put them to sleep on beds improvised upstairs by Madame Arvers. They ate together in the kitchen at a long table, together with two men from the farm and a black-haired Jewish-looking boy whom Madame called Marjan, and who said little or nothing during the meal.

The meal over, Arvers escorted Nicole and Howard back to the salon; presently he produced a set of dominoes and proposed a game. Howard settled down to it with him. The horse-dealer played carelessly, his mind on other things.

Presently he returned to the subject that was on his mind. 'Are many children going to America, monsieur? I cannot comprehend how you can be so positive that they will be welcomed. America is very far away. They do not bother about our difficulties here.'

Howard shrugged his shoulders. 'They are a generous people. These children will be quite all right if I can get them there, because my daughter will look after them. But even without her, there would be many people in America willing to provide for them. Americans are like that.'

The other stared at him incredulously. 'It would cost a great deal of money to provide for a child, perhaps for years. One does not do that lightly for a foreign child of which one knows nothing.'

'It's just the sort of thing they *do* do,' said the old man. 'They would pour out their money in a cause like that.'

The horse-dealer stared at him keenly and thoughtfully. 'Would they provide for Marjan Estreicher?' he enquired at last. 'No doubt they would not do that for a Jew.'

'I don't think it would make the slightest difference in the case of a child. It certainly would make no difference to my daughter.'

Nicole moved impulsively beside him. 'Monsieur . . .' she said, but he stopped her with a gesture. She subsided into silence again, watchful.

Howard said steadily: 'I would take him with me, if that is what you want. I would send him to the United States with the other children. But before that, I should want help to get them all away.'

'Jean Henri?'

'Assuredly, Monsieur.'

The other got up, displacing the unheeded game of dominoes with his sleeve. He went and fetched the Pernod, the glasses, and the water, and poured out a drink for Howard. He offered one to the girl, but she refused.

'The risk is enormous,' he said stubbornly. 'Think what it would mean to my daughter if you should be caught.'

'Think what it would mean to that boy, if he should be caught,' the old man said. 'They would take him for a slave, put him in the mines and work him till he died. That's what the Germans do with Polish children.'

Arvers said: 'I know that. That is what troubles me.'

Nicole said suddenly: 'Does Marjan want to go? You cannot make him if he does not want to. He is old, that one.'

'He is only ten,' said Arvers.

'Nevertheless,' she said, 'he is quite grown up. We cannot take him if he does not want to go.'

Arvers went out of the room; in a few minutes he returned, followed by the boy. He said to him: 'This is the matter, Marjan. This monsieur here is going to England if he can escape the Germans, and from England the children with him are going to America. In America they will be safe. There are no Germans there. Would you like to go with them?'

The boy stood silent. They explained it to him again. At last he said in almost unintelligible French: 'In America, what should I work at?'

Howard said: 'For a time you would have to go to school, to learn English and the American way of living. At school they would teach you to earn your living in some trade. What do you want to do when you grow up?'

Without any hesitation the boy said: 'I want to kill Germans.'

There was a momentary silence. Arvers said: 'That is enough about the Germans. Tell Monsieur here what trade you wish to learn in America, if he should be so kind as to take you there.'

There was a silence.

Nicole came forward. 'Tell us,' she said gently. 'Would you like to grow up with horses? Or would you rather buy things and sell them for a profit?' After all, she thought, it would be difficult for him to go against the characteristics of his race. 'Would you rather do that?'

The boy looked up at her. 'I want to learn to shoot with a rifle from a very long way away,' he said, 'because you can do that from the hills when they are on the road. And I want to learn to throw a knife hard and straight. That is

202

best in the darkness, in the narrow streets, because it does not make a noise.'

Arvers smiled a little ruefully. 'I am sorry, monsieur,' he said. 'I am afraid he is not making a very good impression.'

The old man said nothing.

Marjan said: 'When do we start?'

Howard hesitated, irresolute. This lad might be a great embarrassment to them; at the best he could only be described as a prickly customer. On the other hand, a deep pity for the child lurked in the background of his mind.

'Do you want to come with us?' he asked.

The boy nodded his black head.

'If you come with us, you will have to forget all this about the Germans,' said the old man. 'You will have to go to school and learn your lessons, and play baseball, and go fishing, like other boys.'

The lad said gravely: 'I could not kill a German for another two or three years because I am not strong enough. Not unless I could catch one asleep and drive a pitchfork into his belly as he slept, and even then he might reach out before he died and overcome me. But in America I could learn everything, and come back when I am fifteen years old, and big and strong.'

Howard said gently: 'There are other things to learn in America besides that.'

The boy said: 'I know there is a great deal to learn, monsieur. One thing, you should always go for the young women – not the men. If you get the young women, then they cannot spawn, and before long there will be no more Germans.'

'That is enough,' said Arvers sharply. 'Go back to kitchen and stay there till I call you.'

The boy left the room. The horse-dealer turned to

Nicole. 'I am desolated that he should have said such things,' he said.

The girl said: 'He has suffered a great deal. And he is very young.'

Arvers nodded. 'I do not know what will become of him,' he said morosely.

Howard sat down in the silence which followed and took a sip of Pernod. 'One of two things will happen to him,' he said. 'One is, that the Germans will catch him very soon. He may try to kill one of them, in which case they might shoot him out of hand. They will take him to their mines. He will be rebellious the whole time, and before long he will be beaten to death. That is the one thing.'

The horse-dealer dropped into the chair on the opposite side of the table, the bottle of Pernod between them. There was something in the old man's tone that was very familiar to him. 'What is the other thing?' he asked.

'He will escape with us to England,' said Howard. 'He will end up in America, kindly treated and well cared for, and in a year or two these horrors will have faded from his mind.'

Arvers eyed him keenly. 'Which of those is going to happen?'

'That is in your hands, monsieur. He will never escape the Germans unless you help him.'

There was a long, long silence in the falling dusk.

Arvers said at last: 'I will see what I can do. Tomorrow I will drive Mademoiselle to Le Conquet and we will talk it over with Jean Henri. You must stay here with the children and keep out of sight.'

9

Howard spent most of the next day sitting in the paddock in the sun, while the children played around him. His growing, stubbly beard distressed him with a sense of personal uncleanliness, but it was policy to let it grow. Apart from that, he was feeling well; the rest was welcome and refreshing.

Madame dragged an old cane reclining chair from a dusty cellar and wiped it over with a cloth for him; he thanked her and installed himself in it. The children had the kitten, Jo-Jo, in the garden and were stuffing it with copious draughts of milk and anything that they could get it to eat. Presently it escaped and climbed up into the old man's lap and went to sleep.

After a while he found himself making whistles on a semi-production basis, while the children stood around and watched.

From time to time the Polish boy, Marjan, appeared by the paddock gate and stood looking at them, curious, inscrutable. Howard spoke to him and asked him to come in and join them, but he muttered something to the effect that he had work to do, and sheered away shyly. Presently he would be back again, watching the children as they played. The old man let him alone, content not to hurry the friendship.

In the middle of the afternoon, suddenly, there was a series of heavy explosions over in the west. These mingled with the sharp crack of gunfire; the children stopped their games and stared in wonder. Then a flight of three single-engined fighter aeroplanes got up like partridges from some field not very far away and flew over them at about two thousand feet, heading towards the west and climbing at full throttle as they went.

Ronnie said wisely: 'That's bombs, *I* know. They go whee . . . before they fall, and then they go boom. Only it's so far off you can't hear the whee part.'

'Whee . . . Boom!' said Sheila. Pierre copied her, and presently all the children were running round wheeing and booming.

The real detonations grew fewer, and presently died in the summer afternoon.

'That was the Germans bombing someone, wasn't it, Mr Howard?' asked Ronnie.

'I expect so,' he replied. 'Come and hold this bark while I bind it.' In the production of whistles the raid faded from their minds.

In the later afternoon Nicole returned with Arvers. Both were very dirty, and the girl had a deep cut on the palm of one hand, roughly bandaged. Howard was shocked at her appearance.

'My dear,' he said, 'whatever happened? Has there been an accident?'

She laughed a little shrilly. 'It was the British,' she said. 'It was an air raid. We were caught in Brest – this afternoon. But it was the British, monsieur, that did this to me.'

Madame Arvers came bustling up with a glass of brandy. Then she hustled the girl off into the kitchen. Howard was left in the paddock, staring out towards the west.

The children had only understood half of what had happened. Sheila said: 'It was the bad aeroplanes that did that to Nicole, monsieur, wasn't it?'

'That's right,' he said. 'Good aeroplanes don't do that sort of thing.'

The child was satisfied with that. 'It must have been a very, *very* bad aeroplane to do that to Nicole.'

There was general agreement on that point. Ronnie said: 'Bad aeroplanes are German aeroplanes. Good aeroplanes are English ones.'

He made no attempt to unravel that one for them.

Presently Nicole came out into the garden, white-faced and with her hand neatly bandaged. Madame hustled the children into the kitchen for their supper.

Howard asked after her hand. 'It is nothing,' she said. 'When a bomb falls, the glass in all the windows flies about. That is what did it.'

'I am so sorry.'

She turned to him. 'I would not have believed that there would be so much glass in the streets,' she said. 'In heaps it was piled. And the fires – houses on fire everywhere. And dust, thick dust that smothered everything.'

'But how did you come to be mixed up in it?'

She said: 'It just happened. We had been to Le Conquet, and after *déjeuner* we set out in the motor-car to return here. And passing through Brest, Aristide wanted to go to the Bank, and I wanted tooth-powder and some other things – little things, you understand. And it was while Aristide was in the Bank and I was in the shops in the Rue de Siam that it happened.'

'What did happen?' he asked.

She shrugged her shoulders. 'It was an aeroplane that came racing low over the roofs – so low that one could see the number painted on the body; the targets on the

207

wings showed us that it was English. It swung round the Harbour and dropped its bombs near the Port Militaire, and then another of them came, and another – many of them. It was the German ships in the harbour, I think, that they were bombing. But several of them dropped their bombs in a long line, and these lines spread right into the town. There were two bombs that hit houses in the Rue de Siam, and three or more in the Rue Louis Pasteur. And where a bomb fell, the house fell right down, not five feet high, Monsieur – truly, that was all that could be seen. And there were fires, and clouds of smoke and dust, and glass – glass everywhere . . .'

There was a little silence. 'Were many people hurt?' he asked at last.

She said: 'I think very many.'

He was very much upset. He felt that something should have happened to prevent this. He was terribly concerned for her, and a little confused.

She said presently: 'You must not distress yourself on my account, Monsieur Howard. I assure you, I am quite all right, and so is Aristide.' She laughed shortly. 'At least, I can say that I have seen the Royal Air Force at work. For many months I longed to see that.'

He shook his head, unable to say anything.

She laid her hand upon his arm. 'Many of the bombs fell in the Port Militaire,' she said gently. 'One or two went wide, but that was not intended. I think they may have hit the ships.' She paused and then she said: 'I think John would have been very pleased.'

'Yes,' he said heavily, 'I suppose he would have been.'

She took his arm. 'Come in the salon and we will drink a Pernod together, and I will tell you about Jean Henri.'

They went together into the house. Aristide was not about; in the salon Howard sat down with the girl. He was still distressed and upset; Nicole poured out a Pernod for him and added a little water. Then she poured a smaller one for herself.

'About Jean Henri,' she said. 'He is not to appear in this himself. Aristide will not have that, for the sake of Marie. But in Le Conquet there is a young man called Simon Focquet, and he will take a boat across with you.'

The old man's heart leaped, but all he said was: 'How old is this young man?'

She shrugged her shoulders. 'Twenty – twenty-two, perhaps. He is de Gaullist.'

'What is that, mademoiselle?'

She said: 'There is a General de Gaulle in England with your armies, one of our younger Generals. In France nobody knew much about him, but now he will carry on the battle from England. He is not approved by our Government of Vichy, but many of our young men are slipping away to join him, some by way of Spain and others in boats across the Manche. That is how Simon Focquet wishes to go, because he is a fishing-boy, and knows boats very well.'

'But the Germans will stop that, surely.'

She nodded. 'Already all traffic has been stopped. But the boats are still allowed to fish around the coast and by Ushant. It will be necessary to devise something.

He said: 'Where will he get the boat?'

'Aristide has arranged that for us. Jean Henri will hire one of his boats for fishing to this young man, and Simon then will steal it when he leaves for England. Jean Henri will be the first to complain to the gendarmerie, and to the Germans, that his boat has been stolen. But Aristide will pay him for it secretly. You should pay Aristide, if you have so much money.'

He nodded. 'How much will it be?'

She said: 'Five thousand five hundred francs.'

He thought for a moment. Then he pulled out his wallet from his hip pocket, opened with the deliberation of age, and studied a document. 'I seem to have forty pounds left on my letter of credit,' he said. 'Will that be enough?'

She said: 'I think so. Aristide will want all the payment that you can make because he is a peasant, Monsieur, you understand. But he wishes to help us, and he will not stop the venture for that reason.'

Howard said: 'I would see that he got the difference when the war is over.'

They talked of this for a little time. Then Nicole got up from the table. 'I must go and see the children in their beds,' she said. 'Madame Arvers has been very kind, but one should not leave everything to her.'

'I will come too,' he said. 'They have been very good children all day, and no trouble.'

The children were all sleeping in one room, the two girls in the bed and the three little boys upon a mattress on the floor, covered with rough blankets. The peasant woman was tucking them up; she smiled broadly as Nicole and the old man came in, and disappeared back into the kitchen. Ronnie said: 'My blanket smells of horses.'

Nothing was more probable, the old man thought. He said: 'I expect you'll dream that you're going for a ride all night.'

Sheila said: 'May I go for a ride, too?'

'If you're very good.'

Rose said: 'May we stay here now?'

Nicole sat down on her bed. 'Why?' she said. 'Don't you want to see your father in London?'

La petite Rose said: 'I thought London was a town.'

'So it is. A very big town.'

'I like being in the country like this,' Rose said. 'This is like it was where we used to live.'

Ronnie said: 'But we're all going to London.'

'Not all of you,' the old man said. 'You and Sheila are going to live with your Aunt Margaret at Oxford.'

'Are we? Is Rose going to live with Aunt Margaret, too?'

'No. Rose is going to live with her daddy in London.'

Sheila said: 'Is Pierre going to live with Aunt Margaret?'

'No,' he said. 'Pierre and Willem are going to America to live with my daughter. Did you know I had a grown-up daughter, older than Nicole? She's got a little boy of her own.'

They stared at him incredulously. 'What's his name?' Ronnie asked at last.

'Martin,' the old man said. 'He's the same age as Pierre.'

Pierre stared at them. 'Won't you be coming with us?'

'I don't think so,' Howard said. 'I think I shall have work to do in England.'

His lip trembled. 'Won't Rose be coming?'

Nicole slipped down by his bed. 'It's going to be lovely in America,' she said gently. 'There will be bright lights at night-time, not like the black-out we have here. There is no bombing, nor firing guns at people from the air. There will be plenty to eat, and nice, sweet things like we all used to have. You will live at a place called "Coates Harbor" on Long Island, where Madame Costello has a great big house in the country. And there is a pony for you to ride, and dogs to make friends with, like we all used to have before the war when we had food for dogs. And you will learn to sail a boat, and to swim and dive like the English and Americans do, and to catch fish for pleasure. And you will feel quite safe then, because there is no war in America.'

Pierre stared up at her. 'Will you be coming with me to America?'

211

She said quietly: 'No, Pierre. I must stay here.'

The corners of his mouth dropped. 'I don't want to go alone.'

Howard said: 'Perhaps Rose's father will want her to go too. Then she would go with you. You'd like that, wouldn't you?'

Sheila said: 'May Ronnie and I go, Mr Howard? Can we all go with Pierre?'

He said: 'I'll have to see about that. Your Aunt Margaret may want you in England.'

Ronnie said: 'If she doesn't want us, may we go to Coates Harbor with Pierre?'

'Yes,' he said. 'If she wants you out of England you can all go to Coates Harbor together.'

'Coo,' said the little boy, unfeelingly. 'I do hope she doesn't want us.'

After a time they got the children settled down to sleep; they went downstairs again and out into the garden until supper was ready. The old man said:

'You know a good deal about my daughter's house in America, mademoiselle.'

She smiled. 'John used to tell me about it,' she said. 'He had been out there, had he not, monsieur?'

He nodded. 'He was out there with Enid for a time in 1938. He thought a great deal of her husband, Costello.'

She said: 'He told me all about it very early one morning, when we could not sleep. John loved America. He was *aviateur*, you understand – he loved their technique.'

Not for the first time the old man wondered doubtfully about the nature of that week in Paris. He said absently: 'He enjoyed that visit very much.'

He roused himself. 'I am a little worried about Pierre,' he said. 'I had not thought of sending anybody over with him to America.'

She nodded. 'He is sensitive, that one. He will be lonely and unhappy at first, but he will get over it. If Rose could go too it would be all right.'

He faced her. 'Why not go yourself?' he suggested. 'That would be best of all.'

'Go to America? That is not possible at all, monsieur.'

A little fear stole into his heart. 'But you are coming to England, Nicole?'

She shook her head. 'No, monsieur. I must stay in France.'

He was suddenly deeply disappointed. 'Do you really think that is the best thing to do?' he said. 'This country is overrun with Germans, and there will be great hardships as the war goes on. If you came with us to England you could live with me in my house in Essex, or you could go on to America with the children. That would be much better Nicole.'

She said: 'But monsieur, I have my mother to consider.'

He hesitated. 'Would you like to try to get hold of her, and take her with us? Life in France is going to be very difficult, you know.'

She shook her head. 'I know that things are going to be difficult. But she would not be happy in England. Perhaps I should not be happy either – now.'

'Have you ever been to England?' he asked curiously.

She shook her head. 'We had arranged that I should visit John in England in October, when he could get leave again. I think he would have taken me to see you then, perhaps. But the war came, and there was no more leave . . . And travelling was very difficult. I could not get a visa for my passport.'

He said gently: 'Make that trip to England now, Nicole.'

She shook her head. 'No, monsieur.'

'Why not?'

She said: 'Are you going to America with the children, yourself?'

He shook his head. 'I would like to, but I don't think I shall be able to. I believe that there'll be work for me to do when I get back.'

She said: 'Nor would I leave France.'

He opened his mouth to say that that was quite different, but shut it again without speaking. She divined something of his thought, because she said:

'Either one is French or one is English, and it is not possible that one should be both at the same time. And in times of great trouble, one must stay with one's own country and do what one can to help.'

He said slowly: 'I suppose so.'

Pursuing her train of thought, she said: 'If John and I –' she hesitated – 'if we had married, I should have been English and then it would be different. But now I am not to be English, ever. I could not learn your different ways, and the new life, alone. This is my place that I belong to, and I must stay here. You understand?'

He said: 'I understand that, Nicole.' He paused for a minute, and then said: 'I am getting to be an old man now. When this war is over I may not find it very easy to get about. Will you come and stay with me in England for a little? Just for a week or two?'

She said: 'Of course. Immediately that it is possible to travel, I will come.'

They walked beside each other in silence for the length of the paddock. Presently she said: 'Now for the detail of the journey. Focquet will take the boat tonight from Le Conquet to go fishing up the Chenal as far as Le Four. He will not return to Le Conquet, but tomorrow night he will put into l'Abervrach to land his fish, or to get bait, or on some pretext such as that. He will sail again at midnight of tomorrow night and you must then be in the boat with him, for he will go direct to England. Midnight is the latest time that he can sail, in order that he may be well away from the French coast before dawn.'

Howard asked: 'Where is this place l'Abervrach, mademoiselle? Is it far from here?'

She shrugged her shoulders. 'Forty kilometres, no more. There is a little town behind it, four miles inland, called Lannilis. We must go there tomorrow.'

'Are there many Germans in those parts?'

'I do not know. Aristide is trying to find out the situation there, and to devise something for us.'

The boy Marjan passed through the paddock on his way to the house. Howard turned and called to him; he hesitated, and then came to them.

The old man said; 'We are leaving here tomorrow, Marjan. Do you still want to come with us?'

The boy said: 'To America?'

'First we are going to try to get away to England. If we do that successfully, I will send you to America with Pierre and Willem, to live with my daughter till the war is over. Do you want to go?'

The boy said in his awkward French: 'If I stay with M. Arvers the Germans will find me and take me away. Presently they will kill me, as they killed my mother and as my father will be killed, because we are Jews. I would like to come with you.'

The old man said: 'Listen to me. I do not know if I shall take you, Marjan. We may meet Germans on the way from this place to the coast; we may have to mix with them, eat at their canteens perhaps. If you show that you hate them, they may arrest us all. I do not know if it is safe to take you, if it is fair to Rose and Ronnie and Sheila and Willem and to little Pierre.'

The boy said: 'I shall not make trouble for you. It will be better for me to go to America now; that is what I want to do. It would only be by great good luck that I could kill a German now; even if I could creep up to one in the darkness and rip him open with a sharp knife, I should be caught and killed. But in a few years' time I shall be able to kill many hundreds of them, secretly, in the dark streets. That is much better, to wait and to learn how these things should be managed properly.'

Howard felt slightly sick. He said: 'Can you control yourself, if Germans are near by?'

The boy said: 'I can wait for years, monsieur, till my time comes.'

Nicole said: 'Listen, Marjan. You understand what Monsieur means? If you are taken by the Germans all these little boys and girls will also be taken, and the Germans will do to them what they will do to you. It would be very wrong of you to bring that trouble on them.'

He said: 'Have no fear. I shall be good, and obedient, and polite, if you will take me with you. That is what one must practise all the time, so that you win their confidence. In that way you can get them at your mercy in the end.'

Howard said: 'All right, Marjan. We start in the morning; be ready to come with us. Now go and have your supper and go up to bed.'

He stood watching the boy as he made his way towards the house. 'God knows what sort of world we shall have when this is all over,' he said heavily.

Nicole said: 'I do not know. But what you are doing now will help us all, I think. To get these children out of Europe must be a good thing.'

Presently they were called to the kitchen for their supper. Afterwards, in the salon, Arvers talked to them.

'Listen,' he said, 'and I will tell you what I have arranged.'

He paused. 'Lannilis is full of Germans. That is four miles from the coast, and the places at the coast itself, l'Abervrach and Portsall and places of that sort, are very lightly held or even not occupied at all. They do not interfere with the traffic of the country, and this is what I have devised for you.'

He said: 'Three miles this side of Lannilis there is a farmer called Quintin, and he is to send a load of manure tomorrow to a fisherman called Loudeac, the captain of the lifeboat at l'Abervrach, because Loudeac has a few fields on the hills and wants manure. I have arranged all that. The manure will be delivered in a cart with one horse, you understand? You, m'sieur, will drive the cart. Mademoiselle and the children will accompany you for the ride.'

Howard said: 'That seems sound enough. Nobody would suspect that.'

Aristide glanced at him. 'It will be necessary that you should wear poorer clothes. That I can arrange.'

Nicole said: 'How do we get into touch with Focquet tomorrow night?'

The horse-dealer said: 'Tomorrow night, Focquet will come at nine o'clock to the *estaminet* upon the quayside. He will appear to be slightly drunk, and he will ask for Pernod des Anges. There is no such drink. In that way you will know him. The rest I will leave to you.'

Howard nodded: 'How can we get to Quintin's farm?'

'I will take you myself so far in the car. That will be safe enough, for it is this side of Lannilis and there will be no questions asked. But there I must leave you.' He thought for a minute. 'It will be better that you should not start from Quintin's farm much before five o'clock,' he said. 'That will make it reasonable that you should be in l'Abervrach at nightfall, and even that you should spend the night there, with Loudeac.'

Nicole said: 'What about Loudeac and Quintin, monsieur? Do they know that Monsieur Howard and the children will escape?'

The man said: 'Have no fear, mademoiselle. This is not so uncommon, in these times. They know all that they wish to know, and they have been paid. They are good friends of mine.'

Howard said: 'I must now pay you, monsieur.'

They settled down together at the table.

Soon after that they went to bed; refreshed by a restful day Howard slept well. In the morning he went down for coffee feeling better than he had felt for some days.

Aristide said: 'We leave after *déjeuner*. That will be time enough. Now, I have borrowed clothes for m'sieur. You will not like them, but they are necessary.'

The old man did not like the clothes at all. They were very dirty, a coarse, stained flannel shirt, a pair of torn blue cotton trousers, a dirty canvas pullover that had once been rusty pink in colour, and a black, floppy Breton casque. Wooden sabots were the footgear provided with this outfit, but the old man struck at those, and Arvers produced a torn and loathsome pair of boots.

It was some days since he had shaved. When he came down to the kitchen Nicole smiled broadly. 'It is very good,' she said. 'Now, Monsieur Howard, if you walk with the head hanging down, and your mouth open a little – so. And walk slowly, as if you were a very, very old man. And be very deaf and very stupid. I will talk for you.'

Arvers walked round him, studying him critically. 'I do not think the Germans will find fault with that,' he said.

They spent the rest of the morning studying appearances. Nicole kept her black frock, but Arvers made her dirty it a little, and made her change to a very old pair of low-heeled shoes belonging to his wife. With a shawl belonging to Madame Arvers over her head, he passed her too.

The children needed very little grooming. During the morning they had been playing at the duck-pond, and were sufficiently dirty to pass muster without any painting of the lily. Ronnie and Willem were scratching themselves a good deal, which added verisimilitude to the act.

They started after *déjeuner*. Howard and Nicole thanked Madame Arvers for her kindness; she received their thanks with calm, bovine smiles. Then they all got into the little old de Dion van that Arvers kept for the farm and drove off down the road.

Ronnie said: 'Are we going to the train that we're going to sleep in, Mr Howard?'

'Not just yet,' he said. 'We shall get out of the car presently and say good-bye to Monsieur Arvers, and then we have a ride in a cart. You must all be very careful to speak French only, all the time.'

Sheila said: 'Why must we speak French? I want to speak English, like we used to.'

Nicole said gently: 'We shall be among the Germans. They do not like people who speak English. You must be very careful to speak only in French.'

Rose said suddenly: 'Marjan says the Germans cut his mother's hands off.'

Howard said gently: 'No more talk about the Germans now. In a little time we shall get out, and have a ride in a horse and cart.' He turned to Pierre. 'What sort of noise does a horse make?' he asked.

Pierre said shyly: 'I don't know.'

La petite Rose bent over him. 'Oh, Pierre, of course you know!

'My great-aunt lives in Tours,
In a house with a cherry tree
With a little mouse (squeak, squeak)
And a big lion (roar, roar)
And a wood-pigeon (coo, coo) . . .'

That lasted them all the way through Landerneau, of which they caught only glimpses through the windows at the back of the old van, and half-way to Lannilis.

Presently the van slowed, turned off the road, and bumped to a standstill. Arvers swung round to them from the driving-seat. 'This is the place,' he said. 'Get out quickly, it is not wise to linger here.'

They opened the door at the back of the van and got out. They were in a very small farmyard, the farmhouse itself little more than a workman's cottage of grey stone. The air was fresh and sweet after the van, with a clear savour of the sea. In the warm sun, and looking at the grey stone walls and roofs, Howard could have thought himself in Cornwall.

There was a cart and horse, the cart half loaded with manure, the old grey horse tied to the gate. Nobody was to be seen.

Arvers said: 'Now quickly, monsieur, before a German passes on the road. There is the cart. You have everything quite clear? You take the dung to Loudeac, who lives up on the hill above l'Abervrach, half a mile from the port. There you unload it; Mademoiselle Rougeron must bring back the cart tomorrow to this place. Focquet will be in the *estaminet* tonight at nine o'clock, and he will be expecting you. He will ask for Pernod des Anges. It is all clear?'

'One thing,' the old man said. 'This road leads straight to Lannilis?'

'Assuredly.' The horse-dealer glanced nervously around.

'How do we get through Lannilis? How do we find the road out of the town to l'Abervrach?'

The hot sun beat down on them warmly from a cloudless sky; the scent of briar mingled with the odour of manure about them. Arvers said: 'This road leads straight to the great church in the middle of the town. From the west end of the church a road runs westwards; follow that. Where it forks at the outskirts of the town, by an advertisement for Byrrh, take the right-hand fork. From there to l'Abervrach is seven kilometres.'

Nicole said: 'I have been that way before. I think I know the road.'

The horse-dealer said: 'I will not linger, mademoiselle. And you, you must move off from here at once.' He turned to Howard. 'That is all that I can do for you, monsieur. Good luck. In happier days, we may meet again.'

The old man said: 'I shall look forward to thanking you again for so much kindness.'

Arvers swung himself into the seat of the old van, reversed out into the road, and vanished in a white cloud of dust. Howard looked around; there was no movement from the house, which stood deserted in the afternoon sun.

Nicole said: 'Come, children, up you go.'

Willem and Marjan swung themselves up into the cart; the English children, with Pierre and Rose, hung back. Ronnie said doubtfully: 'Is this the cart you said we were going to have a ride in?'

Rose said: 'It is a dung-cart. It is not correct to ride in a cart full of horse-dung, mademoiselle. My aunt would be very cross with me if I did that.'

Nicole said brightly: 'Well, I'm going to. You can walk with monsieur and help lead the horse, if you like.' She bustled the other children into the cart before her; it was only half full and there was room for all of them to stand and sit upon the edges of the sides in front of the load.

Pierre said: 'May I walk with Rose and lead the horse?'

Nicole said: 'No, Pierre, you're too small for that and the horse walks too quickly. You can stroke his nose when we get there.'

Howard untied the bridle from the gate and led the horse out into the road. He fell into a steady, easy shamble beside the horse, head hanging down.

For an hour and a half they went on like that before they reached the first houses of Lannilis. In the cart Nicole kept the children happy and amused; from time to time the old man heard a little burst of laughter above the clop, clop of the hooves of the old horse. *La petite* Rose walked on beside him, barefoot, treading lightly.

They passed a good deal of German transport on the road. From time to time lorries would come up behind them and they would pull in to the right to let them pass; the grey-faced, stolid soldiers staring at them incuriously. Once they met a platoon of about thirty infantry marching towards them down the road; the *Oberleutnant* in charge looked them over, but did not challenge them. Nobody showed much interest in them until they came to Lannilis.

On the outskirts of the town they were stopped. There was a barricade of an elementary nature, of two old motor-cars drawn half across the road, leaving only a small passage between. A sentry strolled out sleepily in the hot afternoon and raised his hand. Howard pulled up the horse and stared at him, and mumbled something with head hanging and mouth open. An *Unteroffizier* came from the guard-house and looked them over.

He asked in very bad French: 'Where are you taking this to?'

The old man raised his head a little and put his hand to one ear. 'Eh?'

The German repeated his question in a louder tone.

'Loudeac,' the old man said. 'Loudeac, outside l'Abervrach.'

The *Unteroffizier* looked at Nicole. 'And madame goes too?'

Nicole smiled at him and put her hand upon Pierre's shoulder. 'It is the little one's birthday,' she said. 'It is not easy to make fête these days. But as my uncle has to make this trip this afternoon, and as the load is only half and therefore easy for the horse, we make this little journey for an outing for the children.'

The old man nodded. 'It is not easy to make a treat for children in times like these.'

The *Unteroffizier* smiled. 'Proceed,' he said lazily. 'Many happy returns of the day.'

Howard jerked up the old horse, and they passed up the street. There was little traffic to be seen, partly because the French were keeping within doors, partly, no doubt, because of the heat of the afternoon. A few houses were evidently requisitioned by the Germans; there were German soldiers lounging at the windows of bare rooms cleaning their equipment, in the manner of soldiers all over the world. None of them paid any attention to the dung-cart.

By the great church in the middle of the town three tanks were drawn up in the shade of the plane-trees, with half a dozen lorries. From one large house the Swastika flag floated lazily in the hot summer afternoon from a short staff stuck out of a first-floor window.

They paced steadily through the town, past shops and residences, past German officers and German soldiers. At the outskirts of the town they took the right fork at the advertisement for Byrrh, and left the last houses behind them. Presently, blue and hazy in a dip between two fields, the old man saw the sea.

His heart leaped when he saw it. All his life he had taken pleasure from the sight and savour of the sea. In its misty blueness between the green fields it seemed to him almost like a portion of his own country; England seemed very close. By tomorrow evening, perhaps, he would have crossed that blue expanse; he would be safe in England with the children. He trudged on stolidly, but his heart was burning with desire to be at home.

Presently Rose became tired; he stopped the cart and helped her into it. Nicole got down and walked beside him.

'There is the sea,' she said. 'You have not very far to go now, monsieur.'

'Not very far,' he said.

'You are glad?'

He glanced at her. 'I should be very, very glad, but for one thing,' he said. 'I would like you to be coming with us. Would you not do that?'

She shook her head. 'No, monsieur.'

They walked on in silence for a time. At last he said: 'I shall never be able to thank you for what you have done for us.'

She said: 'I have benefited the most.'

'What do you mean?' he asked.

She said: 'It was a very bad time when you came. I do not know if I can make you understand.' They walked on in the hot sun in silence for a time. 'I loved John very much,' she said simply. 'Above all things, I wanted to be an Englishwoman. And I should have been one but for the war. Because we meant to marry. Would you have minded that very much?'

He shook his head. 'I should have welcomed you. Don't you know that?'

She said: 'I know that now. But at the time I was terribly afraid of you. We might have been married if I had not been so foolish, and delayed.' She was silent for a minute. 'Then John – John was killed. And at the same time nothing went right any more. The Germans drove us back, the Belgians surrendered, and the English ran back to their own country from Dunkerque and France was left to fight alone. Then all the papers, and the radio, began to say bad things of the English, that they were treacherous, that they had never really meant to share the battle with us. Horrible things, monsieur.'

'Did you believe them?' he asked quietly.

She said: 'I was more unhappy than you could believe.'

'And now? Do you still believe those things?'

She said: 'I believe this, that there was nothing shameful in my love for John. I think that if we had been married, if I had become an Englishwoman, I should have been happy for the remainder of my life.'

She paused. 'That is a very precious thought, monsieur. For a few weeks it was clouded with doubts and spoilt. Now it is clear once more; I have regained the thing that I had lost. I shall not lose it again.'

They breasted a little rise, and there before them lay the river, winding past the little group of houses that was l'Abervrach, through a long lane of jagged reefs out to the open sea. The girl said: 'That is l'Abervrach. Now you are very near the end of your journey, Monsieur Howard.'

They walked in silence, leading the horse, down the road to the river and along the water-front, past the cement factory, past the few houses of the village, past the lifeboat-house and the little quay. Beside the quay there was a German E-boat apparently in trouble with her engines, for a portion of her deck amidships was removed and was lying on the quay beside a workshop lorry; men in overalls were busy upon her. A few German soldiers lounged upon the quay, watching the work and smoking.

They went on past the *estaminet* and out into the country again. Presently they turned up the hill in a lane full of sweet-briar, and so came to the little farm of Loudeac.

A peasant in a rusty red canvas pullover met them at the gate.

Howard said: 'From Quintin.'

The man nodded and indicated the midden. 'Put it there,' he said. 'And then go away quickly. I wish you good luck, but you must not stay here.'

'That is very well understood.'

The man vanished into the house, nor did they see him again. It was getting towards evening; the time was nearly eight o'clock. They got the children down out of the cart and backed the horse till the load was in the right place to tip; then they tipped the wagon and Howard cleared it with a spade. In a quarter of an hour the job was done.

Nicole said: 'There is time enough, and to spare. If we go now to the *estaminet*, we can get supper for the little ones – coffee, perhaps, and bread and butter.'

Howard agreed. They got into the empty cart and he jerked up the horse; they moved out of the stable yard and down the road towards the village. At a turn of the road the whole entrance to the harbour lay before them, sunny and blue in the soft evening light. In the long reach between the jagged rocks there was a fishing-boat with a deep brown lug sail coming in from the sea; faintly they heard the putter of an engine.

The old man glanced at the girl. 'Focquet,' he said.

She nodded. 'I think so.'

They went on down to the village. At the *estaminet*, under the incurious glances of the German soldiers, they got out of the cart; Howard tied the bridle of the old horse to a rail.

Ronnie said in French: 'Is that a torpedo-boat? May we go and see it?'

'Not now,' said Nicole. 'We're going to have supper now.'

'What are we going to have for supper?'

They went into the *estaminet*. There were a few fishermen there standing by the bar, who looked at them narrowly; it seemed to Howard that they had divined his secret as soon as they set eyes on him. He led the children to a table in a far corner of the room, a little way away from the men. Nicole went through to the kitchen of the place to speak to Madame about supper for the children.

Supper came presently, bread and butter and coffee for the children, red wine mixed with water for Nicole and the old man. They ate uneasily, conscious of the glances at them from the bar, speaking only to assist the children in their meal. It seemed to Howard that this was the real crux of their journey; this was the only time when he had felt his own identity in question. The leaden time crept on, but it was not yet nine o'clock.

Their meal finished, the children became restless. It was still not nine o'clock, and it was necessary to spin out time. Ronnie said, wriggling in his chair: 'May we get down and go and look at the sea?'

It was better to have them out of the way than calling fresh attention to the party in the *estaminet*. Howard said: 'Go on. You can go just outside the door and lean over the harbour wall. Don't go any farther than that.'

Sheila went with him; the other children stayed quiet in their seats. Howard ordered another bottle of the thin red wine.

At ten minutes past nine a big, broad-shouldered young man in fisherman's red poncho and sea boots rolled into the *estaminet*. One would have said that he had visited

227

competitive establishments on the way, because he reeled a little at the bar. He took in all the occupants of the *estaminet* in one swift, revolving glance like a light-house.

'Ha!' he said. 'Give me a Pernod des Anges, and to hell with the *sale Boche*.'

The men at the bar said: 'Quietly. There are Germans outside.'

The girl behind the bar wrinkled her brows. 'Pernod des Anges? It is a pleasantry, no doubt? Ordinary Pernod for m'sieur.'

The man said: 'You have no Pernod des Anges?'

'No, m'sieur. I have never heard of it.'

The man remained silent, holding to the bar with one hand, swaying a little.

Howard got up and went to him. 'If you would like to join us in a glass of the rouge,' he said.

'Assuredly.' The young man left the bar and crossed with him to the table.

Howard said quietly: 'Let me introduce you. This is my daughter-in-law, Mademoiselle Nicole Rougeron.'

The young man stared at him. 'You must be more careful of your French idiom,' he said softly out of the corner of his mouth. 'Keep your mouth shut and leave the talking to me.'

He slumped down into a seat beside them. Howard poured him out a glass of the red wine; the young man added water to it and drank. He said quietly: 'Here is the matter. My boat lies at the quay, but I cannot take you on board here, because of the Germans. You must wait here till it is dark, and then take the footpath to the Phare des Vaches – that is an automatic light on the rocks, half a mile towards the sea, that is not now in use. I will meet you there with the boat.'

Howard said: 'That is clear enough. How do we get on to the footpath from here?'

Focquet proceeded to tell him. Howard was sitting with his back to the *estaminet* door facing Nicole. As he sat listening to the directions, his eye fell on the girl's face, strained and anxious.

'Monsieur . . .' she said, and stopped.

There was a heavy step behind him, and a few words spoken in German. He swung round in his chair; the young Frenchman by his side did the same. There was a German soldier there, with a rifle. Beside him was one of the engineers from the E-boat by the quay in stained blue dungarees.

The moment remained etched upon the old man's memory. In the background the fishermen around the bar stood tense and motionless; the girl had paused, cloth in hand, in the act of wiping a glass.

It was the man in dungarees who spoke. He spoke in English with a German-American accent.

'Say,' he said. 'How many of you guys are Britishers?'

There was no answer from the group.

He said: 'Well, we'll all just get along to the guard-room and have a lil' talk with the *Feldwebel*. And don't let any of you start getting fresh, because that ain't going to do you any good.'

He repeated himself in very elementary French.

IO

There was a torrent of words from Focquet, rather cleverly poured out with well-simulated alcoholic indignation. He knew nothing, he said, of these others; he was just taking a glass of wine with them – there was no harm in that. He was about to sail, to catch the tide. If he went with them to the guard-room there would be no fish for *déjeuner* tomorrow, and how would they like that? Landsmen could never see farther than their own noses. What about his boat, moored at the quay? Who would look after that?

The sentry prodded him roughly in the back with the butt of his rifle, and Focquet became suddenly silent.

Two more Germans, a private and a *Gefreiter*, came hurrying in; the party were hustled to their feet and herded out of the door. Resistance was obviously useless. The man in dungarees went out ahead of them, but he reappeared in a few minutes bringing with him Ronnie and Sheila. Both were very much alarmed, Sheila in tears.

'Say,' he said to Howard, 'I guess these belong to you. They talk English pretty fine, finer 'n anyone could learn it.'

Howard took one of them hand in hand with him on each side, but said nothing. The man in dungarees stared oddly at him for a minute, and remained standing staring after them as they were shepherded towards the guard-room in the gathering dusk.

Ronnie said, frightened: 'Where are we going to now, Mr Howard? Have the Germans got us?'

Howard said: 'We're just going with them for a little business. Don't be afraid; they won't do anything to hurt us.'

The little boy said: 'I told Sheila you would be angry if she talked English, but she would do it.'

Nicole said: 'Did she talk English to the man in the overall?'

Ronnie nodded. Then he glanced up timorously at the old man. 'Are you angry, Mr Howard?' he ventured.

There was no point in making more trouble for the children than they had already coming to them. 'No,' he said. 'It would have been better if she hadn't, but we won't say any more about it.'

Sheila was still crying bitterly. 'I *like* talking English,' she wailed.

Howard stooped and wiped her eyes; the guards, considerately enough, paused for a moment while he did so. 'Never mind,' he said. 'You can talk as much English as you like now.'

She walked on with him soberly, in sniffing, moist silence.

A couple of hundred yards up the road to Lannilis they were wheeled to the right and marched into the house that was the guard-room. In a bare room the *Feldwebel* was hastily buttoning his tunic as they came in. He sat down behind a bare trestle table; their guards ranged them in front of him.

He glanced them up and down scornfully. 'So,' he said at last. '*Geben Sie mir Ihre legitimationspapiere.*'

Howard could understand only a few words of German,

231

the others nothing at all. They stared at him uncertainly. *'Cartes d'identité,'* he said sharply.

Focquet and Nicole produced their French identity-cards; the man studied them in silence. Then he looked up. Howard put down his British passport on the bare table in the manner of a man who plays the last card of a losing hand.

The *Feldwebel* smiled faintly, took it up, and studied it with interest. 'So!' he said. *'Engländer.* Winston Churchill.'

He raised his eyes and studied the children. In difficult French he asked if they had any papers, and appeared satisfied when told that they had not.

Then he gave a few orders in German. The party were searched for weapons, and all they had was taken from them and placed on the table – papers, money, watches, and personal articles of every sort, even their handkerchiefs. Then they were taken to another room with a few palliasses laid out upon the floor, given a blanket each, and left. The window was barred over roughly with wooden beams; outside it in the road a sentry stood on guard.

Howard turned to Focquet. 'I am very sorry this has happened,' he said. He felt that the Frenchman had not even had a run for his money.

The young man shrugged his shoulders philosophically. 'It was a chance to travel and to see the world with de Gaulle,' he said. 'Another chance will come.' He threw himself down on one of the palliasses, pulled the blanket round him, and composed himself to sleep.

Howard and Nicole arranged the palliasses in two pairs to make beds for the little boys and the little girls, and got them settled down to sleep. There remained one mattress over.

'You take that,' he said. 'I shall not sleep tonight.'

She shook her head. 'Nor I either.'

232

Half an hour later they were sitting side by side leaning against the wall, staring out of the barred window ahead of them. It was practically dark within the room; outside the harbour showed faintly in the starlight and the last glow of evening. It was still quite warm.

She said: 'They will examine us in the morning. What shall we say?'

'There's only one thing we can say. Tell them the exact truth.'

She considered this for a moment. 'We must not bring in Arvers, nor Loudeac or Quintin if we can avoid it.'

He agreed. 'They will ask where I got these clothes. Can you say that you gave them to me?'

She nodded. 'That will do. Also, I will say that I knew Focquet and arranged with him myself.'

She crossed to the young man, now half asleep, and spoke earnestly to him for a few minutes. He grunted in agreement; the girl came back to Howard and sat down again.

'One more thing,' he said. 'There is Marjan. Shall I say that I picked him up upon the road?'

She nodded. 'On the road before you came to Chartres. I will see that he understands that.'

He said doubtfully: 'That should be all right so long as they don't cross-examine the children.'

They sat in silence for a long time after that. Presently she stirred a little by him, shifting to a more comfortable position.

'Go and lie down, Nicole,' he said. 'You must get some sleep.'

'I do not want to sleep, monsieur,' she said. 'Truly I am better sitting here like this.'

'I've been thinking about things,' he said.

'I also have been thinking.'

He turned to her in the darkness. 'I am so very sorry to

have brought you into all this trouble,' he said quietly. 'I did want to avoid that, and I thought that we were going to.'

She shrugged her shoulders. 'It does not matter.' She hesitated. 'I have been thinking about different things to that.'

'What things?' he asked.

'When you introduced Focquet – you said I was your daughter-in-law.'

'I had to say something,' he remarked. 'And that's very nearly true.'

In the dim light he looked into her eyes, smiling a little. 'Isn't it?'

'Is that how you think of me?'

'Yes,' he said simply.

There was a long silence in the prison. One of the children, probably Willem, stirred and whimpered uneasily in his sleep; outside the guard paced on the dusty road.

At last she said: 'What we did was wrong – very wrong.' She turned towards him. 'Truly, I did not mean to do wrong when I went to Paris, neither did John. We did not go with that in mind at all. I do not want that you should think it was his fault. It was nobody's fault, neither of us. Also, it did not seem wrong at the time.'

His mind drifted back fifty years. 'I know,' he said. 'That's how these things happen. But you aren't sorry, are you?'

She did not answer that, but she went on more easily. 'He was very, very naughty, monsieur. The understanding was that I was to show him Paris, and it was for that that I went to Paris to meet him. But when the time came, he was not interested in the churches or in the museums, or the picture-galleries at all.' There was a touch of laughter in her voice. 'He was only interested in me.'

'Very natural,' he said. It seemed the only thing to say.

'It was very embarrassing, I assure you, I did not know what I should do.'

He laughed. 'Well, you made your mind up in the end.'

She said reproachfully: 'Monsieur – it is not a matter to laugh over. You are just like John. He also used to laugh at things like that.'

He said: 'Tell me one thing, Nicole. Did he ask you if you would marry him?'

She said: 'He wanted that we should marry in Paris before he went back to England. He said that under English law that would be possible.'

'Why didn't you?' he asked curiously.

She was silent for a minute. Then she said: 'I was afraid of you, monsieur.'

'Of me?'

She nodded. 'I was terrified. It now sounds very silly, but – it was so.'

He struggled to understand. 'What were you frightened of?' he asked.

She said: 'Figure it to yourself. Your son would have brought home a foreign girl, that he had married very suddenly in Paris. You would have thought that he had been foolish in a foreign city, as young men sometimes are. That he had been trapped by a bad woman into an unhappy marriage. I do not see how you could have thought otherwise.'

'If I had thought that at first,' he said, 'I shouldn't have thought it for long.'

'I know that now. That is what John told me at the time. But I did not think that it was right to take the risk. I told John, it would be better for everybody that we should be a little more discreet, you understand.'

'I see. You wanted to wait a bit.'

She said: 'Not longer than could be helped. But I wanted very much that everything should be correct, that we should start off right. Because, to be married, it is for all one's life, and one marries not only to the man but to the relations also. And in a mixed marriage things are certain to be difficult, in any case. And so, I said that I would come to England for his next leave, in September or October, and we would meet in London, and he could then take me to see you in your country home. And then you would write to my father, and everything would be quite in order and correct.'

'And then the war came,' he said quietly.

She repeated: 'Yes, monsieur, then the war came. It was not then possible for me to visit England. It would almost have been easier for John to visit Paris again, but he could get no leave. And so I went on struggling to get my *permis* and the visa month after month.

'And then,' she said, 'they wrote to tell me what had happened.'

They sat there for a long time, practically in silence. The air grew colder as the night went on. Presently the old man heard the girl's breathing grow more regular and knew she was asleep, still sitting up upon the bare wooden floor.

After a time she stirred and fell half over. He got up stiffly and led her, still practically asleep, to the palliasse, made her lie down, and put a blanket over her. In a short time she was asleep again.

For a long time he stood by the window, looking out over the harbour mouth. The moon had risen; the white plumes of surf upon the rocks showed clearly on the blackness of the sea. He wondered what was going to happen to them all. It might very well be that he would be taken from the children and sent to a concentration camp; that for him would be the end, before so very long. The thought of what might happen to the children distressed him terribly. At all costs, he must do his best to stay at liberty. If he could manage that it might be possible for him to make a home for them, to look after them till the war was over. A home in Chartres, perhaps, not far from Nicole and her mother. It would take little money to live simply with them, in one room or in two rooms at the most. The thought of penury did not distress him very much. His old life seemed very, very far away.

Presently, the blackness of the night began to pale towards the east, and it grew colder still. He moved back to the wall and, wrapped in a blanket, sat down in a corner. Presently he fell into an uneasy sleep.

At six o'oclock the clumping of the soldiers' boots in the corridor outside woke him from a doze. He stirred and sat upright; Nicole was awake and sitting up, running her fingers through her hair in an endeavour to put it into order without a comb. A German *Oberschütze* came in and made signs to them to get up, indicating the way to the toilet.

Presently, a private brought them china bowls, some hunks of bread and a large jug of bitter coffee. They breakfasted, and waited for something to happen. They were silent and depressed; even the children caught the atmosphere and sat about in gloomy inactivity.

Presently the door was flung open, and the *Feldwebel* was there with a couple of privates. '*Marchez*,' he said. '*Allez, vite.*'

They were herded out and into a grey, camouflaged motor-lorry with a closed, van-like body. The two German privates got into this with them and the doors were shut and locked upon them. The *Feldwebel* got into the seat beside the driver, turned and inspected them through a little hatchway to the driver's compartment. The lorry started.

They were taken to Lannilis, and unloaded at the big house opposite the church, from the window of which floated the Swastika flag. Here they were herded into a corridor between their guards. The *Feldwebel* went into a door and closed it behind him.

They waited thus for over half an hour. The children, apprehensive and docile at the first, became bored and restless. Pierre said, in his small voice: 'Please, monsieur, may I go out and play in the square?'

Sheila and Ronnie said in unison, and very quickly: 'May I go too?'

Howard said: 'Not just now. You'll have to stay here for a little while.'

Sheila said mutinously: 'I don't want to stay here. I want to go out in the sun and play.'

Nicole stooped to her and said: 'Do you remember Babar the Elephant?'

The little girl nodded.

'And Jacko the Monkey? What did he do?'

Laughter, as at a huge, secret joke. 'He climbed up Babar's tail, right up on to his back!'

'Whatever did he do that for?'

The stolid, grey-faced Germans looked on mirthlessly, uncomprehending. For the first time in their lives they were seeing foreigners, displaying the crushing might and power of their mighty land. It confused them and perplexed them that their prisoners should be so flippant as to play games with their children in the corridor outside the very office of the Gestapo. It found the soft spot in the armour of their pride; they felt an insult which could not be properly defined. This was not what they had understood when their Führer last had spoken from the Sport-Palast. This victory was not as they had thought it would be.

The door opened, the sentries sprang to attention, clicking their heels. Nicole glanced upwards, and then stood up, holding Sheila in one hand. From the office *Feldwebel* cried, '*Achtung!*' and a young officer, a *Rittmeister* of the Tank Corps came out. He was dressed in a black uniform not unlike the British battle-dress; on his head he wore a black beret garnished with the eagle and swastika, and a wreath-like badge. On his shoulder-straps an aluminium skull and crossbones gleamed dull upon the black cloth.

Howard straightened up and Focquet took his hands out of his pockets. The children stopped chattering to stare curiously at the man in black.

He had a notebook and a pencil in his hand. He spoke to Howard first. '*Wie heissen Sie?*' he asked. '*Ihr Familien-name und Taufname? Ihr Beruf?*'

Somebody translated into indifferent French and the particulars of all the party were written down. As regards nationality, Howard declared himself, Sheila, and Ronnie to be English; there was no use denying it. He said that Willem and Marjan were of nationality unknown.

The young officer in black went into the office. In a few minutes the door was flung open again and the party were called to attention. The *Feldwebel* came to the door.

'*Folgen Sie mir!* Halt! *Rührt Euch!*' They found themselves in the office, facing a long table. Behind this sat the officer who had interrogated them in the passage. By his side was an older man with a square, close-cropped head and a keen, truculent expression. He held himself very straight and stiff, as if he were in a straight waistcoat, and he also wore a black uniform, but more smartly cut, and with a shoulder-belt in black leather resembling the Sam Browne. This man, as Howard subsequently learned, was Major Diessen of the Gestapo.

He stared at Howard, looking him up and down, noting

the clothes he wore, the Breton casque upon his head, the stained rust-coloured poncho jacket, the dirty blue overall trousers.

'So,' he said harshly, but in quite good English. 'We still have English gentlemen travelling in France.' He paused. 'Nice and Monte Carlo,' he said. 'I hope that you have had a very nice time.'

The old man was silent. There was no point in trying to answer the taunts.

The officer turned to Nicole. 'You are French,' he said, fiercely and vehemently. 'You have been helping this man in his secret work against your country. You are a traitor to the Armistice. I think you will be shot for this.'

The girl stared at him, dumbfounded. Howard said: 'There is no need to frighten her. We are quite ready to tell you the truth.'

'I know your English truth,' the Gestapo officer replied. 'I will find my own, even if I have to whip every inch of skin from her body and pull out every finger-nail.'

Howard said quietly: 'What do you want to know?'

'I want to know what means you used to make her help you in your work.'

There was a small, insistent tug at the old man's sleeve. He glanced down and it was Sheila, whispering a request.

'Presently,' he said gently. 'You must wait a little.'

'I can't wait,' she said. 'I want to go now.'

The old man turned to the Gestapo officer. 'There is a small matter that requires attention,' he said placidly. He indicated Rose. 'May this one take this little girl outside for a minute? They will come back.'

The young Tank Corps officer smiled broadly; even the Gestapo man relaxed a little. The *Rittmeister* spoke to the sentry, who sprang to attention and escorted the two little girls from the room.

Howard said: 'I will answer your question so far as I can. I have no work in France, but I was trying to get back to England with these children. As for this young lady, she was a great friend of my son, who is now dead. We have known each other for some time.'

Nicole said: 'That is true. Monsieur Howard came to us in Chartres when all travelling to England had been stopped. I have known Focquet here since I was a little girl. We were trying to induce him to take monsieur and these children back to England in his boat, but he was unwilling on account of the regulations.'

The old man stood silent, in admiration of the girl. If she got away with that one it let Focquet out completely.

The officer's lips curled. 'I have no doubt that Mister Howard wanted to return to England,' he said dryly. 'It is getting quite too hot here for fellows of his sort.'

He said suddenly and sharply: 'We captured Charenton. He is to be executed tomorrow, by shooting.'

There was a momentary silence. The German eyed the party narrowly, his keen eyes running from one to the other. The girl wrinkled her brows in perplexity. The young *Rittmeister* of the Tank Corps sat with an impassive face, drawing a pattern on his blotting-pad.

Howard said at last: 'I am afraid I don't understand what you mean. I don't know anybody called Charenton.'

'No,' said the German. 'And you do not know your Major Cochrane, nor Room 212 on the second floor of your War Office in Whitehall.'

The old man could feel the scrutiny of everybody in the room upon him. 'I have never been in the War Office,' he said, 'and I know nothing about the rooms. I used to know a Major Cochrane who had a house near Totnes, but he died in 1924. That is the only Cochrane that I ever knew.'

The Gestapo officer smiled without mirth. 'You expect me to believe that?'

'Yes, I do,' the old man said. 'Because it is the truth.'

Nicole interposed, speaking in French. 'May I say a word. There is a misunderstanding here, truly there is. Monsieur Howard has come here directly from the Jura, stopping only with us in Chartres. He will tell you himself.'

Howard said: 'That is so. Would you like to hear how I came to be here?'

The German officer looked ostentatiously at his wrist-watch and leaned back in his chair, insolently bored. 'If you must,' he said indifferently. 'I will give you three minutes.'

Nicole plucked his arm. 'Tell also who the children are and where they came from,' she said urgently.

The old man paused to collect his thoughts. It was impossible for him, at his age, to compress his story into three minutes; his mind moved too slowly. 'I came to France from England in the middle of April,' he said. 'I stayed a night or two in Paris, and then I went on and stayed a night in Dijon. You see, I had arranged to go to a place called Cidoton in the Jura, for a little fishing holiday.'

The Gestapo officer sat up suddenly, galvanised into life. 'What sort of fish?' he barked. 'Answer me – quick!'

Howard stared at him. 'Blue trout,' he said. 'Sometimes you get a grayling, but they aren't very common.'

'And what tackle to catch them with – quickly!'

The old man stared at him, nonplussed, not knowing where to start. 'Well,' he said, 'you need a nine-foot cast, but the stream is usually very strong, so 3X is fine enough. Of course, it's all fishing wet, you understand.'

The German relaxed. 'And what flies do you use?'

A faint pleasure came to the old man. 'Well,' he said

with relish, 'a Dark Olive gets them as well as anything, or a large Blue Dun. I got one or two on a thing called a Jungle Cock, but –'

The German interrupted him. 'Go on with your story,' he said rudely. 'I have no time to listen to your fishing exploits.'

Howard plunged into his tale, compressing it as much as seemed possible to him. The two German officers listened with growing attention and with growing incredulity. In ten minutes or so the old man reached the end.

The Gestapo officer, Major Diessen, looked at him scornfully. 'And now,' he said. 'If you had been able to return to England, what would you have done with all these children?'

Howard said: 'I meant to send them to America.'

'Why?'

'Because it is safe over there. Because this war is bad for children to see. It would be better for them to be out of it.'

The German stared at him. 'Very fine words. But who was going to pay to send them to America, may I ask?'

The old man said: 'Oh, I should have done that.'

The other smiled, scornfully amused. 'And what would they do in America? Starve?'

'Oh no. I have a married daughter over there. She would have made a home for them until the war was over.'

'This is a waste of time,' the German said. 'You must think me a stupid fellow to be taken in with such a tale.'

Nicole said: 'Nevertheless, m'sieur, it is quite true. I knew the son and I have known the father. The daughter would be much the same. American people are generous to refugees, to children.'

Diessen turned to her. 'So,' he sneered, 'mademoiselle comes in to support this story. But now for mademoiselle herself. We learn that mademoiselle was a friend of the old English gentleman's son. A very great friend . . .'

He barked at her suddenly. 'His mistress, no doubt?'

She drew herself up. 'You may say so if you like,' she said quietly. 'You can call a sunset by a filthy name, but you do not spoil its beauty, monsieur.'

There was a pause. The young Tank officer leaned across and whispered a word or two to the Gestapo officer. Diessen nodded and turned back to the old man.

'By the dates,' he said, 'you could have returned to England if you had travelled straight through Dijon. But you did not do so. That is the weak point of your story. That is where your lies begin in earnest.'

He said sharply: 'Why did you stay in France? Tell me now, quickly, and with no more nonsense. I promise you that you will talk before tonight, in any case. It will be better for you to talk now.'

Howard was puzzled and distressed. 'The little girl,' he turned and indicated Sheila, 'fell ill in Dijon. I told you so just now. She was too ill to travel.'

The German leaned across the table to him, white with anger. 'Listen,' he said. 'I warn you once again, and this for the last time. I am not to be trifled with. That sort of lie would not deceive a child. If you had wanted to return to England you would have gone.'

'These children were in my care,' the old man said. 'I could not have done that.'

The Gestapo officer said: 'Lies . . . lies . . . lies.' He was about to say something more, but checked himself. The young man by his side leaned forward and whispered deferentially to him again.

Major Diessen leaned back in his chair. 'So,' he said, 'you refuse our kindness and you will not talk. As you wish. Before the evening you will be talking freely, Mister

Englishman, but by then you will be blind, and in horrible pain. It will be quite amusing for my men. Mademoiselle, too, shall be there to see, and the little children also.'

There was a silence in the office.

'Now you will be taken away,' the German said. 'I shall send for you when my men are ready to begin.' He leaned forward. 'I will tell you what we want to know, so that you may know what to say even though you be blind and deaf. We know you are a spy, wandering through the country in disguise and with this woman and the children as a cover. We know you have been operating with Charenton – you need not tell us about that. We know that either you or Charenton sent information to the English of the Führer's visit to the ships in Brest, and that you caused the raid.'

He paused. 'But what we do not know, and what this afternoon you shall tell us, is how the message was passed through to England, to that Major Cochrane' – his lip sneered – 'that died in 1924, according to your story. That is what you are going to tell, Mister Englishman. And as soon as it is told the pain will stop. Remember that.'

He motioned to the *Feldwebel*. 'Take them away.'

They were thrust out of the room. Howard moved in a daze; it was incredible that this thing should be happening to him. It was what he had read of and had found some difficulty in crediting. It was what they were supposed to do to Jews in concentration camps. It could not be true.

Focquet was taken from them and hustled off on his own. Howard and Nicole were bundled into a downstairs prison room, with a heavily-barred window; the door was slammed on them and they were left alone.

Pierre said, in French: 'Are we going to have our dinner here, mademoiselle?'

Nicole said dully: 'I expect so, Pierre.'

Ronnie said: 'What are we going to have for dinner?'

She put an arm around his shoulder. 'I don't know,' she said mechanically. 'We'll see when we get it. Now, you run off and play with Rose. I want to talk to Monsieur Howard.'

She turned to Howard. 'This is very bad,' she said. 'We are involved in something terrible.'

He nodded. 'It seems to be that air raid that they had on Brest. The one that you were in.'

She said: 'In the shops that day they were saying that Adolf Hitler was in Brest, but one did not pay attention. There is so much rumour, so much idle talk.'

There was a silence. Howard stood looking out of the window at the little weeded, overgrown garden outside. As he stood the situation became clear to him. In such a case the local officers of the Gestapo would have to make a show of energy. They would have to produce the spies who had been instrumental in the raid, or the mutilated bodies of people who were classed as spies.

Presently he said: 'I cannot tell them what I do not know, and so things may go badly with me. If I should be killed, you will do your best for the children, Nicole?'

She said: 'I will do that. But you are not going to be killed, or even hurt. Something must be possible.' She made a little gesture of distress.

Pursuing his thought, he said: 'I shall have to try and get them to let me make a new will. Then, when the war is over and you could get money from England, you would be able to keep the children and to educate them, those of them that had no homes. But in the meantime you'll just have to do the best you can.'

The long hours dragged past. At noon an orderly brought them an open metal pan with a meal of meat and vegetables piled on it, and several bowls. They set the children down to that, who went at it with gusto.

Nicole ate a little, but the old man practically nothing.

The orderly removed the tray and they waited again. At three o'clock the door was flung open and the *Feldwebel* was there with a guard.

'*Le Vieux*,' he said, '*Marchez*.' Howard stepped forward and Nicole followed him. The guard pushed her back.

The old man stopped. 'One moment,' he said. He took her hand and kissed her on the forehead. 'There, my dear,' he said. 'Don't worry about me.'

They hustled him away, out of that building and out into the square. Outside the sun was bright; a car or two passed by and in the shops the peasants went about their business. In Lannilis life went on as usual; from the great church the low drone of a chant broke the warm summer air. The women in the shops looked curiously at him as he passed by under guard.

He was taken into another house and thrust into a room on the ground floor. The door was shut and locked behind him. He looked around.

He was in a sitting-room, a middle-class room furnished in the French style with uncomfortable, gilded chairs and rococo ornaments. A few poor oil paintings hung upon the walls in heavy, gilded frames; there was a potted palm, and framed, ancient photographs upon the side tables, with a few ornaments. There was a table in the middle of the room, covered over with a cloth.

At this table a young man was sitting, a dark-haired, pale-faced young man in civilian clothes, well under thirty. He glanced up as Howard came into the room.

'Who are you?' he asked in French. He spoke almost idly, as if the matter was of no great moment.

The old man stood by the door, inwardly beating down his fears. This was something strange and therefore dangerous.

247

'I am an Englishman,' he said at last. There was no point any longer in concealment. 'I was arrested yesterday.'

The young man smiled without mirth. This time he spoke in English, without any trace of accent. 'Well,' he said, 'you'd better come on and sit down. There's a pair of us. I'm English too.'

Howard recoiled a step. 'You're *English?*'

'Naturalised,' the other said carelessly. 'My mother came from Woking, and I spent most of my life in England. My father was a Frenchman, so I started off as French. But he was killed in the last war.'

'But what are you doing here?'

The young man motioned to the table. 'Come on and sit down.'

The old man drew a chair up to the table and repeated his question. 'I did not know there was another Englishman in Lannilis,' he said. 'Whatever are you doing here?

The young man said: 'I'm waiting to be shot.'

There was a stunned, horrible pause. At last, Howard said: 'Is your name Charenton?'

The young man nodded. 'Yes,' he said, 'I'm Charenton. I see they told you about me.'

There was a long silence in the little room. Howard sat dumb, not knowing what to say. In his embarrassment his eyes fell upon the table, upon the young man's hands. Sitting with his hands before him on the table, Charenton had formed his fingers in a peculiar grip, the fingers interlaced, the left hand palm up and the right hand palm down. The thumbs were crossed. As soon as he observed the old man's scrutiny he glanced at him sharply, then undid the grasp.

He sighed a little.

'How did you come to be here?' he asked.

Howard said: 'I was trying to get back to England, with a few children.' He rambled into his story. The young man listened to him quietly, appraising him with keen, curious eyes.

In the end he said: 'I don't believe that you've got much to worry about. They'll probably let you live at liberty in some French town.'

Howard said: 'I'm afraid they won't do that. You see, they think that I'm mixed up with you.'

The young man nodded. 'I thought that must be it. That is why they've put us together. They're looking for a few more scapegoats, are they?'

Howard said: 'I am afraid they are.'

The young man got up and walked over to the window. 'You'll be all right,' he said at last. 'They've got no evidence against you – they can't have. Sooner or later you'll get back to England.'

There was a tinge of sadness in his voice.

Howard said: 'What about you?'

Charenton said: 'Me? I'm for the high jump. They got the goods on me all right.'

It seemed incredible to Howard. It was as if he had been listening to a play.

'We both seem to be in difficulties,' he said at last. 'Yours may be more serious than mine; I don't know. But you can do one thing for me.' He looked around. 'If I could get hold of a piece of paper and a pencil, I would redraft my will. Would you witness it for me?'

The other shook his head. 'You must write nothing here without permission from the Germans; they will only take it from you. And no document that had my signature upon it would get back to England. You must find some other witness, Mr Howard.'

The old man sighed. 'I suppose that is so,' he said. And presently he said: 'If I should get out of this and you should not, is there anything I can do? Any message you would like me to take?'

Charenton smiled ironically. 'No messages,' he said definitely.

'There is nothing I can do?'

The young man glanced at him. 'Do you know Oxford?'

'I know Oxford very well,' the old man said. 'Were you up there?'

Charenton nodded. 'I was up at Oriel. There's a place up the river that we used to walk to – a pub by a weir pool, a very old grey stone house beside a little bridge. There is the sound of running water all the time, and fish swimming in the clear pool, and flowers, flowers everywhere.'

'You mean the "Trout Inn," at Godstow?'

'Yes – the "Trout." You know it?'

'I know it very well indeed. At least, I used to, forty years ago.'

'Go there and drink a pint for me,' the young man said. 'Sitting on the wall and looking at the fish in the pool, on a hot summer day.'

Howard said: 'If I get back to England, I will do that.' He glanced around the shabby, garishly furnished room. 'But is there no message I can take to anyone?'

Charenton shook his head. 'No messages,' he said. 'If there were, I would not give them to you. There is almost certainly a microphone in this room, and Diessen listening to every word we say. That is why they have put us here together.' He glanced around. 'It's probably behind one of those oil paintings.'

'Are you sure of that?'

'As sure as I'm sitting here.'

He raised his voice and said, speaking in German: 'You are wasting your time, Major Diessen. This man knows nothing about my affairs.' He paused and then continued:

'But I will tell you this. One day the English and Americans will come, and you will be in their power. They will not be gentle as they were after the last war. If you kill this old man you will be hung in public on a gallows, and your body will stay there rotting as a warning to all other murderers.'

He turned to Howard: 'That ought to fetch him,' he said placidly, speaking in English.

The old man was troubled. 'I am sorry that you spoke like that,' he said. 'It will not do you any good with him.'

'Nor will anything else,' the young man said. 'I'm very nearly through.'

There was a quiet finality about his tone that made Howard wince.

'Are you sorry?' he enquired.

'No, by God I'm not,' Charenton said, and he laughed boyishly. 'We didn't succeed in getting Adolf, but we gave him the hell of a fright.'

Behind them the door opened. They swung round; there was a German *Gefreiter* there with a private. The private marched into the room and stood by Howard. The *Gefreiter* said roughly: '*Kommen Sie.*'

Charenton smiled as Howard got up. 'I told you so,' he said. 'Good-bye. All the best of luck.'

'Good-bye,' said the old man. He was hustled out of the room before he had time to say more. As he passed down the corridor to the street he saw through an open door the black uniformed Gestapo officer, his face dark with anger. With a sick heart Howard walked out into the sunlit square between his guards.

They took him back to Nicole and the children. Ronnie rushed up to him. 'Marjan has been showing us how to stand on our heads,' he said excitedly. 'I can do it and so can Pierre. Willem can't, and none of the girls. Look, Mr Howard. Just look!'

In a welter of children standing on their heads Nicole looked anxiously at him. 'They did nothing?' she enquired.

The old man shook his head. 'They used me to try to make a young man called Charenton talk,' he said. He told her briefly what had happened.

'That is their way,' she said. 'I have heard of that in Chartres. To gain their end through pain they do not work upon the body. They work upon the mind.'

The long afternoon dragged into evening. Cooped in the little prison room it was very hot and difficult to keep the children happy. There was nothing for them to do, nothing to look at, nothing to read to them. Nicole and Howard found themselves before long working hard to keep the peace and to stop quarrels, and this in one way was a benefit to them in that it made it difficult for them to brood upon their own position.

At last the German orderly brought them another meal, a supper of bitter coffee and long lengths of bread. This caused a diversion and a rest from the children; presently, the old man and the girl knew very well, the children would grow sleepy. When the orderly came back for the supper things they asked for beds.

He brought them straw-filled palliasses, with a rough pillow and one blanket each. They spent some time arranging these; by that time the children were tired and willing to lie down.

The long hours of the evening passed in bored inactivity. Nicole and Howard sat on their palliasses, brooding; from time to time exchanging a few words and relapsing into silence. At about ten o'clock they went to bed; taking off their outer clothes only, they lay down and covered themselves with the blanket.

Howard slept fairly well that night, the girl not so well. Very early in the morning, in the half-light before dawn, the door of their prison opened with a clatter. The *Gefreiter* was there, fully dressed and equipped with bayonet at his belt and steel helmet on his head.

He shook Howard by the shoulder. '*Auf!*' he said. He indicated to him that he was to get up and dress himself.

Nicole raised herself on one arm, a little frightened. 'Do they want me?' she asked in French. The man shook his head.

Howard, putting on his coat, turned to her in the dim light. 'This will be another of their enquiries,' he said. 'Don't worry. I shall be back before long.'

She was deeply troubled. 'I shall be waiting for you, with the children,' she said simply. 'They will be safe with me.'

'I know they will,' he said. '*Au revoir.*'

In the cold dawn they took him out into the square and along to the big house with the swastika flag, opposite the church, where they had first been interrogated. He was not taken to the same room, but to an upstairs room at the back. It had been a bedroom at one time and some of the bedroom furniture was still in place, but the bed had been removed and now it was some kind of office.

The black uniformed Gestapo officer, Major Diessen, was standing by the window. 'So,' he said, 'we have the Englishman again.'

Howard was silent. The German spoke a few words in his own language to the *Gefreiter* and the private who had brought Howard to the room. The *Gefreiter* saluted and withdrew, closing the door behind him. The private remained standing at attention by the door. The cold, grey light was now strong in the room.

'Come,' said the German at the window. 'Look out. Nice garden, is it not?'

253

The old man approached the window. There was a garden there, entirely surrounded by high old red-brick walls covered with fruit trees. It was a well-kept, mature garden, such as he liked to see.

'Yes,' he said quietly. 'It is a nice garden.' Instinctively he felt the presence of some trap.

The German said: 'Unless you help him, in a few minutes your friend Mr Charenton will die in it. He is to be shot as a spy.'

The old man stared at him. 'I don't know what is in your mind that you have brought me here,' he said. 'I met Charenton for the first time yesterday, when you put us together. He is a very brave young man and a good one. If you are going to shoot him, you are doing a bad thing. A man like that should be allowed to live, to work for the world when this war is all over.'

'A very nice speech,' the German said. 'I agree with you; he should be allowed to live. He shall live, if you help him. He shall be a prisoner to the end of the war which will not be long now. Six months at the most. Then he will be free.'

He turned to the window. 'Look,' he said. 'They are bringing him out.'

The old man turned and looked. Down the garden path a little cordon of six German soldiers, armed with rifles, were escorting Charenton. They were under the command of a *Feldwebel*; an officer rather behind Charenton, who walked slowly, his hands in his trousers-pockets. He did not seem to be pinioned in any way, nor did he seem to be particularly distressed.

Howard turned to the German. 'What do you want?' he asked. 'Why have you brought me to see this?'

'I have had you brought here,' said the German, 'to see if you would not help your friend, at a time when he needs help.'

254

He leaned towards the old man. 'Listen,' he said softly. 'It is a very little thing, that will not injure either of you. Nor will it make any difference to the war, because in any case your country now is doomed. If you will tell me how he got the information out of France and back to England, to your Major Cochrane, I will stop this execution.'

He stepped back. 'What do you think?' he said. 'You must be realist. It is not sensible to let a brave young man die, when he could be saved to work for your country when the war is over. And further, nobody can ever know. Charenton will stay in prison till the war is over, in a month or two; then he will be released. You and your family of children will have to stay in France, but if you help us now you need not stay in prison at all. You can live quietly in Chartres with the young woman. Then, when the war is over, in the autumn, you shall all go home. There will be no enquiries about this from England, because by that time the whole organisation of British spies will have become dispersed. There is no danger for you in this at all, and you can save that young man's life.' He leaned towards Howard again. 'Just a few little words,' he said softly. 'How did he do it? He shall never know you told.'

The old man stared at him. 'I cannot tell you,' he replied. 'Quite truthfully, I do not know. I have not been concerned in his affairs at all.' He said it with a sense of relief. If he had had the information things would have been more difficult.

The Gestapo officer stepped back. 'That is mere nonsense,' he said harshly. 'I do not believe that. You know sufficient to assist an agent of your country if he needs your help. All travellers in any foreign country know that much. Do you take me for a fool?'

Howard said: 'That may be so with German travellers.

255

In England ordinary travellers know nothing about espionage. I tell you, I know literally nothing that could help this man.'

The German bit his lip. He said: 'I am inclined to think you are a spy yourself. You have been wandering round the country in disguise, nobody knows where. You had better be careful. You may share his fate.'

'Even so,' the old man said, 'I could not tell you anything of value to you, because I do not know.'

Diessen turned to the window again. 'You have not got very much time,' he said. 'A minute or two, not more. Think again before it is too late.'

Howard looked out into the garden. They had put the young man with his back against the wall in front of a plum-tree. His hands now were bound behind his back, and the *Feldwebel* was blindfolding him with a red cotton handkerchief.

The German said: 'Nobody can ever know. There is still time for you to save him.'

'I cannot save him in that way,' the old man said. 'I have not got the information. But this is a bad, wicked thing that you are going to do. It will not profit you in the long run.'

The Gestapo officer swung round on him suddenly. He thrust his face near to the old man's. 'He gave you messages,' he said fiercely. 'You think you are clever, but you cannot deceive me. The "Trout Inn" – beer – flowers – fish! Do you think I am a fool? What does all that mean?'

'Nothing but what he said,' Howard replied. 'It is a place that he is fond of. That is all.'

The German drew back morosely. 'I do not believe it,' he said sullenly.

In the garden the *Feldwebel* had left the young man by the wall. The six soldiers were drawn up in a line in front of him, distant about ten yards. The officer had given them a command and they were loading.

'I am not going to delay this matter any longer,' said Diessen: 'Have you still nothing to say to save his life?'

The old man shook his head.

In the garden the officer glanced up to their window. Diessen lifted his hand and dropped it. The officer turned, drew himself up and gave a sharp word of command. An irregular volley rang out. The old man saw the body by the plum-tree crumple and fall, twitch for a little and lie still.

He turned away, rather sick. Diessen moved over to the middle of the room. The sentry still stood impassive at the door.

'I do not know whether I should believe your story or not,'the German said heavily at last. 'If you are a spy you are at least a clever one.'

Howard said: 'I am not a spy.'

'What are you doing in this country, then? Wandering round disguised as a French peasant?'

'I have told you that,' the old man said wearily, 'many times. I have been trying to get these children back to England, to send them to their homes or to America.'

The German burst out: 'Lies – lies! Always the same lies! You English are the same every time! Stubborn as mules!' He thrust his face into the other's. 'Criminals, all the lot of you!' He indicated the garden beyond the window. 'You could have prevented that, but you would not.'

'I could not have prevented you from killing that young man. That was your own doing.'

The Gestapo officer said, gloomily: 'I did not want to kill him. He forced me to do it, you and he between you. You are both to blame for his death. You left me with no other course.'

There was a silence. Then the German said: 'All your time

you spend lying and scheming against us. Your Churchill and your Chamberlain, goading us on, provoking us to war. And you are just another one.'

The old man did not answer that.

The German pulled himself together, crossed the room, and sat down at a table. 'This story of yours about sending these children to America,' he said. 'I do not believe a word of it.'

The old man was very, very tired. He said, indifferently: 'I can't help that. That is what I meant to do with them.'

'You still say that you would have sent them to your married daughter?'

'Yes.'

'Where does she live in America?'

'At a place called Coates Harbor, on Long Island.'

'Long Island. That is where the wealthy live. Is your daughter very wealthy?'

The old man said: 'She is married to an American business man. Yes, they are quite well off.'

The German said incredulously: 'You still wish me to believe that a wealthy woman such as that would make a home in her own house for all these dirty little children that you have picked up?'

Howard said: 'She will do that.' He paused, and then he said, 'You do not understand. Over there, they want to help us. If they make a home for children, refugees from Europe, they feel that they are doing something worth while. And they are.'

The German glanced at him curiously. 'You have travelled in America?'

'A little.'

'Do you know a town called White Falls?'

Howard shook his head. 'That sounds like quite a common name, but I don't recollect it. What state is it in?'

'In Minnesota. Is that far from Long Island?'

'It's right in the middle. I should think it's about a thousand miles.' This conversation was becoming very odd, the old man thought.

The German said: 'Now about mademoiselle. Were you going to send her to America also? Is she one of your children, may I ask?'

The old man shook his head. 'I would like her to go there,' he replied. 'But she will not leave France. Her father is a prisoner in your hands; her mother is alone in Chartres. I have tried to persuade her to come with us to England, but she will not do so. You have nothing against her.'

The other shrugged his shoulders. 'That is a matter of opinion. She has been helping you in your work.'

The old man said wearily: 'I tell you over and over again, I have no secret work. I know that you do not believe me.' He paused. 'The only work that I have had for the last fortnight has been to get these children into safety.'

There was a little silence.

'Let them go through to England,' he said quietly. 'Let the young man Focquet sail with them for Plymouth in his boat, and let Mademoiselle Rougeron go with them to take them to America. If you let them go, like that, I will confess to anything you like.'

The Gestapo man stared at him angrily. 'You are talking nonsense,' he replied. 'That is an insult to the German nation that you have just made. Do you take us for a pack of dirty Russians, to make bargains of that sort?'

Howard was silent.

The German got up and walked over to the window. 'I do not know what to make of you,' he said at last. 'I think that you must be a very brave man, to talk as you have done.'

Howard smiled faintly. 'Not a brave man,' he said. 'Only a very old one. Nothing you can do can take much from me, because I've had it all.'

The German did not answer him. He spoke in his own language to the sentry, and they took Howard back to the prison room.

11

Nicole greeted him with relief. She had spent an hour of unbearable anxiety, tortured by the thought of what might be happening to him, pestered by the children. She said: 'What happened?'

He said wearily: 'The young man, Charenton, was shot. Then they questioned me a lot more.'

She said gently: 'Sit down and rest. They will bring us coffee before very long. You will feel better after that.'

He sat down on his rolled-up mattress. 'Nicole,' he said. 'I believe there is a chance that they might let the children go to England without me. If so, would you take them?'

She said: 'Me? To go alone to England with the children? I do not think that that would be a good thing, Monsieur Howard.'

'I would like you to go, if it were possible.'

She came and sat by him. 'Is it for the children that you want this, or for me?' he asked.

He could not answer that. 'For both,' he said at last.

With clear logic she said: 'In England there will be many people, friends of yours and the relations of the English children, who will care for them. You have only to write a letter, and send it with them if they have to go without you. But for me, I have told you, I have no business in England – now. My country is this country, and my parents are here and in trouble. It is here that I must stay.'

He nodded ruefully. 'I was afraid that you would feel like that.'

Half an hour later the door of their room was thrust open, and two German privates appeared outside. They were carrying a table. With some difficulty they got it through the door and set it up in the middle of the room. Then they brought in eight chairs and set them with mathematical exactitude around the table.

Nicole and Howard watched this with surprise. They had eaten all their meals since they had been in captivity from plates balanced in their hands, helped from a bowl that stood upon the floor. This was something different in their treatment, something strange and suspicious.

The soldiers withdrew. Presently, the door opened again, and in walked a little French waiter balancing a tray, evidently from some neighbouring café. A German soldier followed him and stood over him in menacing silence. The man, evidently frightened, spread a cloth upon the table and set out cups and saucers, a large pot of hot coffee and a jug of hot milk, new rolls, butter, sugar, jam, and a plate of cut rounds of sausage. Then he withdrew quickly, in evident relief. Impassively, the German soldier shut the door on them again.

The children crowded round the table, eager. Howard and Nicole helped them into their chairs and set to work to feed them. The girl glanced at the old man.

'This is a great change,' she said quietly. 'I do not understand why they are doing this.'

He shook his head. He did not understand it either. Lurking in his mind was a thought that he did not speak, that this was a new trick to win him into some admission. They had failed with fear; now they would try persuasion.

The children cleared the table of all that was on it and got down, satisfied. A quarter of an hour later the little waiter reappeared, still under guard; he gathered up the cloth and cleared the table, and retired again in silence. But the door did not close.

One of the sentries came to it and said: '*Sie können in den Garten gehen.*' With difficulty Howard understood this to mean that they might go into the garden.

There was a small garden behind the house, completely surrounded by a high brick wall, not unlike another garden that the old man had seen earlier in the day. The children rushed out into it with a carillon of shrill cries; a day of close confinement had been a grave trial to them. Howard followed with Nicole, wondering.

It was another brilliant, sunlit day, already growing hot. Presently, two German soldiers appeared carrying arm-chairs. These two chairs they set with mathematical exactitude precisely in the middle of a patch of shade beneath a tree. '*Setzen Sie sich,*' they said.

Nicole and Howard sat down side by side, self-consciously, in silence. The soldiers withdrew, and a sentry with a rifle and a fixed bayonet appeared at the only exit from the garden. There he grounded his rifle and stood at ease, motionless and expressionless. There was something sinister about all these developments.

Nicole said: 'Why are they doing this for us, monsieur? What do they hope to gain by it?'

He said: 'I do not know. Once, this morning, I thought perhaps that they were going to let us go – or at any rate, let the children go to England. But even that would be no reason for giving us arm-chairs in the shade.'

She said quietly: 'It is a trap. They want something from us; therefore they try to please us.'

He nodded. 'Still,' he said, 'it is more pleasant here than in that room.'

Marjan, the little Pole, was as suspicious as they were. He sat aside upon the grass in sullen silence; since they had been taken prisoner he had barely spoken one word. Rose, too was ill at ease; she wandered round the garden, peering at the high walls as if looking for a means to escape. The younger children were untouched; Ronnie and Pierre and Willem and Sheila played little games around the garden or stood, finger in mouth, looking at the German sentry.

Presently Nicole, looking round, saw that the old man was asleep in his arm-chair.

They spent the whole day in the garden, only going back into their prison room for meals. *Déjeuner* and *diner* were served in the same way by the same silent little waiter under guard; good, plentiful meals, well cooked and attractively served. After dinner the German soldiers removed the table and the chairs, and indicated that they might lay out their beds. They did so and put all the children down to sleep.

Presently Howard and Nicole went to bed themselves.

The old man had slept only for an hour when the door was thrust open by a German soldier. He bent and shook the old man by the shoulder. '*Kommen Sie,*' he said. '*Schnell – zur Gestapo.*'

Howard got up wearily and put on his coat and shoes in the darkness. From her bed Nicole said: 'What is it? Can I come too?'

He said: 'I don't think so, my dear. It's just me that they want.'

She expostulated: 'But what a time to choose!'

The German soldier made a gesture of impatience.

Howard said: 'Don't worry. It's probably another inter-rogation.'

He was hustled away and the door closed behind him. In the dark room the girl got up and put on her skirt, and sat waiting in the darkness, sitting on her bed among the sleeping children, full of forebodings.

Howard was taken to the room in which they had first been interviewed. The Gestapo officer, Major Diessen, was there sitting at the table. An empty coffee cup stood beside him, and the room was full of his cigar-smoke. The German soldier who brought Howard in saluted stiffly. The officer spoke a word to him, and he withdrew, closing the door behind him. Howard was left alone in the room with Major Diessen.

He glanced at the clock. It was a little after midnight. The windows had been covered over with blankets for a blackout.

Presently the German looked up at the old man standing by the wall. 'So,' he said. 'The Englishman again.' He opened a drawer beside him and took out a large, black automatic pistol. He slipped out the clip and examined it; then put it back again and pulled the breech to load it. He laid it on the blotting-pad in front of him. 'We are alone,' he said. 'I am not taking any chances, as you see.'

The old man smiled faintly. 'You have nothing to fear from me.'

The German said: 'Perhaps not. But you have much to fear from me.'

There was a little silence. Presently he said: 'Suppose I were to let you go to England after all? What would you think then, eh?'

The old man's heart leapt and then steadied again. It was probably a trap. 'I should be very grateful, if you let me take the children,' he said quietly.

'And mademoiselle too?'

He shook his head. 'She does not want to come. She wants to stay in France.'

The German nodded. 'That is what we also want.' He paused, and then said: 'You say that you would be grateful. We will see now if that is just an empty boast. If I were to let you go to England with your children, so that you could send them to America, would you do me a small service?'

Howard said: 'It depends what it was.'

The Gestapo man flared out: 'Bargaining! Always the same, you English! One tries to help you, and you start chaffering! You are in no position to drive bargains, Mr Englishman!'

The old man persisted: 'I must know what you want me to do.'

The German said: 'It is a matter of no difficulty . . .'

There was a short pause.

His hand strayed to the black automatic on the desk before him, and began fingering it. 'There is a certain person to be taken to America,' he said deliberately. 'I do not want to advertise her journey. It would be very suitable that she should travel with your party of children.'

The gun was now in his hand, openly.

Howard stared at him across the table. 'If you mean that you want to use my party as a cover for an agent going to America,' he said, 'I will not have it.'

He saw the forefinger snap round the trigger. He raised his eyes to the German's face and saw it white with anger. For a full half-minute they remained motionless, staring at each other.

The Gestapo officer was the first to relax. 'You would drive me mad,' he said bitterly. 'You are a stubborn and obstinate people. You refuse the hand of friendship. You are suspicious of everything we do.'

Howard was silent. There was no point in saying more than was necessary. It would not help.

'Listen to me,' the German said, 'and try to get this into your thick head. This is not an agent who is travelling to America. This is a little girl.'

'A little girl?'

'A little girl of five years old. The daughter of my brother, who has been killed.'

The gun was firmly in his hand, resting upon the desk but pointing in the direction of the old man.

Howard said: 'Let me understand this fully. This is a little German girl that you want me to take to America, with all the other children?'

'That is so.'

'Who is she, and where is she going?'

The German said: 'I have told you who she is. She is the daughter of my brother Karl. Her name is Anna Diessen, and at present she is in Paris.'

He hesitated for a minute. 'You must understand,' he said, 'that there were three of us. My oldest brother Rupert fought in the World War, and then went to America. He now has a business, what you would call a grocery, in White Falls. He is an American citizen now.'

'I see,' said Howard thoughtfully.

'My brother Karl was *Oberleutnant* in the 4th Regiment Tanks, in the Second Panzer Division. He was married some years ago, but the marriage was not a success.' He hesitated for a moment and then said quickly: 'The girl was not wholly Aryan, and that never works. There was trouble, and she died. And now Karl, too, is dead.'

He sat brooding for a minute. Howard said gently: 'I am very sorry.' And he was.

267

Diessen said sullenly: 'It was English treachery that killed him. He was driving the English before him, from Amiens to the coast. There was a road cluttered up with refugees, and he was clearing it with his guns to get his tank through. And hiding in amongst these refugees were English soldiers that Karl did not see, and they threw bottles of oil on top of his cupola so they dripped down inside, and then they threw a flame to set the oil alight. My brother threw the hatch up to get out, and the English shot him down before he could surrender. But he had already surrendered, and they knew it. No man could go on fighting in a blazing tank.'

Howard was silent.

Diessen said: 'So there is Anna who must be provided for. I think it will be better if she goes to live with Rupert in America.'

The old man said: 'She is five years old?'

'Five and a half years.'

Howard said: 'Well, I should be very glad to take her.'

The German stared at him thoughtfully. 'How quickly after you reach England will the children go? How many of them are you sending to America? All of them?'

Howard shook his head. 'I doubt that. Three of them will certainly be going, but of the six two are English and one is a French girl with a father in London. I don't suppose that they would want to go – they might. But I shall send the other three within a week. That is, if you let us go.'

The German nodded. 'You must not wait longer. In six weeks we shall be in London.'

There was a silence. 'I do not want that you should think I am not confident about the outcome of this war,' Diessen said. 'We shall conquer England, as we have conquered France; you cannot stand against us. But for many years there will be war with your Dominions, and while that is going on there will be not much food for children, here or in Germany. It will be better that little Anna should be in a neutral country.'

Howard nodded. 'Well, she can go with my lot if you like to send her.'

The Gestapo officer eyed him narrowly. 'There must be no trickery. Remember, we shall have Mademoiselle Rougeron. She may return to Chartres and live with her mother, but until I have a cable from my brother Rupert that little Anna is safe with him, we shall have our eye on mademoiselle.'

'As a hostage,' said the old man quietly.

'As a hostage.' The German stared at him arrogantly. 'And another thing, also. If any word of this appears, it is the concentration camp for your young lady. I will not have you spreading lies about me as soon as you reach England. Remember that.'

Howard thought quickly. 'That has another side to it,' he said. 'If Mademoiselle Rougeron gets into trouble with the Gestapo and I should hear of it in England, this story shall be published in my country and quoted in the German news upon the radio, mentioning you by name.'

Diessen said furiously: 'You dare to threaten me!'

The old man smiled faintly. 'Let us call off this talk of threats,' he said. 'We are in each other's hands, and I will make a bargain with you. I will take your little girl and she shall travel safely to White Falls, even if I have to send her by the Clipper. On your side, you will look after Mademoiselle Rougeron and see that she comes to no harm. That is a bargain that will suit us both, and we can part as friends.'

The German stared at him for a long time, 'So,' he said at last. 'You are clever, Mr Englishman. You have gained all that you want.'

'So have you,' the old man said.

The German released the automatic and reached out for a slip of paper. 'What address have you in England? I shall send for you when we visit London in August.'

They settled to the details of the arrangement. A quarter of an hour later the German got up from the table. 'No word of this to anyone,' he said again. 'Tomorrow in the evening you will be moved from here.'

Howard shook his head. 'I shall not talk. But I would like you to know one thing. I should have been glad to take your little girl with me in any case. It never entered my head to refuse to take her.'

The German nodded. 'That is good,' he said. 'If you had refused I should have shot you dead. You would have been too dangerous to leave this room alive.'

He bowed stiffly. '*Auf Wiedersehen*,' he said ironically. He pressed a button on his desk; the door opened and the sentry took Howard back through the quiet, moonlit streets to his prison.

Nicole was sitting on her bed, waiting for him. As the door closed she came to him and said: 'What happened? Did they hurt you?'

He patted her on the shoulder. 'It's all right,' he said. 'They did nothing to me.'

'What happened, then? What did they want you for?'

He sat down on the bed and she came and sat down opposite him. The moon threw a long shaft of silver light in through the window; faintly, somewhere, they heard the droning of a bomber.

'Listen, Nicole,' he said. 'I can't tell you what has happened. But I can tell you this, and you must try to forget what I am telling you. Everything is going to be all right. We shall go to England very soon, all of the children – and I shall go too. And you will go free, and travel back to Chartres to live with your mother, and you will have no trouble from the Gestapo. That is what is going to happen.'

She said breathlessly: 'But – I do not understand. How has this been arranged?'

He said: 'I cannot tell you that. I cannot tell you any more, Nicole. But that is what will happen, very soon.'

'You are not tired, or ill? This is all true, but you must not tell me how it has been done?'

He nodded. 'We shall go tomorrow or the next day,' he replied. There was a steady confidence in his tone which brought conviction to her.

'I am very, very happy,' she said quietly.

There was a long silence. Presently she said: 'Sitting here in the darkness while you were away, I have been thinking, monsieur.' In the dim light he could see that she was looking away from him. 'I was wondering what these children would grow up to be when they were old. Ronnie – I think he will become an engineer, and Marjan a soldier, and Willem – he will be a lawyer or a doctor. And Rose will be a mother certainly, and Sheila – she may be a mother too, or she may become one of your English women of business. And little Pierre – do you know what I think of him? I think that he will be an artist of some sort, who will lead many other men with his ideas.'

'I think that's very likely,' said the old man.

The girl went on. 'Ever since John was killed, monsieur, I have been desolate,' she said quietly. 'It seemed to me that there was no goodness in the world, that everything had gone mad and crazy and foul – that God had died or gone away, and left the world to Hitler. Even these little children were to go on suffering.'

There was a pause. The old man did not speak.

'But now,' she said, 'I think I can begin to see the pattern. It was not meant that John and I should be happy, save for a week. It was intended that we should do wrong. And now, through John and I, it is intended that these children should escape from Europe to grow up in peace.'

Her voice dropped. 'This may have been what John and I were brought together for,' she said. 'In thirty years the world may need one of these little ones.' She paused. 'It may be Ronnie or it may be Willem, or it may be little Pierre who does great things for the world,' she said. 'But when that happens, monsieur, it will be because I met your son to show him Paris, and we fell in love.'

He leaned across and took her hand, and sat there in the dim light holding it for a long time. Presently they lay down upon their beds, and lay awake till dawn.

They spent the next day in the garden, as the day before. The children were becoming bored and restless with the inactivity; Nicole devoted a good deal of her time to them, while Howard slept in his arm-chair beneath the tree. The day passed slowly. Dinner was served to them at six; after the meal the table was cleared by the same waiter.

They turned to put down beds for the children. The *Gefreiter* stopped them; with some difficulty he made them understand that they were going away.

Howard asked where they were going to. The man shrugged his shoulders. '*Nach Paris?*' he said doubtfully. Evidently he did not know.

Half an hour later they were taken out and put into a covered van. Two German soldiers got in with them, and they moved off. The old man tried to ask the soldiers where they were being taken to, but the men were uncommunicative. Presently, from their conversation, Howard gathered that the soldiers were themselves going on leave to Paris; it seemed that while proceeding on leave they were to act as a guard for the prisoners. That looked as if the Paris rumour was correct.

He discussed all this with Nicole in a low tone as the van swayed and rolled inland from the coast through the leafy lanes in the warm evening.

Presently they came to the outskirts of a town. Nicole peered out. 'Brest,' she said presently. 'I know this street.'

One of the Germans nodded. 'Brest,' he said shortly.

They were taken to the railway station; here they got out of the van. One of the soldiers stood guard over them while the other went to see the RTO; the French passengers looked at them curiously. They were passed through the barrier and put into a third-class carriage with their guards, in a train which seemed to be going through to Paris.

Ronnie said: 'Is this the train we're going to sleep in, Mr Howard?'

He smiled patiently. 'This isn't the one I meant, but we may have to sleep in this one,' he said.

'Shall we have a little bed, like you told us about?'

'I don't think so. We'll see.'

Rose said: 'I do feel thirsty. May I have an orange?'

There were oranges for sale upon the platform. Howard had no money. He explained the requirements to one of the German soldiers, who got out of the carriage and bought oranges for all of them. Presently they were all sucking oranges, the children vying with the German soldiers in the production of noise.

At eight o'clock the train started. It went slowly, stopping at every little local halt upon the line. At eight-twenty it drew up at a little place called Lanissant, which consisted of two cottages and a farm. Suddenly Nicole, looking out of the window, turned to Howard.

'Look!' she said. 'Here is Major Diessen.'

The Gestapo officer, smart and upright in his black uniform and black field boots, came to the door of their carriage and opened it. The German sentries got up quickly and stood to attention. He spoke to them incisively in German. Then he turned to Howard.

'You must get out,' he said. 'You are not going on in this train.'

Nicole and Howard got the children out of the carriage on to the platform. Over the hill the sun was setting in a clear sky. The Gestapo officer nodded to the guard, who shut the carriage door and blew a little toot upon his horn. The train moved forward, the carriages passed by them, and went on slowly up the line. They were left standing on this little platform in the middle of the country with the Gestapo officer.

'So,' he said. 'You will now follow me.'

He led the way down the wooden steps that gave on to the road. There was no ticket-collector and no booking-office; the little halt was quite deserted. Outside, in the lane, there was a grey car, a Ford van with a utility body. In the driver's seat there was a soldier in black Gestapo uniform. Beside him was a child.

Diessen opened the door and made the child get out. '*Komm, Anna*,' he said. '*Hier ist Herr Howard, und mit ihm wirst du zu Onkel Ruprecht gehen*.'

The little girl stared at the old man, and his retinue of children, and at the dishevelled girl beside him. Then she stretched out a little skinny arm, and in a shrill voice exclaimed: 'Heil Hitler!'

The old man said gravely: '*Guten abend, Anna*.' He turned to the Gestapo officer, smiling faintly. 'She will have to get out of that habit if she's going to America,' he said.

Diessen nodded. 'I will tell her.' He spoke to the little girl, who listened to him round-eyed. She asked a question, puzzled; Howard caught the word Hitler. Diessen explained to her again; under the scrutiny of Howard and Nicole he flushed a little. The child said something in a clear, decisive tone which made the driver of the car turn in his seat and glance towards his officer for guidance.

Diessen said: 'I think she understands.' To the old man he seemed a little embarrassed.

He asked: 'What did she say?'

The officer said: 'Children do not understand the Führer. That is reserved for adults.'

Nicole asked him in French: 'But, monsieur, tell us what she said.'

The German shrugged his shoulders. 'I cannot understand the reasoning of children. She said that she is glad that she has not got to say "Heil Hitler" any more, because the Führer wears a moustache.'

Howard said with perfect gravity: 'It is difficult to understand the minds of children.'

'That is so. Now, will you all get into the car. We will not linger in this place.' The German glanced around suspiciously.

They got into the car. Anna got into the back seats with them; Diessen seated himself beside the driver. The car moved down the road. In the front seat the Gestapo officer turned, and passed back a cotton bag tied with a string to Howard, and another to Nicole.

'Your papers and your money,' he said briefly. 'See that it is all in order.'

The old man opened it. Everything that had been taken from his pockets was there, quite intact.

In the gathering dusk they drove through the countryside for an hour and a half. From time to time the officer said something in a low tone to the driver; the old man got the impression once that they were driving round merely to kill time till darkness fell. Now and again they passed through villages, sometimes past barricades with German posts on guard. At these the car stopped and the sentry came and

275

peered into the car. At the sight of the Gestapo uniform he stepped quickly back and saluted. This happened two or three times.

Once Howard asked: 'Where are we going to?'

The German said: 'To l'Abervrach. Your fisherman is there.'

After a pause the old man said: 'There was a guard upon the harbour.'

Diessen said: 'There is no guard tonight – that has been arranged. Do you take me for a fool?'

Howard said no more.

At ten o'clock, in the first darkness, they ran softly to the quay at l'Abervrach. The car drew up noiselessly and the engine stopped at once. The Gestapo officer got out and stood for half a minute, staring around. All was quiet and still.

He turned back to the car. 'Come,' he said. 'Get out quickly – and do not let the children talk.' They helped the children from the car. Diessen said to Nicole: 'There is to be no trickery. You shall stay with me. If you should try to go with them, I shall shoot down the lot of you.'

She raised her head. 'You need not draw your gun,' she said. 'I shall not try to go.'

The German did not answer her, but pulled the big automatic from the holster at his waist. In the dim light he went striding softly down the quay; Howard and Nicole hesitated for a moment and then followed him with the children; the black-uniformed driver brought up the rear. At the end, by the water's edge, Diessen turned.

He called to them in a low tone. 'Hurry.'

There was a boat there, where the slip ran down into the water. They could see the tracery of its mast and rigging outlined against the starry sky; the night was very quiet.

They drew closer and saw it was a half-decked fishing-boat. There were two men there, besides Diessen. One was standing on the quay in the black uniform they knew so well. The other was in the boat, holding her to the quay by a rope rove through a ring.

'In with you, quickly,' said Diessen. 'I want to see you get away.'

He turned to Focquet, speaking in French. 'You are not to start your engine till you are past Le Trepied,' he said. 'I do not want the countryside to be alarmed.'

The young man nodded. 'There is no need,' he said in the soft Breton dialect. 'There is sufficient wind to steer by, and the ebb will take us out.'

They passed the seven children one by one down into the boat. 'You now,' the German said to Howard. 'Remember to behave yourself in England. I shall send for you in London in a very few weeks' time. In September.'

The old man turned to Nicole. 'This is good-bye, my dear,' he said. He hesitated. 'I do not think this war will be over in September. I may be old when it is over, and not able to travel very well. You will come and visit me, Nicole? There is so much that I shall want to say to you. So much that I wanted to talk over with you, if we had not been so hurried and so troubled in the last few days.'

She said: 'I will come and stay with you as soon as we can travel. And you shall talk to me about John.'

The German said: 'You must go now, Mr Englishman.'

He kissed the girl; for a minute she clung to him. Then he got down into the boat among the children.

Pierre said: 'Is this the boat that's going to take us to America?'

The old man shook his head. 'Not this boat,' he said, with mechanical patience. 'That will be a bigger boat than this.'

'How big will that one be?' asked Ronnie. 'Twice as big?'

Focquet had slipped the warp out of the ring and was thrusting vigorously with an oar against the quay-side. The stretch of dark water that separated them from France grew to a yard, to five yards wide. The old man stood motionless, stricken with grief, with longing to be back upon the quay, with the bitter loneliness of old age.

He saw the figure of the girl standing with the three Germans by the water's edge, watching them as they slid away. The ebb caught the boat and hurried her quietly out into the stream; Focquet was heaving on a halliard forward and the heavy nut-brown sail crept slowly up the mast. For a moment he lost sight of Nicole as a mist dimmed his eyes; then he saw her again clearly, still standing motionless beside the Germans. Then the gloom shrouded all of them, and all he could see was the faint outline of the hill against the starry sky.

In deep sorrow, he turned and looked forward to the open sea. But tears blinded him, and he could see nothing of the entrance.

Ronnie said: 'May I work the rudder, Mr Howard?'

The old man did not answer him. The little boy repeated his question.

Rose said: 'I do feel sick.'

He roused himself and turned to their immediate needs with heavy heart. They had no warm clothes and no blankets to keep off the chill of the night sea. He spoke a few sentences to Focquet and found him mystified at their deliverance; he found that the young man intended to cross straight over to Falmouth. He had no compass and no chart for the sea crossing of a hundred miles or so, but said he knew the way. He thought that it would take a day and a night, perhaps a little longer. They had no food with them, but he had a couple of bottles of red wine and a beaker of water.

They pulled a sail out from the forepeak and made a resting-place for the children. The old man took Anna and made her comfortable in a corner first, and put her in the charge of Rose. But Rose, for once, displayed little of her maternal instinct; she was preoccupied with her own troubles.

In a very few minutes she was sick, leaning over the side of the boat under the old man's instructions. One by one the children followed her example as they reached the open sea; they passed Le Trepied, a black reef of rock, with so much wailing that they might just as well have had the engine running after all. In spite of the quick motion of the boat the old man did not feel unwell. Of the children, the only one unaffected was Pierre, who stood by Focquet at the stern, gazing at the moonlight on the water ahead of them.

They turned at the Libenter buoy and headed to the north. In a lull between the requirements of the children Howard said to Focquet: 'You are sure that you know which way to steer?'

The young Frenchman nodded. He glanced at the moon and at the dim loom of the land behind them, and at the Great Bear shimmering in the north. Then he put out his hand. 'That way,' he said. 'That is where Falmouth is.' He called it 'Fallmoot.' 'In the morning we will use the engine; then we will get there before evening.'

A fresh wailing from the bows drew the old man away. An hour later most of the children were lying exhausted in an uneasy doze; Howard was able to sit down himself and rest. He glanced back at the land. It was practically lost to sight; only a dim shadow showed where France lay behind them. He stared back at Brittany with deep regret, in bitter lonely sadness. With all his heart he wished that he was back there with Nicole.

Presently he roused himself. They were not home yet; he must not give way to depression. He got up restlessly and stared around. There was a steady little night breeze from the south-east; they were making about four knots.

'It is going well,' said Focquet. 'If this wind holds we shall hardly need the engine.'

The young fisherman was sitting on a thwart smoking a *caporal*. He glanced back over his shoulder. 'To the right,' he said, without moving. 'Put it this way. So. Keep her at that, and look always at your star.'

The old man became aware that little Pierre was at the helm, thrusting with the whole weight of his body on the big tiller. He said to Focquet: 'Can that little one steer a boat?'

The young man spat into the sea. 'He is learning. He is quick, that one. It prevents sea-sickness, to sail the ship. By the time that we reach England he will be a helmsman.'

The old man turned to Pierre. 'You can do that very well,' he said. 'How do you know which way to go?'

In the dim light of the waning moon he saw Pierre staring straight ahead. 'Focquet told me,' he replied. The old man had to strain to catch his little voice above the lapping of the waves. 'He said, to sail at those square stars up there.' He raised his little arm and pointed at the Bear. 'That is where we are going to, m'sieur. That is the way to America, under those stars. There is so much food there that you can give some to a dog and have him for your friend. Mademoiselle Nicole told me so.'

Presently he grew tired; the boat began to wander from the Bear. Focquet threw the stump of his cigarette into the sea and routed out a heap of sacking. Howard took the helm and the young man arranged a sleepy little boy upon the floor beside their feet. After a time Focquet lay down himself on the bare boards and slept for an hour while the old man sailed the boat on through the starlight.

All night they saw no ships at all upon the sea. Ships may have been near them, but if so they were sailing without lights and did not trouble them. But in the half-light of dawn, at about half-past four, a destroyer came towards them from the west, throwing a deep feathery bow wave of white foam aside as she cut through the water, bearing down on them.

She slowed a quarter of a mile away and turned from a grey, menacing spear into rather a battered, rusty ship, menacing still, but worn with much hard work. A young man in duffle coat and service cap shouted at them from the bridge, megaphone in hand: *'Vous êtes Français?'*

Howard shouted back: 'Some of us are English.'

The young man waved at him cheerfully. 'Can you get to Plymouth all right?'

'We want to go to Falmouth.' The whine of the destroyer's fans and the lapping of the waves made conversation difficult.

'You've got to go to Plymouth. Plymouth! Is that all right for you?'

Howard spoke quickly to Focquet, and then nodded to the ship. The young officer waved at him again and stepped back. There was a sudden foaming of the stern and the destroyer shot away upon her course up-Channel. They were left tossing in the creamy effervescence of her wake.

They altered course two points towards the east and started up the engine, giving them about six knots of speed. The children roused, and in failing misery began to vomit again. They were all cold, and very tired, and desperately hungry.

Presently the sun came up and the day grew warm.

The old man gave them all a little drink of wine and water.

All morning they plugged on over a sunlit, summer sea. Now and again the young Frenchman asked Howard the time, studied the sun, and made a correction to his course. At noon a thin blue line of land appeared ahead of them to the north.

At about three o'clock a trawler closed them, and asked who they were, and, as they tossed beside her, showed them the high land of Rame Head on the horizon.

At about half-past five they were off Rame Head. A motor-launch, a little yacht in time of peace, ranged up alongside them; an RNVR lieutenant questioned them again. 'You know the Cattewater?' he shouted to Howard. 'Where the flying boats are? That's right. Go up there and into the basin on the north side. All refugees land at the fish quay in the basin. Got that? Okay.'

The launch sheered off and went upon her way. The fishing-boat nosed in past Rame Head, past Cawsand, past the breakwater into the shelter of the Sound. Ahead of them lay Plymouth on its hills, grey and peaceful by its harbour in the evening sunlight. Howard stared at it and sighed a little. It seemed to him that he had been happier in France than he would be in his own land.

The sight of the warships in the Sound, the land, and the calmer water revived the children a little; they began to look about and take an interest again. Under the old man's guidance Focquet threaded his way through the warships; off Drake's Island they came to the wind and lowered the brown sail. Then, under engine only, they made their way to the fish quay.

There were other boats before them at the quay, boats full of an assortment of mixed nationalities, clambering ashore and into England. They lay off for a quarter of an hour before they could get to the steps, while the gulls screamed around them, and stolid men in blue jerseys looked down upon them, and holiday girls in summer cotton frocks took photographs of the scene.

At last they were all stumbling up the steps to join the crowd of refugees in the fish-market. Howard was still in the clothes of a Breton labourer, unshaven, and very, very tired. The children, hungry and exhausted, clustered round him.

A masterful woman, trim and neat in the uniform of the WVS, shepherded them to a bench. '*Asseyez vous là*,' she said in very bad French, '*jusqu'on peut vous attendre*.'

Howard collapsed on to the seat and sat there half in coma, utterly exhausted. Once or twice women in uniform came to them and asked them questions, which he answered mechanically. Half an hour later a young girl brought them cups of tea, which they took gratefully.

Refreshed, the old man took more interest in his surroundings. He heard a cultured Englishwoman's voice.

'There's that lot over there, Mrs Dyson. All those children with the two men.'

'What nationality are they?'

'They seem to be a mixed lot. There's rather an attractive little girl there who speaks German.'

'Poor little thing! She must be Austrian.'

Another voice said: 'Some of those children are English.'

There was an exclamation of concern. 'I had no idea! But they're in such a *state*! Have you seen their poor little heads? My dear, they're *lousy*, every one of them.' There was a shocked pause. 'That horrible old man – I wonder how he came to be in charge of them.'

The old man closed his eyes, smiling a little. This was the England that he knew and understood. This was peace.

12

The last bomb had fallen, the last gun had fired; over in the east the fires were dying down. Then came the long notes of the 'All Clear' from different quarters of the town.

We got up stiffly from our chairs. I went over to the long window at the far end of the room, pulled back the curtains and threw back the shutters. The glass from the window fell in on the carpet with a crash; the wind blew fresh into our faces with a bitter, acrid smell of burning.

Down in the streets below tired men in raincoats, gum-boots, and tin-hats were tending a small motor-pump. There was a noise like a thousand jangling cut-glass chandeliers as men in the houses opposite poked the remains of broken windows from the frames, letting the glass fall on the pavements, going methodically from room to room.

A cold, grey light was spreading over London. It was raining a little.

I turned from the window. 'Did you get them over to the States?' I asked.

'Oh yes,' he said. 'They all went together. I sent a wireless telegram to the Cavanaghs offering to send Sheila and Ronnie, and Tenois asked if he might send Rose. I got a woman that I know to go with them, and take them to Coates Harbor.'

'And Anna too?'

He nodded. 'Anna went too.' We moved towards the door. 'I had a letter this week from her uncle in White Falls. He said that he had sent a cable to his brother in Germany, so that ought to be all right.'

'Your daughter must have had a bit of a shock when they arrived,' I said.

He laughed. 'Well, I don't know. I sent a cable asking if she'd have them, and she said she would. She'll be all right with them. Costello seems to be reorganising the whole place for them. He's building a swimming-pool and a new boat-house for their boats. I think that they'll be very happy there.'

We went downstairs in the grey dawn and parted in the hall. He went out a few steps ahead of me; I paused to ask the night porter about damage to the club. He said that they had had a fire-bomb on the roof, but that young Ernest had kicked it about till it went out. He said there was no gas or water coming to the building, but that the electricity had survived the blitz.

I yawned. 'I spent the night up in the smoking-room talking to Mr Howard,' I said.

The man nodded. 'I looked in once or twice and saw you sitting with him,' he said. 'I said to the steward, I said – quite a good thing you was with him. He's got to look a great deal older recently.'

'Yes,' I said. 'I'm afraid he has.'

'He went away for a long holiday a month or two ago,' the porter said. 'But I don't know as it did him a great deal of good.'

I went out, and the glass crunched tinkling beneath my feet.

A TOWN LIKE ALICE

It was in occupied Malaya where Jean Paget became inured to illness, cruelty and death. Yet it was there that she first heard of Alice Springs and fell in love with the gentle Australian and his strange tales. Then something so terrible occurred she knew she would never see Joe Harman again – or so she believed . . .

One of the best-loved of Nevil Shute's novels, *A Town Like Alice* is his masterpiece of love, enterprise and triumph over the ravages of war.

'Nevil Shute is an accomplished storyteller . . . He has contrived a gripping novel of an English girl's courage and unflagging faith in humanity' *The Scotsman*

'A very well told tale, bound to hold the attention of everyone who reads it. Mr Shute is a born narrator, a talent enjoyed by very few indeed' *Tatler*